A Girl Called Violet

Kay Seeley

Published by Enterprise Books
Copyright © 2020 Kay Seeley
All rights reserved.
ISBN: 978-1-9164282-2-5

To Lorraine and Liz

With thanks

.

Kay Seeley's books

Novels
The Water Gypsy
The Watercress Girls
The Guardian Angel

The Hope Series
A Girl Called Hope (Book 1)
A Girl Called Violet (Book 2)

All Kay's novels are also available in Large Print

Box Set (ebook only)
The Victorian Novels Box Set

Short Stories
The Cappuccino Collection
The Summer Stories
The Christmas Stories

Please feel free to contact Kay through her website
www.kayseeleyauthor.com She'd love to hear from
you.
Or follow Kay on her Facebook Page
https://www.facebook.com/kayseeley.writer/

Chapter One

London July 1905

Violet hurried along the road. She was tempted to lift her skirts and run, but that would only draw attention to her, something she wished to avoid at all cost. It would upset the children too, who were hurrying along beside her. She glanced from side to side at the empty street as she walked, wary in case she may be being followed, or may be seen by someone who might recognise her and want to stop to chat. Her breath came in short gasps. She wasn't used to hurrying.

It was early Sunday morning. Too early for all but the costers and market traders trundling their barrows over the cobbles. Her mind spiralled back to the May Day bank holiday, month or so ago.

In the kitchen they were clearing away the breakfast things and she'd asked her sister-in-law, Alice, if she'd like to come over the park with her. "There's a funfair," she said. "And a breath of fresh air will do us all good."

The twins had been so excited. "Can we go on the merry-go-round?" William said. "I love the merry-go-round."

"I like the horses. Can we ride on the ponies?" Rose had asked.

"Will there be candy? And can we go on all the rides?"

"We'll see," Violet told them. "You have to wait and see."

Alice sighed. "You go. I've got the books to do and John wants me to go through the orders." Although Violet's older brother John held the licence of the Hope and Anchor, the pub he'd run since their parents died, they all took turns working in the bar. Paperwork wasn't his strong point so he relied on Alice to do it.

"John works you too hard," Violet said, seeing the dark shadows beneath Alice's eyes.

"Bank holiday is our busiest time," she said. "Why don't you ask Hope to go with you? She enjoys spending time with the children."

Hope, her older, married sister, had no children of her own, so spending time with Violet's five-year-old twins and Amy, Alice and John's three-year-old, was precious to her. In the end Violet had called on Hope and she'd been delighted to go along with her and their younger brother Alfie.

They'd been there a while and the children had gone on all the rides. She'd tried her luck on some of the stalls and come away with a plaster cast of a lady with a crinoline. "I'll put it on the mantelshelf," she said. "It will be a reminder of a happy day out."

They'd walked around the fairground for the best part of the afternoon when she saw him. A fleeting glance. She wasn't even sure it was him but it made her heart jump so suddenly it almost stopped beating.

She persuaded herself she'd imagined it. It couldn't have been him. Her mind was playing tricks. Still, the man she saw bore a striking resemblance. Older, heavier, shabbier, as though the years had not been kind to him. Lank strands of greying hair poked out from his straw boater to curl untidily on the collar of his blazer. Gone was the boyish charm she remembered, the shock of blonde hair that fell casually onto his forehead. The wide smile and twinkling blue eyes. The straw hat and stripped blazer were him all over. Ever the showman. It had been nearly six years. Why would he come back?

Then she thought perhaps he was here working, doing his magic tricks for the punters at the funfair. She'd hurried the children away with the promise of ice cream. Hope had agreed when she said she was dying for a cup of tea, so they left the park.

A few days later when Violet took some of the costumes she'd been working on to the theatre for their latest performance, costumes that had to be finished by hand, Florrie, the cleaner, mentioned that she'd seen him.

"He was asking after you," she said and a great black cloud descended over Violet as her mind filled with memories of their time together.

She'd been sixteen, naive and stupidly trusting. She dreamed of fame and fortune, going places, seeing the world. She was pretty too, she knew that. He said beautiful. She had a voice. She could sing, everyone said so. He said he'd make her a star.

"Really?" she said to Florrie. "He knows where I live." Yes, she thought, if he wanted to find her he'd know where to look. Still, she doubted he'd dare show his face at the pub. All the same her fists curled and her stomach churned. She felt sick at the thought of seeing him again and her brother John wouldn't be too pleased either.

She sighed as the memories of the past played through her mind. It wasn't all bad. They'd had good times, at the beginning. He'd go on stage and do his magic tricks, then she'd sing a couple of songs. Those days were long gone. The only singing she did now was at the Hope and Anchor on Saturday nights. Her regular singing spot brought the customers in making it the best night of the week. Last night was no exception, that's when she saw him again.

She'd been singing all the old Music Hall songs the audience loved in the function room as usual. A good crowd too. They'd clapped, cheered and joined in with the songs that were their favourites. The room filled with chatter, laughter and singing. Then, towards the end of the evening, she slipped out to get a drink and thought she saw him making his way through the public bar. She wasn't sure at first, she only caught a glimpse and it had been years… but the churning in her stomach told her she wasn't mistaken. He was back, and he'd come looking for her.

Her stomach churned. She struggled to finish the next song and left the stage, pushing past Alice who was serving behind the bar. Her heart pounded as she rushed upstairs.

She sat on the bed for what felt like hours, trying to figure out what it was he wanted. He wasn't stupid enough to think there was anything for him here, surely? If John saw him she'd not be responsible for his actions.

Her hands shook as she unbuttoned her dress, changed into her night shift and put on her dressing gown. The pub would be closed by now. Slowly she made her way down to the kitchen where John and Alice were having a nightcap before retiring to their beds.

"Can I have one of those?" she said nodding at the bottle of brandy on the table.

John lifted the bottle to pour one for her. "What happened to you? You left a bit sudden. Alice thought you weren't feeling well."

Violet gulped back the drink. "I thought I saw someone I knew," she said.

Before John could enquire further Alice jumped up. "Oh there was someone. He left a note for you, Violet." She dashed into the bar and returned with an envelope with Violet's name on it. "Sorry. I almost forgot. It was just before closing."

Violet opened the letter and read it. As she did so the blood drained from her face, nausea rose up in her throat and her knees buckled. She would have hit the floor if it hadn't been for Alice, catching her and guiding her to a chair.

"Are you alright?" Alice said. "You look like you've had a bit of a shock."

John poured her another brandy.

"No," she said. "I'm fine." she picked up the glass, swigged back the rest of the warming, mellow liquid and made her way unsteadily upstairs.

She read the note over and over:

Hello, Violet, I see you've landed on your feet. Time for us to get reacquainted and for me to meet my children, the children you've kept from me. You

didn't know I knew about them did you? But I made it
my business to know.
Bring them to The Palace of Varieties, Shoreditch,
tomorrow at opening time.
Don't disappoint me, Violet. You know how I hate
being disappointed.
Your ever-loving Bert.

'Ever-loving Bert'? Well he'd never been that. On stage he was The Magnificent Merlin, Master of Magic and Mystery, who could keep you spellbound with his tricks. Well he was full of tricks all right, but not the ones you saw on stage. And he'd tricked her hadn't he? Tricked her into believing that he loved her. Tricked her into an unwanted pregnancy. There was nothing magnificent or magic about that. What a fool she'd been. She'd fallen for his charms and come to regret it. Thanks to her family those days were gone and she had no intention or desire to see him ever again.

She thought of her children, Rose and William. Children he didn't want and had told her to 'get rid' of. She'd adored them from the first moment they drew breath and there was nothing in the world she wouldn't do for them. Her mind filled with memories of the day they were born, their first smiles, their first steps, how proud she was of them. The first time she held them she thought her heart would burst with love. Nothing in life had prepared her for the rush of emotion she felt holding them in her arms. The deepest feelings of pride and joy had filled her whole body. She loved them more than life itself, now their father wanted to see them.

Memories of his drinking, the beatings and the bruises filled her mind. If he thought he could turn up after all these years and take them from her he could think again. She vowed then that he'd never see them. She'd protect them whatever it took.

They were her children, children who'd have never been born if Bert Shadwick had had his way. Tears filled her eyes as the memories rose around her. She recalled his anger when she told him she was expecting, and the beating that followed when she refused to get rid of it. That was nearly six years ago. Six years during which he'd never seen them, never called to ask about them, she wasn't even sure he knew about them, until now. Until she got that note.

She'd overheard the gossip about him at the theatre over the years. Performers who'd worked in theatres all over the country talked about him, recalling how she used to work with him. They'd say how his fortunes had gone from pretty terrible to even worse. His magic tricks had fallen out of favour. Modern audiences wanted more baffling illusions, cleverer tricks, more subtle and refined. They'd moved on, he hadn't. Even his agent had dropped him. That must have been hard for him to bear.

Whatever he wanted now it was sure to be to his advantage, no one else's. He'd always had a streak of crafty meanness about him. Well, she wasn't going to give in to him, not this time, not like she had in the past, following him around the country, eager to perform with him whatever the cost, and there was a cost. She knew that now.

It was exciting at first, travelling around the country, appearing on stage with him. It was as though her dreams were coming true. He was a magician, he could do anything, at least that's what she believed. He said he loved her, made her feel special. He promised

7

her the world. Of course it didn't last. Oh they did well enough if his act went well, a run of good bookings at classy theatres and they'd be drinking champagne. He'd even let her sing. But if things went badly, then there'd be the beatings, the other women, the midnight flits from lodgings without paying the bill. It was a life she'd left behind and not one she wanted to return to.

She rose before dawn and started to gather her things together. She'd take only one bag; that was all she'd be able to manage with the children. She'd pack each of them a small case of essentials. Most of their things could be replaced, they grew out of them so quickly she'd have to replace them anyway. It would be like a holiday, she'd be taking them on an adventure.

She moved quietly around the room putting her most precious things into a canvas carrier, then tiptoed along to where William and Rose slept, along with John and Alice's daughter, Amy. She gazed at their pale angel faces as they slept lost in dreams. William had his father's fine blond hair and air of innocence, belying his confident, mischievous nature. Rose had her mother's unruly auburn curls and practicality. They were the one good thing she'd got from Bert and she couldn't imagine life without them now.

She put their favourite toys and some of their clothes into a bag for each of them. A glass fronted cupboard on the wall held silver cups and other Christening gifts. She put them into her bag along with her jewellery. Then she gently woke them.

Rose grumbled in her sleep as she shook her awake, but she had to shush William, who always woke bright as a button, ready for the excitement of the day. He was a chatterbox too, so Violet was afraid he'd wake Amy, then she'd have to explain to Alice and John what she was doing.

She pulled a sleepy Rose and curious William into her arms. "We're going on an adventure," she whispered. "It's a secret, so we have to be really quiet and creep out without waking the rest of the house. Can you both do that?"

William nodded. "I can," he said so Violet had to shush him again.

"What for?" Rose asked. "Where are we going?"

She got out their best clothes, the ones she could least afford to leave behind, and ushered them into her room to dress. "Come downstairs as soon as you're dressed," she told them. "And remember, no noise."

Downstairs she made her way into the bar. She'd need money. As much money as she could find. What she had in her purse wouldn't get them very far but there was always a float left in the till. That'd be enough for a start. She'd sell her jewellery and the children's silver Christening gifts if she had to.

The sound of the till opening seemed to fill in the empty bar. She cursed under her breath and glanced around in time to see John appear from the cellar.

"Good heavens," he said. "Violet. What on earth are you doing this early and…?" He frowned. "Was that the till I heard being opened?"

Violet blushed to the roots of her auburn hair. She swallowed. "I'm sorry," she said. "I wouldn't have, but…" She could no longer hold back her fear, an avalanche of anguish overtook her and she collapsed sobbing into John's arms. He guided her to a chair and the whole story came tumbling out. She showed him the note.

He took the paper from her hand and read it. "It's from Bert Shadwick, the no good idle swine. He's got a nerve, showing his face in here. If I'd seen him he wouldn't have walked out the same way he walked in." Anger flared in his eyes. He turned to Violet. "You're not going to see him are you? Is that why you're taking money from the till? For that swine Bert Shadwick?" His face filled with fury.

"No. No, of course I'm not. I've learned my lesson, but he's asked to see the twins. I can think of no good reason he'd want to do that. He never wanted them in the first place. Told me to 'get rid' or he'd do it for me. Had a jolly good try 'an all." Venom filled her voice as she said, "I'd die before I let him near Rose and William. I'm taking them away, somewhere safe, somewhere he won't be able to find us."

"Running away, Violet? Is that your answer? Running away never solved anything. I thought you knew that." He glanced again at the note. His jaw set. "If you want I'll round up some lads from the market. Well go and sort 'im out. He won't come back in a hurry."

Violet shook her head. "No, John. It's not your problem. You've taken us in and looked after us, but your responsibility is to Alice and Amy. Bert's not stupid, he'd hear you were coming and be prepared for you, then he'd start on them."

"If you're sure. You know I'd stand by you whatever you decide. Help in any way I can. You're family too."

"Thanks, but it's just until I can sort something out. Find somewhere safe for them. I've heard the gossip and rumours about Bert. He's got into debt and he's the sort would sell his grandmother if there was a few bob in it for him. I dread to think what plans he has for Rose and William, but he'll never get them, not as long as I've breath in my body."

John's expression softened. "Where will you go?"

"I can't tell you. If you know Bert'll try to get it out of you. Once he's made up his mind to do something he won't stop until he's done it."

"I'm not stupid. I'd never tell him."

"No? Not if he threatened your family, Alice and Amy? He would you know. As long as you know where I am they're in danger."

"Well, at least let me know when you get there. Let me know you're safe."

Violet smiled. "I'll do my best," she said, "but don't bank on it."

Rose and William burst into the bar full of excitement. "Where are we going? Is it a holiday? When will we come back?" They stopped short when they saw John. "Oh hello, Uncle John, are you coming too?" William said.

John shook his head. "Wait here a minute," he said and dashed into his office behind the bar. When he returned he gave Violet a bag of money. "Saturday's takings," he said. "You'll need it more than me."

Violet smiled and kissed him. "Thanks," she said and ushered the children out.

Chapter Two

By the time Violet picked up the bags and ushered the children into the street, shushing them as she went, the early sun was just rising over the rooftops. It was going to be a bright sunny day.

Hurrying along the street Violet kept glancing around. William was skipping along in front of her. Even at that early hour he was full of energy, bouncing along while Rose walked sedately by her mother's side.

"Where are we going?" Rose asked, her thin voice almost lost in the rumble of wheels of a passing carriage.

"We're going to stay with a friend of mine at the seaside," Violet said, crossing her fingers that her friend Nesta still ran her boarding house in Great Yarmouth. "It'll be fun."

She forced her lips into a smile and tried to sound more convincing than she felt. She slowed at the crossroads to catch her breath and caught sight of a hackney carriage coming towards them. She waived it down and sighed with relief as the driver pulled the horses to a halt. A ride to the station would be quicker and less noticeable than walking.

It was a short journey, during which the children bubbled with excitement. William plied her with questions. "Will there be a beach with sand? Can we make sandcastles? Will there be pony rides? And ice cream?" Even Rose's eyes shone. Once they were away from London she'd be able to make sure they had a good time without having the worry of Bert appearing.

When they boarded the train Violet relaxed a little. It was hot and stuffy. She wished she could remove her hat which was giving her a headache. William was his usual restless self, chattering, looking out of the window, jumping up and down, wanting to walk about. "Sit still, William. You're wearing me out just watching you," Violet said.

William pouted. "How far is it to the seaside? When will we get there?"

"Last time we went to the seaside you were sick," Rose reminded him. They'd both been on an outing with the local Licensed Victuallers Association and William had been sick on the way home.

"It was the jiggling of the coach," he said. "I'll be all right as long as we don't go on a coach."

"It was the seven sausage rolls and three bags of toffee you ate," Rose said. "It was, wasn't it, Ma?"

"Be quiet and stop arguing," Violet said. "Can't you just read your books or look out of the window?"

The children quietened and Violet watched as the train left the city and the grimy buildings gave way to green countryside filled with trees. Even the sky was a cloudless blue. She'd been mortified when John caught her raiding the till, but he had been a diamond once he saw Bert's note and the money he'd given her was a godsend.

Running away had been an impulse. She'd only thought to get away from any chance of Bert seeing her or the children. She wanted to put as much distance as she could between them. Now she was beginning to realise the enormity of what she was doing, uprooting her children from the only home they'd ever known.

She glanced out of the window and watched as the miles slipped by. Supposing they can never go back?

Never see the rest of their family or their friends again? She was casting them out into a world of uncertainty. But the alternative was worse. Whatever Bert planned for them no good would come of it. She knew that much. Nothing good ever came from being with Bert. She'd learned that to her cost. She was determined that he wouldn't find them. She'd do whatever it took to make sure he never saw them.

Then she remembered her arrangement with Hope. They were supposed to be going on a picnic. She felt bad about that too, letting Hope down. She knew how much she enjoyed seeing the children. She'd send her a note when they arrived, but then she'd risk them knowing where she was from the postmark. She sighed. All she hoped was that her sister wouldn't think badly of her. They hadn't always got along in the past, but since the twins were born they'd become fonder of each other. Violet hoped that hadn't changed.

After a while Rose spoke again. "Why couldn't Amy come with us?" she asked. "She's never been to the seaside."

Violet smiled. Amy was three and Rose treated her like a doll, always wanting to take her out or brush her ginger hair. "She's too little and she'd miss her ma wouldn't she?" Violet said.

"I'll miss her," Rose said, pouting.

"I know, I'll miss her too," Violet said.

"And Uncle John and Aunty Alice," Rose said. "It's a pity they couldn't come with us isn't it?"

"Yes, a great pity," Violet said. Amy would miss them too, another thing to feel guilty about. "It's only for a little while. We'll see them all again soon. And you'll have lots of exciting things to tell her." She felt a stab of guilt as she said it, but it was quickly dismissed.

Rushing through the countryside Violet relaxed as the distance behind them lengthened. The warmth of the day and the rhythm of the train lulled her senses. Her mind began to wander.

She recalled what John had said about running away. He was right, running away never solved anything. The problem of Bert would still be there. Wherever she went he'd find her. And as long as she had the children with her they'd be in danger too. She vowed that, as soon as she got them settled, she'd return to London and sort Bert out once and for all. She wasn't afraid of him for herself, just for the children. No, she could stand up to him now and tell him just what she thought of him.

That decided she calmed down and enjoyed the rest of the journey.

By the time the train pulled into the station at Great Yarmouth it was nearly lunchtime. The train shuddered to a stop with a great deal of noise and smoke. The hissing of the brakes and release of steam filled the air. "We're here," Violet said. "Come on, William, where's your bag?" William had dropped his bag on the floor of the carriage and some of his marbles had rolled under the seat. He dived onto the floor and scrabbled around to find them.

"Oh William, get up, you'll get your clothes filthy." Violet pulled him up. She'd only brought one change of clothes and she'd been hoping the ones he was wearing would last at least a couple of days before she had to find somewhere to get them cleaned.

Eventually she managed to usher them off the train onto the station concourse. A crowd of travellers pushed past them making their way to the exit. Violet glanced around. It was several years since she'd seen

Nesta and everything looked different from the way she remembered it. She wasn't sure which way to go. She had the address. She'd find a cab. Together they made their way out into the road and she looked around. The last of the cabs outside the station was just pulling away. She dropped her bag onto the pavement. She looked both ways and saw the road rapidly emptying.

As the last cab disappeared around the corner William pulled impatiently at her skirt. "Are we there? Which way is it? This bag's too heavy, can you carry it?"

She tutted. "No, William. Rose is carrying her bag. You shouldn't have brought so much if you can't carry it. Now, wait here while I find us some transport."

A tall man in a grey suit standing behind her lifted his top hat. "You'll be lucky," he said, in an accent she found difficult to place. "Cabs around here disappear faster than a field of corn besieged by locusts when the London train comes in."

She turned around. He smiled, a warm spontaneous gesture that lit up his thin, intelligent features.

"Then we'll take the omnibus," she said.

"Not today," he said. "It's Sunday. And the cabs won't come back once the London train has gone."

"Oh," she said. Suddenly coming at short notice on a Sunday didn't seem such a good idea. She'd stayed with Nesta before but couldn't recall how they got there. On tour all the transport had been arranged for them and she couldn't remember where the guest house was, except that it was at the end of the Promenade.

16

"Allow me to introduce myself. Gabriel Stone at your service." He executed a perfect bow. "Where are you heading? Perhaps I can help?"

"Only if you happen to have a handy carriage standing by," Violet said, irritated by his presumption.

"Better than that. I have a motor car parked around the corner. If you'd care for a ride?"

William's eyes widened. "Really? A motor car? Can we, Ma? Please, Ma?" He almost bounced with excitement.

Violet glanced around at the empty street. There were no cabs in sight. She noticed that the shops were all closed too. It was hot and she was wearing her best green velvet suit, which was quite unsuitable for the warm weather. She'd been loath to leave it behind as she knew she looked good in it and it had cost a fortune to make, but now she found it overbearingly hot.

"I can assure you you'll be quite safe. I'm not in the habit of picking up young ladies, but you looked a little lost and you're children look tired."

"We are," William piped up. "Aren't we, Rose?" He gave an exaggerated yawn, tapping his mouth with his hand and nudged Rose to do the same. She did, but hers came out more like a giggle. "We'd like a ride, wouldn't we, Rose?" he pestered.

"Do you live around here?" Violet asked. "We're going to stay at a friend's boarding house, the Sea View. It's at the end of the Promenade. Do you know it?"

"I'm staying at a hotel just off the Promenade," he said. "I'm going that way so I'll be happy to take you."

Gabriel Stone looked presentable. His suit was expertly tailored and, if he could afford a motor car, he must be a man of substance. She'd mentioned staying with a friend to give the impression that they were expected. It seemed that they were stranded unless she took up his offer of a lift. What could he do with two children along in broad daylight? The look in his slate grey eyes, his steady smile and his air of quiet determination convinced her. Her resistance caved in. "Well, perhaps we'll have a look at this motor car and see. Where is it?"

Gabriel offered his arm and with his other hand picked up Violet's bag, also gathering William's bag from his hands. "This way," he said.

They followed him around the corner to where the motor was parked. Open topped, with yellow painted wheels and bonnet and two rows of seats Violet couldn't fail to be impressed.

"Climb aboard," Gabriel said. The children didn't need second telling.

"This really is most kind of you," Violet said. "She crossed her fingers that Nesta still ran the boarding house where she'd stayed all those years ago when she was on tour with Bert. They'd become good friends then, she only hoped Nesta would remember her.

Despite her reservations about this stranger who'd picked them up in a quite outrageous fashion, Violet climbed aboard. She sat on the back seat with the children. Gabriel took a large handle from the front seat and walked around to the front of car. Violet watched fascinated as he swung the handle and the motor sprang into life. He climbed in behind the wheel, took off his top hat and replaced it with a flat cap. He then pulled on a pair of string-backed driving gloves, glanced round to see they were all right, and with a honk of the horn they set off.

Soon they were bowling along narrow streets towards the Promenade. The drive was exhilarating. Violet felt quite daring. They must have been travelling at least ten miles an hour, she thought. The wind in their faces felt cool. Perhaps the heavier suit hadn't been such a bad idea after all but she had to hang on to her hat. William leaned out at the side, looking at the road ahead, the breeze bringing colour to his cheeks and ruffling his blond curls. Rose leaned into her mother, to shelter from the wind, but both their faces beamed with delight.

Chapter Three

Violet's older sister, Hope, stood staring out of her first-floor drawing room window. Morning sunbeams filled the large, airy room. She'd taken her coffee there after breakfast to enjoy the view which she loved. The elegant, five storey, Georgian town house, named 'Peacehaven' although far from peaceful, overlooked the river. Small boats honked and hooted as they made their way to and from the nearby docks. The noise of the ships loading and unloading carried over on the breeze. Hope often sat watching the boats on the river. She never tired of the water and its ever-changing mood.

Today bright sunlight sparkled on the waves, the passing crafts leaving rippling patterns in their wake. It would be a fine day for a picnic in the park with Violet and the children. She wondered about asking Alfie, their youngest brother, if he'd like to come too, then decided the walk might be too much for him. His crippled leg had strengthened as he grew older and at fourteen he stood a good inch taller than Hope, but he'd been with them before and she knew he found it tiring. Anyway, her husband Silas was home and there was nothing Alfie liked more than spending a day with Silas, who'd become a father figure for him since he'd come to live with them.

Alfie had done so well at school that he'd gained a place on a training course at an accountancy firm in Liverpool. He'd be leaving at the end of the week. Hope was so proud of him but she'd miss him. The house wouldn't be the same without him.

A knock on the door brought her out of her reverie. Daisy the maid came in to clear away the coffee tray. "Is there anything else, ma'am?" she asked as she gathered up the crockery. "Mrs B says there's cold cuts, pies, fruit and cake packed for your picnic. If there's anything else..."

"Thank you, Daisy. Nothing else," Hope said. "You go off and give my regards to your mother. I hope she's quite recovered." Daisy's mother had been poorly the week before and Hope had given Daisy time off to look after her.

"Thank you, ma'am," Daisy said, bobbing a curtsy before hurrying out of the door.

Hope had an hour or two to kill before it would be time to get ready to meet Violet and the children. Silas had left his newspaper and she picked it up to read until it was time to get ready to go out. She'd only been sat for about five minutes when she heard a loud, insistent knocking on the front door. Putting down her paper Hope wondered who could be calling so urgently on a Sunday morning. She hurried downstairs to open the door and gasped in shock.

"John?" she said. "What on earth?"

A clearly disgruntled John barged past her, a scowl on his face. She closed the door and followed him back to the room she'd just left.

"Is Silas in? I wanted to ask his advice."

"He's in the study with Alfie," she said. "Is there anything I can do?" It still irked her that John, although a year younger than her, had been considered head of the family until she married. Now he often consulted Silas over family matters.

"I thought you ought to know," he said. "Bert Shadwick's back and Violet has run away – again."

"Violet's run away with Bert Shadwick – again?" she asked, her brow furrowed. "I don't believe it!"

John shook his head. "No, not with Bert – away from him. And she's taken the children with her. I caught her this morning taking money from the till. She showed me this." He handed Hope the note Violet had shown him before bursting into tears and telling him she was taking the children away.

Hope read the note.

She gasped. Of course she knew he was the father of Violet's children, but she'd never expected to hear from him again. Her mind flew back to the day Violet reappeared after running away with him when she was just sixteen. She'd been beaten black and blue and was five months pregnant.

"But what could he possibly want with William and Rose?"

John shook his head. "Nothing good."

"But Violet – is she all right?"

John smiled. "Yes. I heard the till being opened. She was after money so I gave her Saturday's takings. Should be enough for her to find a place somewhere."

"But where? Where will she go?"

John shrugged. "She wouldn't say. Said it's best we don't know. She's terrified of him. If I find him first he'll be sorry he ever met us. Me and the lads from the market'll soon sort 'im out." He glanced around. "That's why I need to talk to Silas."

True, Silas had wealth, power, influence and ran a successful business, but even so, John was her brother, Violet was her sister. Surely she should be the one he came to for advice? "I don't know what you expect Silas to do," she said. "Violet's over twenty-one and they're her children. I suppose she can take them wherever she pleases." The old irritation she always felt when Violet did something impulsive and unwise rose up inside her. She swallowed it back down.

Just then Silas appeared. "What's the commotion?" he said. Then, seeing John, he stepped towards him hand held out. "John. Good to see you. How are the family?"

"Violet's run off with the children," Hope said, tears beginning to well up in her eyes as she realised that if Violet had taken them she may never see them again. It would feel like the most terrible loss.

Silas gazed at John, waiting for his explanation. John appeared to have recovered from his earlier panic and explained calmly to Silas what had happened the previous evening and that morning.

"I think she's frightened what he'll do to them. He left her a note."

"You mean he threatened her?"

John handed Silas the note. His brow darkened as he read it.

"I think he wants to take them away from her," John said. "It's the sort of spiteful, malicious, mean thing he would do."

Silas stroked his chin, deep in thought. "He is their father," he said. "I see no threat here, just a father wanting to see his children. That's only natural."

"Natural!" Hope's shrill outburst shattered Silas's calm reasoning. "This is Bert Shadwick we're talking about. The swindler, drunk and woman beater. I dread to think what he'd do to the children if he got hold of them. And why would he want them anyway?" She stared at him, wide-eyed.

"Violet says it'll be for no good purpose," John said. "And I agree with her. I was all for going to see him and sorting him out once and for all. According to the note he'll be at The Palace of Varieties in Shoreditch at opening time. Me and the lads…"

"And risk losing your licence into the bargain?" Hope said. "What will become of your family then?" Hope thought of Alice and little Amy who'd have no say in the matter.

"Hope's right," Silas said. "Violence isn't the answer. I suppose his name is on the birth certificate?"

Hope and John exchanged glances as a tumble of memories cascaded through Hope's mind. "Yes," she said. "It is."

"Then he has rights. I fear, if it came to a matter of law, Violet could be accused of kidnapping them—"

"Kidnapping her own children?"

"As I said, he has rights and there's nothing we can do until we find out what he has in mind for them."

John shook his head. "I'll swing for 'im if he touches them kids."

"Well, if Violet's gone away as you say he'll be unlikely to see them won't he? I'll make some enquiries around town. See if I can find out anything about what he's into these days. If there's any chance it's illegal, which is a distinct possibility knowing his reputation, we can let the law deal with him in the proper way."

John looked decidedly uncomfortable but agreed to leave it to Silas to find out what he could.

"I'll walk back with you," Hope said, although her heart was pumping with rage. "Perhaps I can take Amy to the park for a while, give Alice a break."

"Thank you," John said. Hope wasn't sure he'd leave it at that.

She put on a light coat and straw boater garlanded with flowers for the walk with John back to the Hope and Anchor. She collected the picnic basket from Mrs B and went out with John. Inside her stomach was churning. "Just like Violet to run away from things," she said as they walked in the warm sunshine. "I wish she'd come to us. We may have been able to find another way of dealing with Bert. As Silas says, preferably something involving the law. How did she think she'd be able to manage on her own with two young children?"

"Knowing Violet I doubt she was thinking at all," John said. "She knows what Bert's like better than any of us. We've seen the results of his drinking and bad temper, but she's experienced it. She didn't want Rose and William to suffer in the same way. Personally I don't blame her. When you're a parent you'd do anything for your kids."

"I know," Hope said, although she didn't miss the dig about her not having any children of her own. The pain felt real. There was nothing in the world she longed for more than to have children with Silas. She dreamed of the house being filled with the laughter of children, children who looked at her with Silas's striking blue eyes, seeing his features in their faces and running her fingers through hair as dark as and shiny as his. Children who'd run into her arms for comfort and love. Children whose lives she could share with the man she loved more than anything else in the world. Surely John knew that.

"She told me she'd die before she let him near William and Rose," John said. "What else could she do?"

Hope softened. She knew Violet, despite her faults, was a good mother who cared deeply for her children. She'd taken them away to protect them, but as an unmarried mother with two young children and no means of support it wouldn't be easy. But then Violet had never gone for easy had she?

Chapter Four

When they got to the end of the Promenade Gabriel pulled the car to a stop by the kerb. "I'm afraid we'll have to walk from here," he said, pulling on the brake handle. He jumped out and ran round to help Violet alight. Once she was safely deposited on the pavement he took the cap off his head and replaced it with his grey topper. "Sea View Guest House is at the other end of the Promenade but I can't drive any closer."

The children clambered out after Violet and they made their way along the narrow road between the buildings to the seafront. As they turned the corner the sea came into view. The sudden brightness was like stepping into a burst of sunshine. A brilliant new world, like a picture postcard, spread out before them. The sun blazed in a vast, cloudless sky. Music from the barrel organs playing on the pier ahead of them floated across the water on a light, salty breeze.

Violet caught her breath. It looked wonderful. Both children yelped in delight. Alongside the Promenade the sandy beach stretched for miles. Waves from the sea gently lapped the shore. Groups of people, all wearing light clothing and straw boaters, sat happily enjoying the beach. Smiling couples walked along the esplanade, sedately linking arms. Violet felt as though she'd come to paradise.

"Can we paddle, please, please," an excited Rose asked, pulling at Violet's skirt.

William didn't wait for permission. "Let's go in the sea," he yelled, dashing off towards the beach.

"William, come back at once," Violet called, but her cries fell on deaf ears.

Gabriel dropped the bags he was carrying and raced after him. With several long strides he caught up with the scampering child, scooped him up and carried his wriggling body back to Violet.

"Over exuberance I'm afraid," he said, putting William down beside his sister. "Perhaps an ice cream would cool his enthusiasm? There's a tea shop further along. It's early in the season but I think they'll be open."

None of them had eaten that day. Hunger nipped at Violet's stomach and she felt sure the children felt the same, although they never complained. The thought of a refreshing cup of tea and perhaps a scone or sandwich was irresistible. "That would be lovely," she said.

"Goody, ice cream," William said. Gabriel picked up the bags and William took his hand to walk with him to the tea shop. Walking behind them Violet noticed the ease with which he moved and his effortless charm as he nodded to the people who passed. An elderly couple came towards them. The gentleman lifted his hat in greeting and the woman smiled. Violet nodded in return. She suppressed a smile. They had obviously mistaken them for a family newly arrived from town for a seaside holiday. Violet found the thought pleasing. If only it were true, she thought.

Flowers in baskets hung outside the white painted tea shop. Inside white clothed tables filled the floor and a raised platform up a few steps. Gabriel chose a table on the platform where the sun shone in through the window and they could enjoy the view over the seafront. He ordered ice creams and small cakes for the children and pots of tea and toasted teacakes for himself and Violet. The waitress scurried off to fill the order.

"So how long are you down for?" Gabriel asked. "Is it just a holiday or something else?"

"Something else?" Violet said. "What do you mean?" The sun through the glass was making her feel hot and the attention of this handsome young man did nothing to cool that feeling.

"Well, I must admit to some curiosity," he said. "An attractive young lady arrives with two children, unaccompanied and wearing what one can only describe as clothing more suited to hill walking in Scotland than for a holiday at the beach. One can't help wondering."

He was right. The children's clothes, like hers, were chosen for durability and usefulness. Not for a holiday in the sun. She blushed, unable to think of a quick response.

Gabriel sipped his tea. "Will your husband be joining you?" he asked, his eyebrows raised and his tone one of interest. His gaze firmly fixed on the ring she wore on her wedding finger.

Violet fingered the ring. It was her mother's, given to her by John shortly after their mother died. "Best you have it," he'd said. "In the circumstances." She had no ring of her own. Oh Bert had promised her one, along with a host of other promises he never intended to keep. She later found out that his wife wore the only wedding ring he'd had cause to purchase. She'd laughed when she heard his wife had left him and gone off with a toff a few years back. Serves him right, Violet thought. She often wondered why his wife put up with his philandering, the drinking, the girls and his violent temper. Well, she'd got out and Violet wished

29

her well. She'd got out too and had no intention of going back.

"No, I'm widowed," she said.

Gabriel brightened visibly, then his brow furrowed and his face reassembled itself into a look of deep concern. "Oh I'm sorry," he said. "I know what it's like to lose someone close. Was it recent?"

Violet suppressed a smile. "Quite recent," she said, but not regretted, she thought. More like wishful thinking.

"So, a short holiday to numb the grief? You have friends who will look after you?"

Violet sighed. This was more difficult than she'd imagined. If only Hope and John were here, she thought. She missed them already. "I have family and friends, yes. Now I really must be getting on. My friend will wonder where I've got to. Thank you for the tea and ice creams, Mr Stone."

She pushed her chair back and rose to go, gathering up the children as she did so. Gabriel rose also. "I'm sorry," he said. "I didn't mean to upset you. It's really none of my business. Please sit and finish you tea. Can we start again?" He looked like a small boy who'd dropped his ice cream and didn't know how to pick it up again. "Please?"

Violet sat. This man had charm and was obviously well educated and well set up. It would be foolish beyond belief not to find out more about him. "You're forgiven," she said and smiled for the first time that day. "But enough about me, now you must tell me all about yourself. I'm afraid William will be pestering you non-stop for another ride in your motor car. It's an obsession of his."

"Oh, it's not my car. I hired it from the local garage to tour the countryside. And please, my friends call me Gabriel. I hope we will be friends."

"Gabriel?" she said. "An unusual name."

"Yes, I think my parents were hoping for an angel, but they got me instead." He smiled a smile that lit up his grey eyes and Violet's heart beat even faster.

By the time they left the tea room Violet felt she knew an awful lot about Gabriel Stone. He was on a short touring holiday around Norfolk and Suffolk. He sold furniture for a living. "Not very glamorous, I'm afraid," he'd said, "but everyone needs furniture." His family had a farm with sheep and cows. He shared William's passion for automobiles and anything mechanical. That was enough to be going on with, but she couldn't help hoping to see him again.

When they reached Sea View Guest House Violet bade him good day and thanked him for the ride in his car. "William will never stop talking about it," she said.

He stood with his hat in his hands. "Perhaps I can take you all out again?" he ventured. "It would be my pleasure. There's some lovely countryside around here and I'm sure the children would like to see the boats on the Broads."

"Yes, please," a grinning William said. "Say yes, Ma. Please."

"Well, you seem to have won them over," Violet said, not ungraciously. "I'm Violet, by the way. Violet Daniels, Mrs." That was as near the truth as she could manage. She had thought to make up a name, after all he didn't know her. She could be anybody she pleased, but then she thought of the children and realised she'd never get away with it.

"Violet. A pleasure to meet you." He bowed and lifted her hand to his lips. "Until we meet again," he said and smiled as he walked away.

Violet's heart was pumping. Not only because of the gallant gentlemen who'd just left, but also as she was hoping against hope that Nesta would still run the guest house and would remember her. They'd been good friends back when she was singing on stage with Bert. She'd seen all their up and downs and helped Violet when she decided to run home to her family, five months pregnant and with no ring on her finger. Nesta held no candle for Bert and Violet was relying on her good nature to let them stay for a while. She couldn't afford to pay much rent either.

She rang the doorbell and waited. It was nearly one o'clock and, being Sunday, Nesta would be busy changing the beds and cleaning the rooms while the guests were out. Violet held her breath.

A few minutes later she heard the sound of footsteps coming along the hall and the door opened. "Hello, Nesta," Violet said.

Nesta Roberts, a well-built woman in her early fifties and landlady of the Sea View Guest House, stared at Violet.

"Don't you remember me?" Violet said, her heart in her mouth. If they couldn't stay here she didn't know what she'd do.

Nesta's puzzled frown turned to a broad grin. "Well," she said as recognition lit up her face. "I'll go to the foot of our stairs. If it isn't The Cockney Songbird." Then she noticed the children. "And two young sprogs to boot. Well, you'd better come in. Don't stand on me doorstep like you're growing there."

Warmth flowed through Violet as she stepped into the hall. It wasn't the smartest hall she'd ever seen, several stains graced the brown wallpaper in places and the carpet appeared worn, but she immediately felt at home. Some of her happiest memories were here, in this shabby place with this down-to-earth woman who'd been like a mother to her all those years ago. If only it hadn't been for Bert.

Over a light lunch of cheese and ham with bread and jam for the children, Violet explained to Nesta about the note from Bert and running away from London on the spur of the moment.

"He always was a bad lot," Nesta said. "I knew you was in the family way, but twins? Well I never."

"I was hoping to stay for a while, until I could sort something out for the children," Violet said. "I don't know what I'll do if Bert tries to take them away from me. I'd die before I'd let him have them."

Nesta frowned. "Take them away from you? I thought he just wanted to see 'em, not that he'd be any sort of father, not with his record."

"Bert never does anything without a reason. I'm terrified he'll take them and use them for his own ends."

"I can understand 'im wanting you back with 'im in the business. You brought in more punter than 'e ever did. But why would he want them? Not his style at all. He spends his time travelling around the country. Last thing he'd want is two little 'uns tagging along."

"That's true enough, but I'm afraid he's got something in mind that won't be for the benefit of me or the children."

"Well I did hear he'd got in with a bad crowd. Some sort of dodgy stuff an all." Nesta looked perturbed then she smiled and poured Violet another cup of tea. "It's probably only rumour and gossip. You know how show people love to talk."

Violet sipped her tea, deep in thought. "I feared he was using them to get at me, or as leverage to get what he wants. I can't see him wanting me back to sing. Never did like competition when it came to performing. No. He's thinking of getting something out of my family."

Nesta's nose wrinkled. "I know your brother runs a pub, but it's not his is it? He's paying rent same as the rest of us. I shouldn't think you've enough to make it worth him trying anything on."

"You're right, I've nothing to speak of but my sister, Hope, is married to a man of wealth and position. Bert could be trying to get to him through me." She put her cup on the saucer and sat back. She remembered Hope's wedding day and the envy she'd felt as she walked down the aisle to wed Silas Quirk. He was a catch in anyone book. She recalled wondering what chance she'd have of ever wearing white and walking down the aisle into the arms of a handsome, wealthy, caring man. No chance. Not with twins born out of wedlock. They'd been six months old then and as they'd grown her love for them had grown too. Today she couldn't imagine life without them. She didn't envy Hope any longer, nor begrudge her the happiness she knew she'd found with Silas. She'd found her own happiness and didn't need anyone else's approval.

A new determination was growing inside her. "I need to see him to let him know he'll get nowt out of me and he's whistling for the moon if he thinks he'll get a brass farthing out of Silas Quirk."

Chapter Five

Sitting in Nesta's back parlour, overlooking her small back garden, brought a kaleidoscope of memories running through Violet's mind. Not just of Nesta's place but all the other boarding houses they stayed at when she was 'on the road' with Bert. Some were better than others. Nesta's was one of the best. They'd stayed in some really dreadful places but to Violet then it had seemed so glamorous. All part of the adventure and working to become a star. She had nothing but admiration for the landladies who put up with all sort of performers coming and going at all hours of the day and night, and many in various states of drunkenness. Bert wasn't the worst, not then, but from what she'd heard he probably would be now.

"Do you still take in performers from the theatre on the pier?" she asked.

Nesta nodded. "A few. I like to keep in touch. It's all changing though, the old place 'as bin done up and they want the big names now, them as stays in the better hotels. All big bands and chorus girls. I did 'ave a couple of girls stay last year. Nice girls they were, but," she sighed, "it's all different these days." She poured Violet another cup of tea.

"Can we go on the beach now?" William asked as soon as he'd finished the jam sandwiches and milk Nesta had laid out for the children.

"I expect you'll want to get washed up and change afore you go to the beach," Nesta said.

"I'm afraid we haven't much to change into," Violet said. "All we have are the clothes I could pack in their small bags. Nothing suitable for the beach I'm afraid."

"That'll never do," Nesta said. Her glance ran over Violet and the children in their unsuitable-for-the-beach clothes. "I've one or two things I've no use for that might fit you," she said. "And Mrs Jones on the corner may be able to help you out with somat for the children. She's got six kids of her own and runs a nursery for the summer visitors who want to leave their offspring for a few hours while they go shopping and haven't brought their own nursery maids or help. Her children are a bit older than yours and no doubt she'll have some cast-offs she could let you have for a few pennies."

"Thank you, that'll be a life-saver," Violet said.

"Come up and I'll show you your room, then you can sort somat out."

Nesta showed them to a room on the second floor which overlooked the beach. "You're lucky it's early in the season," she said. "I'm not yet fully booked."

The guest house had ten rooms set out on three upper floors, four rooms on the first and second floors with a small bathroom on each floor and two rooms in what would at one time have been the attic.

"You don't look after this place all on your own do you, Nesta?" Violet said, realising for the first time how much work would be involved.

"No. I have a girl comes in most days, when she remembers. She does the rooms and I do the cooking. It works out quite well." She went to a cupboard in the hall and came back with an armful of sheets and blankets. "I'm afraid you'll have to make up your own beds. It's her day off."

"That's fine," Violet said, glancing round at the one double and two single beds that almost filled what was obviously a family room. "I'm happy to help you out and do anything I can," she said. "I can't pay much…"

"Aw don't fret about that," Nesta said. "It's good to see an old friend. I'm sure I'll survive without taking owt from you."

Once Violet had unpacked their few belonging she went back downstairs. Nesta took her into a back room and opened up a wardrobe full of cast-off gowns. Violet picked out several light cotton dresses. Frilled at the front and round the neck with puffed out sleeves they were a bit dated, but Violet was glad to have them. They'd be much more suitable for the beach than the suit she'd worn for the journey. Nesta loaned her a straw bonnet too, one with flowers and ribbons on the brim. Violet put it on over her auburn curls and secured it with a hat pin. "How do I look?" she said.

Nesta grinned. "You'll do," she said.

Then she went to see Mrs Jones. When she got there she was delighted to find Mrs Jones had enough of her children's out-grown clothes to fill a small shop. Violet was able to buy at least three dresses for Rose and three shirts and shorts for William. "I keeps 'em for the summer visitors," Mrs Jones said. "You'd be surprised how many turn up with not a clue about the best thing to wear on the beach. I do a good trade an' all." She glanced at the children. "I take kids in when their parents want 'em looked after for a few hours as well. Tuppence an hour each if you're interested."

Violet smiled. "Thanks. I'll bear it in mind."

When she'd got Rose and William changed she put on one of Nesta's cotton dresses. Nesta was more heavily built and taller so her dresses were loose on Violet and skimmed her ankle but she was glad of them. "I can take them in," she said. "They'll do me a turn. I can't thank you enough."

"Keeping them kids out of Bert Shadwick's clutches will be enough thanks for me," Nesta said. "Never could stand the man."

"Thank you. You've been a treasure," she said to Nesta, "just as I knew you would be."

Nesta blushed. "Aw, get away with you twernt nowt." But Violet could see how pleased she was.

It was mid afternoon by the time Violet took the children to the beach. Walking along the sun drenched promenade warmth enveloped them. They'd all changed into lighter clothes and Violet felt her heart grow lighter too. It was as though she'd left her troubles behind in the grime and sweat of London and come to a magical place where all things were possible. She bought the children a bucket and spade each so they could build sandcastles or collect shells. She hired a deckchair for herself.

Sitting watching the children playing in the sand she couldn't prevent a smile touching her lips. They were a million miles away from London and Bert Shadwick. The note, the thought of him taking the children, all faded into the recess of her mind.

Looking around she saw that various cafes and bars lined the promenade. She had experience working in the bar. If she got herself a job she could afford to pay Nesta rent and they could stay here forever. She sighed at the thought. Could she really leave her family and friends behind and start again in a new place? The idea was very tempting.

By the time the children had been in the sea, built their sandcastles and knocked them down, they were both covered in sand but didn't seem to mind. She decided to take them on the pier, the place that held so many memories. They wouldn't go along to the theatre at the end, she didn't want to be recognised, but she bought them each an ice cream and paid for them to go on one of the rides. Then they stood at the railings watching the tide come in. Memories of the times she stayed there with Bert in the early days ran through her mind, but she pushed them away. This was a new start.

They took a turn around the town to see what shops there were, then made their way back to the guest house for tea. The children were tired but happier than she ever seen them. Perhaps this was the beginning of a new life for them all, she thought.

After tea the children played with their toys on the floor until Violet put them to bed, sleepy but happy.

"I like it here," William said. "Can we stay forever?"

"We'll have to see," Violet said, although she knew it was an impossible dream.

Later that evening Nesta and Violet sat on the veranda at the front of the building, looking out over the promenade. Violet sighed. "I wish I could stay here forever," she said. "But I can't. The money I have won't last long. I need to find a job and a way of making a living for me and the children."

"Aye," Nesta said. "Holidays are like that. They make you wonder why you do it all. But you've responsibilities now. You'll need to find your way."

A light breeze caressed Violet's face, blowing tendrils of auburn hair across her cheeks. She'd never felt so at home and settled. If only I'd never met Bert

Shadwick, she thought. But then realised she wouldn't have been to as many places, met as many people or had the children and that would be a greater loss than she could bear.

"Have you ever thought about going back to the singing?" Nesta said. "You were good. You'd get back to it in an instant. 'Course you'd need some new material…"

Nesta gasped as though hit by a sudden thought. She jumped up and ran inside to the heavy mahogany sideboard. A few minutes of foraging and she brought over a pile of papers. "Have a look at these," she said with a wide grin on her face.

Violet stretched out the papers on the table in front of her. Nesta had saved every poster from the theatre over the last ten years. She rummaged through and found one from six years ago. There she was, well, her name anyway *The Cockney Songbird*, and there was Bert, *The Magnificent Merlin, Master of Magic and Mystery*. His fresh face, sparkling blue eyes and radiant smile stared out at her, just the way she remembered. A curl of blond hair flopped over his forehead, making him look more like a freshly scrubbed, innocent schoolboy than ever.

Nesta watched her. "Aye, a looker then weren't he? That face wouldn't be out o' place on a cherub," she said. "He could charm the birds out o' the trees, he could." She sighed. "An' charmed a more 'an a few lasses into 'is bed."

Violet blushed.

"Fallen angels I used to call 'em, them what fell for 'is charms. I think he saw their innocence as a challenge. Never could resist a challenge could Bert."

A misty look came over Violet. "Strange how the past comes back to haunt you," she said. "Feelings you thought were dead and buried can rise up inside you and leave you breathless."

Nesta gasped. "You don't mean you still have feelings for Bert?"

"No, of course not, but I miss the glamour of being on stage, the anticipation, then the thrill of the audience. It wasn't all bad you know. In the beginning it was…"

"Didn't last though did it? Never does. Best to keep it as a once fond memory."

Violet pushed the posters to one side. "Looks a bit different now," she said. "Time hasn't been good to him and it shows."

"That'll be booze. Never could resist it either. Late nights and penny ices. Gets 'em every time."

Violet sat back and sipped her tea which had gone quite cold. "I expect you've seen it all, haven't you, Nesta. The ones who go up in the world and the ones who fall down."

Nesta nodded. "Aye lass. Seen it all. Them were the good old days."

"Do you miss it, the thrill of being on stage?" Violet looked at Nesta. She was still a good looking woman. "You must have been quite something in your day," she said.

Nesta blushed with pleasure then laughed. "Don't be so cheeky – in my day indeed. I can still stir a few hearts if I puts me mind to it."

Violet didn't doubt it. Nesta had a presence about her and a quality you never lose. She'd sung in the Music Halls and could hold an audience enthralled with her voice. Memories filed through Violet's brain as they spent a good couple of hours reminiscing. They laughed, they cried, they had more tea and then they put the children to bed.

Over a nightcap Nesta came back to the subject of Violet taking up singing again.

Violet laughed. "Me appearing at the end of the pier? No surer way for Bert to find me." She paused. "No. I need to do something entirely different. Somewhere he won't think of looking."

The next morning after a breakfast of bacon, eggs, tomatoes, bread and honey, payment for which Nesta waved away when Violet offered, Violet said she'd go into town and look for a summer job. "There must be places looking for staff," she said. "A cafe or something where I can put in a few hours."

"And the children?"

Violet's stomach churned. She needed to work to earn money for their keep, but it was going to be more difficult than she'd thought. "I was hoping…"

Nesta smiled. "All right, I'll keep an eye on 'em this morning, they can help with the beds and sweeping, but only till lunchtime."

Violet jumped up and kissed her cheek. "Thanks, Nesta, you're a treasure."

"Aye, like the Elgin Marbles, only older," she said with a chuckle.

The day was warm although slightly overcast with pearly clouds scattered across the summer sky. "It'll clear later," Nesta said glancing out.

"Beach this afternoon then," Violet said to the children who were anxious to get out. She was putting her bonnet on when there came a knocking at the door.

"I'll go," she said, hoping it wasn't customers for Nesta which would mean she'd have to stay until they were settled in. Nesta wouldn't want the children hanging around while she booked new customers in. Her jaw dropped with surprise when she saw Gabriel Stone standing on the doorstep.

Chapter Six

Mid-morning on Monday Hope was getting ready for her afternoon visit to see her friend Margaret Taylor. They were fund-raising for a school for girls they wanted to set up. They intended the school to teach the sort of skills the pupils would need if they were to have any chance of making a good living. Most of the local girls came from the poorest families and she often despaired what the future might hold for them. Both Hope and Margaret were strong advocates for the education of the fairer sex and couldn't understand why they weren't taught business and accounting skills alongside the boys. They would also include shorthand and typing skills so the girls could work in offices rather than in the sweatshops that passed for factories.

She heard a rumpus downstairs but thought it might be a delivery boy causing a commotion. Daisy's raised voice reached her ears followed by the sound of footsteps pounding up the stairs. She caught her breath and jumped up when Bert Shadwick burst into the room with an anxious Daisy in his wake.

"I'm sorry," Daisy said. "He pushed past me. I tried to stop him."

"It's all right, Daisy," Hope said, regaining her composure. "Has Mr Quirk left yet?"

"A few minutes ago," Daisy said.

Hope forced a smile. Dealing with an angry Bert Shadwick alone was not a prospect she relished. From the way he treated Violet she knew he'd have no hesitation in punching her or slapping her if she annoyed him. He couldn't hold his temper and the fact she was a woman would make no difference. She wished Silas was still there but there was nothing she could do about it.

"Thank you, that'll be all," she said.

Daisy reluctantly withdrew, but Hope felt sure she'd be lurking in the hall outside, in case she was needed.

"Where's Violet and my children?" Bert said, before she could draw breath to ask what he wanted, pushing his way into her house uninvited.

As he spoke a vision of how Bert used to be flashed through Hope's mind. He looked more dashing then, with a boyish charm that had turned Violet's head. He'd always taken care of his appearance too. Now his coat appeared dated, less well pressed and his shoes more scuffed and shabby. His hair was slightly unkempt and dark stubble shadowed his chin. Fortune had not been kind to him. He'd gone down in the world, while she was painfully aware that she'd gone up. She recalled the day they'd all sat in the ambulance on the way to hospital the day her Pa… Tears stung her eyes at the memory. She'd sat with Violet, John, Bert and Silas. Bert had looked after Violet and she remembered hoping he'd care for her. A very different Bert stood before her today.

"I've been to the pub. She's not there. Gone they told me. Gone where? I thought you'd know, you being so close an all."

"You've been to the Hope and Anchor? I can only imagine the sort of reception you got there."

Bert shrugged. His eyes narrowed. "Saw some blousy old woman who smelled of fish and boiled cabbage. She told me Violet had gone."

45

Hope guessed he meant Elsie, the cook. Had John seen him he'd likely be sporting a few bruises and would have been warned off coming to see Hope.

"So then, you decided to come and harangue me because the girl you put in the family way is no longer at your disposal? How dare you?" Hope felt rage rising up inside her. She didn't blame Violet for running away from this vile little man. She should never have got involved with him in the first place, although there was no telling Violet. She recalled how she'd tried to stop her going away with him when Ma lay on her deathbed in hospital, but Violet never listened. Always a dreamer, naive and foolish, Violet gave her heart away so easily and then expressed surprise when it was broken and her dreams turned to ashes. Hope would do everything in her power to make sure she didn't fall into Bert's clutches again, especially as Violet's children were involved. Children she loved as dearly as if they were her own.

Bert's demeanour became conciliatory. "Aw, come on, Hope," he said, turning the hat he carried in his hands. "You know me. Sure I sometimes let me anger get out of hand, but I only ever wanted the best for Violet. An' I didn't know about the twins, not till recently. I only want to see 'em. They are my children, you can't deny that."

"Children you wouldn't have had if you'd had your way and Violet had 'got rid' as you suggested," she said. "Children who are five years old, have a family, a home and a future all no thanks to you. It's a bit late now to come and play the caring father, don't you think?"

Bert's face twisted into a sly grin. "If I didn't know you better, Hope Quirk," he said, "I'd think you

46

was after having them children for your own. From what I hear you and your fancy-pants husband ain't been able to have any." He stepped so close that Hope felt his breath on her face. His eyes burned with hate. "When I get 'em, and I will, it'll be a cold day in hell afore you ever set eyes on 'em again. You dried up old sow."

Hope gasped. Uncontrollable fury raged through her. Her immediate reaction was to slap his leering face. She raised her hand. He grabbed her arm and pushed her away. Reeling backward she fell and, turning, hit her head on the corner of the table.

The last thing she heard before she passed out was a mighty roar as Silas entered the room, grabbed Bert by the shoulders and marched him out, throwing him out of the front door into the gutter.

When she came round she found Silas bending over holding her while he bathed a wound on her forehead. "Oh my darling," he said as she opened her eyes. "Thank God you're all right."

Hope tried to sit up. She felt dizzy so closed her eyes and sank back into his arms taking comfort in his broad shoulders supporting her.

"Daisy, send for Doctor Matthews," Silas said to the girl hovering at the edge of Hope's vision.

"No. Please. Don't make a fuss," Hope said. "I'll be fine in a moment. It's only a bump. It'll heal."

"He could have killed you," Silas said. "I've a good mind to call the police."

"No. No. Please don't," Hope said. "I'll be fine."

After a few minutes the dizziness passed. Her head throbbed a little but she felt a lot better. "I'm afraid I was angry about Bert coming here. He was looking for Violet," she said.

"I've thrown that bastard out. If he ever comes here again I'll have the law on him." Silas's face was granite, but softened when he looked at Hope. His eyes filled with tenderness as he stroked her cheek. "Are you sure you're all right. I could fetch Doctor Matthews in a moment."

"No, really. I'll be fine in a minute or two. Just need to get my breath." She realised that she'd let Bert get the better of her and that made her madder than ever. Silas helped her into a chair.

"I'm more relieved than I can say that you were here," she said. "I thought you'd already left."

He smiled. "I had. I'd got to the end of the road with Abel when Daisy came running after me. When she told me what had happened…" he shook his head. "I can't leave you alone can I? I fear we'll just have to spend every minute together so I can take care of you." He stroked her cheek again.

Hope laughed, which made the pain in her head worse. "Oh don't," she said. "I'm quite capable of taking care of myself. He just caught me off balance. It was an accident." She paused. Then decided to tell Silas the truth. "I tried to slap him. He caught my hand and pushed back. It was my fault. I'll know better next time." She grinned. "Next time I'll hit him with something stronger and heavier than my hand."

Silas shook his head and kissed her. "I'm not sure you're safe to be left alone," he said. "But I doubt he'll have the nerve to come back. Still, I could leave Abel with you if you like."

Abel was Silas's manservant. Although only fifteen he'd been with Silas since he was seven years old and so devoted to him he never left his side, unless Silas insisted.

"No. I'm going out anyway, to meet Margaret, and I'm not sure the ladies in Burton's Cafe and Tea Rooms would appreciate Abel's presence." Even as she said it she knew it wasn't true. The ladies would be delighted to oggle Abel with his muscular build, dark skin and exotic look, but Abel might not enjoy it quite so much.

"If you're sure."

"I'm sure."

Later, when she met Margaret for tea, Margaret noticed the cut and darkening bruise on Hope's forehead, so she had to tell her about Bert's visit.

"He sounds like a terrible man," Margaret said. "What on earth did Violet see in him?"

"He promised he'd make her a star. She was very young."

"He's shown no interest in the children before. What on earth can he want with them now?"

"Spite," Hope said. "Pure spite. I'm afraid he hit a nerve when he said about not having any children of my own."

Margaret nodded. She'd been friends with Hope for many years and they had no secrets between them. Margaret had been there when Violet's twins were born and knew how deeply Hope cared for them and how much she longed for children of her own.

"In that case I hope he rots in hell before he ever gets hold of them," Margaret said, which was strong condemnation coming from Margaret who always saw the best in people.

Chapter Seven

Seeing him standing there all Violet's good intentions flew out of her brain like a flock of migrating swallows.

"I was wondering if you and the children would care for a ride out into the countryside," he said. "It promises to be a beautiful day, too nice to be spending it indoors."

"Yes please. Yes, yes, say yes please, Ma." An excited William had appeared at Violet's side, tugging her skirt and jumping up and down.

"I take it you know this young man," Nesta said, her brow puckered.

"We met yesterday," Violet said. "He was kind enough to give us a lift from the station in his motor car." She turned to Gabriel. "Although I must say I didn't expect to see you again so soon."

"Time and tide wait for no man," he said, "and I was hoping we could become better acquainted." His grey eyes sparkled and Violet's heart stuttered. She glanced at Nesta.

"Go on," Nesta said. "Man's right, time and tide…"

William whooped and rushed to get his coat. "You'll both need your warmest clothes," Violet warned, recalling how cold it was in the open-topped car.

"I can put the hood up if it's too cold," Gabriel said, his face filled with concern.

"Thank you, we'll be fine," Violet said. The clothes they'd arrived in were heavier than the summer ones she'd bought from Mrs Jones so she got the children changed before they set out.

Bowling along country lanes in the Wolseley with Gabriel, Violet saw a different life to the one she was used to. The open roads, bare of traffic, the fields and trees they passed and the freshness of the air that put roses in all their cheeks, a very different world from the grimy streets of London.

The children bounced with joy as they sped along, past picturesque villages and breathtaking scenery. But that wasn't all Violet was watching. Although Gabriel said he worked selling furniture his hands were soft. Gentleman's hands Ma would have called them. "You can always judge a man by his hands," Ma used to say.

She also noticed his manners, his quiet confidence and his easy charm. There wasn't much opportunity for conversation as they drove along, the wind whipping the words from their lips, but he stopped at various places along the route so they could admire the view, explaining to the children what they saw, how the windmills worked and how they came to be built there. He told them about the birds that flew over the coastline. For a while she could forget about Bert and his threats and lose herself in the promise of a different life.

Mid-morning they stopped at one of the villages and found a tea shop where he bought tea and scones for himself and Violet, and apples and lemonade for the children.

"That's very kind of you," Violet said, aware that this was the second time she'd relied upon his generosity to feed Rose and William.

"Not at all," he said. "I enjoy their company... and yours." The twinkle in his eyes made Violet's heart leap again. Warmth flowed through her as she relished being in such well-educated and intelligent company. Very different from the men who frequented the Hope and Anchor. The shopkeepers and their wives were all right, she even liked the costers with their heart of gold, but they paled in comparison to Gabriel Stone, who was as dashing as they were dull. It's about time I had a bit of excitement in my life, Violet thought.

"I see you've had a good time," Nesta said when they returned.

"It was wonderful," Violet said. "I'd forgotten how to have a good time and what fun it could be when you have a man on your arm."

"Oh aye? Getting a bit carried away aren't we? You hardly know 'im. Best not to go getting ideas about 'im. To 'im it's no more 'an a holiday fling he's after. An' a bit more'n that without any commitment if I know men, and I do an' all."

Violet's face fell. "Gabriel's not like that," she said. "He's different."

Nesta's eyebrows rose. "Oh aye, different is 'e. If you asks me they're all the same. I mean, what do you know about him? Really know?"

"I know a lot about him." Violet was defiant.

"Only what's he's told you. You don't know 'is friends, who he goes around with, his family. I'd be very careful if I were you."

Well, you're not me, Violet thought but said, "Oh Nesta, I know you have my interests at heart, but I do know what I'm doing. It's just a pleasant friendship and a bit of light relief for me, but it's good for the children too, to have a man around. Something they sorely miss, with John being so busy with the pub and not having a father." Despite her protestations Violet

52

knew Nesta was right. She minded more about Gabriel and his opinions than she'd care to admit and she really did know very little about him.

"Hmm." Nesta grimaced. "Talking of which, what are you going to do about Bert?"

"If Bert says he wants to take the children from me you can bet that's not what he's after. He's no interest in them. He'll be using them to get at me." Her jaw clenched as she thought about what Bert might be intending to do. She had no doubt he had a mean side to him, she'd seen it often enough. Still, she was stronger now and could face up to him if she had to, especially if the future of her children was in question. It was true what John had said, running away never solved anything. "I suppose I'll have to go and see him sometime and sort things out," she said. "but the children are having such a good time. I'm always going to put them first. He'll have to stew for a while."

Violet could see from Nesta's face that she knew the children weren't the only ones having a good time. "Don't leave it too long," she said. "You can leave 'em with me for a couple of days when you're ready, I don't get busy for a while yet, but once the season starts proper – well, that's a different matter."

Violet nodded. "I quite understand and I'm very grateful."

That evening, when the children were in bed, she went out to find work. The first few places she tried had no vacancies. When she asked they'd smile and say "Try next door." Heavy hearted, she walked into The Tivoli Bar. Customers pressed up to the counter shouting out their orders to a harassed, thick set man in shirt-sleeves doing his best to serve them. Looking round she saw empty glasses on tables and ashtrays overflowing. She gathered up the empty glasses and carried them to the end of the bar. Then she picked up a waste bin and went round emptying the ashtrays, chatting to the customers as she did so. When she took the waste bin back she called out to the barman, who was pulling a pint, "Need any help?"

"You done bar work afore?" he asked.

"For many years," she said.

He paused to look her over. She guessed he was the proprietor. Thin wisps of grey hair surrounded a jovial face which lit up with a smile. He put the pint he'd pulled onto the bar. "Come in," he said walking over to lift the hatch. He put his hand out. "I'm Al," he said.

"Violet." She shook his hand.

"Welcome," he said. Then he ran through the prices calling them out as he walked along the bar. They were much higher than the prices in the Hope and Anchor, but Violet supposed that people on holiday don't mind paying a bit extra for their pleasures.

He watched her as she served the first few customers. When the crush up to the bar lulled she told him she was looking for evening work.

"Two shillings a night plus tips," he said. "Extra on Sundays."

Violet smiled. Fourteen shillings a week would mean she could pay Nesta for their room and have some to spare. It wouldn't be much, but it was enough to be going on with and her days would be free to spend with the children. Often the holidaymakers, in jovial mood, would leave tips that helped to increase her income.

Every day for the next two weeks, Gabriel arrived on the doorstep ready to take her and the children out.

He'd suggest a drive out in the car to visit a farm, a museum or to see the boats. He seemed to know the area well and Violet happily went along with his suggestions. Wherever they went he'd buy them lunch and treat them to sweets or little toys.

Afternoons she'd take the children to the beach and he'd go along too. He'd remove his shoes and socks and paddle with William, help Rose collect shells and wash the sand off William's feet with a bucket of water when he got too sandy. Violet was enthralled. She'd never known men like that existed and wished her pa had been more like Gabriel. She couldn't imagine him washing their feet no matter how dirty they got. They had picnics, they went on the pier where he treated them to ice creams and rides on the carousel or helter-skelter, and Violet would tell Nesta how wonderful it all was, much to Nesta's dismay.

"Don't seem right," she'd say. "You're spending so much time with 'im. And what about the children? Young William's totally enthralled by 'im. What's going to 'appen when 'is 'oliday's over? You'll wake up one morning an' 'e'll be gone, taking somat of yourn along with 'im, no doubt. What you going to do then?"

Violet knew Nesta meant he'd be taking her heart with him, but she wasn't about to admit she'd lost it so easily. "William's enthralled because they share a passion for motor cars and machines," she said. "Gabriel's going to take him to a rally. There'll be lots of cars to look at, that's why he's so excited. Where would he get an opportunity like that in London?"

The thought of trooping through muddy fields looking at cars horrified Violet, but spending time with Gabriel would make it bearable.

Every evening they returned to the guest house in time for tea and for Violet to put the children to bed. They'd be bubbling with excitement talking about their day and what they were planning for tomorrow. It was a special time and Violet loved it. Once they were safely tucked up she'd go to her job secure in the knowledge that Nesta would look after them. She didn't earn much so the treats and outings Gabriel provided made everything more exciting.

Spending time with her children away from the pub and her everyday worries awakened a sense of wonder within her. Getting to know them, each separate individuals with their own likes and dislikes, their own view of the world and their different personalities was a revelation. William was so much like his father, but the good side of him. The side that was cute, cheeky and made her laugh until her sides ached. He could be a charmer too, when it suited him. Rose on the other hand was the epitome of Violet's mother. Caring, practical and undemanding. She'd fit in with William and adored him, letting him lead her into the sort of mischief she'd never dream of getting into by herself.

Sometime she worried that Nesta was right. She was spending too much time with Gabriel. "I'm sure you have other things to do," she said. "Selling your furniture, or whatever it is you do," and he'd laugh and say that he was on holiday and spending time with her and her children was much more fun than spending it alone.

When she asked him about his work or his family or how come he knew so much about the countryside he'd laugh, shrug his shoulders and say, "I just pick things up."

"Like lost young ladies?"

He laughed again. "Not as a rule," he said. "But I'm not sorry I did on one particular occasion." Mirth danced in his eyes. Then he changed the subject and she went along with whatever he suggested they did next.

As the days passed she found she looked forward more and more to seeing him. Wherever they went she'd take his arm as they walked along, looking to the outside world as though they were the perfect couple, or at least that's how Violet saw it. He was attentive too. It gave her a comfortable feeling of belonging, a feeling she could easily get used to.

One afternoon a lady in the cafe where she went to fetch drinks for the children commented saying, "What a handsome family you have." Violet almost burst with pride. "Yes," she replied, "I'm very fortunate." The thought stayed with her for the rest of the day.

Gabriel was a gentleman too. He never took advantage of her, or suggested anything improper. She felt relaxed in his company. He made her laugh and she enjoyed their animated conversations. It was a long time since she'd had such stimulating company and she wasn't about to give it up in a hurry. If only life could always be like this, she thought after one particularly pleasant outing.

One night she was walking back to the guest house after her evening shift at the pub, thinking about nothing in particular, when her problems were brought sharply into focus. A man walking ahead of her looked, from the back, exactly like Bert Shadwick. He wore a striped blazer and straw boater and strode along as though the world owed him a living, just like Bert.

She caught her breath. If he was here he'd soon find her. He only had to go into the bars along the front and he'd soon walk into The Tivoli. Her heart raced. The memory of the note he'd left ran through her mind and the fury she'd felt then fired up inside her again. She'd tell him exactly what he could do if he thought he could ever take her children from her.

She marched up to the man, grabbed his shoulder and spun him around.

A startled stranger stared back at her. The surprise on his face turned to fear and then anger. "What the—"

"Oh sorry," she said. "I thought you were somebody else."

She brushed his collar down, and with her heart still pumping, backed away. "So sorry," she repeated. "Sorry to trouble you."

The encounter shook her. If it had been Bert she was ready to face him, find out what he was really after. She was no longer afraid of him. Perhaps it was time she returned to London.

The next morning, over breakfast, she told Nesta of her plan. "I'll only be away a couple of days," she said.

"What about us?" William said. "Who's going to look after us?"

"I'll be looking after you," Nesta said. "You can 'elp out around the place."

William's face fell. "What about the beach and going on the pier?"

Nesta ruffled his curls. "I dare say these old legs of mine could manage a walk to the beach now an' then," she said, "an' tea on the pier has always been a treat."

"That's all right then," William said his attention going back to his fried egg on toast.

Violet laughed. "I have your permission then?"

He nodded.

"If you're going home can you bring me some of dolly's clothes," Rose asked. Rose spent a great deal of time dressing and undressing her favourite doll. "I forgot to bring them." Sadness filled her little face.

"I'll see what I can do," Violet said. "If I can't find them we'll go out a buy some material to make new."

Rose beamed.

"What about your young man?" Nesta asked, refusing to use his name as a sign of her disapproval.

"His hotel is on the way to the station. I'll pop in and leave him a message. I need to let Al know too. She hugged the children and kissed them goodbye, admonishing them once again to, "be good and don't cause Mrs Roberts any trouble."

"We won't," William said. Violet wished she could believe him. She left Hope's address in case Nesta needed to contact her. She didn't need to call in at Gabriel's hotel as she ran into him on the way and he insisted on seeing her safely onto the train. "Come back soon," he called as the train pulled out of the station.

Chapter Eight

Hope put the last letter asking for support for the school for girls that she and Margaret were planning into the envelope. She'd spent the morning in the small office she shared with Silas catching up with her correspondence while he dealt with accounts from the club he owned. Having worked at the club she was familiar with the paperwork and staff management and he would often refer to her or ask her opinion on particular matters. These days she only visited The Grenadier if there were new staff to interview or be trained but she enjoyed feeling part of it.

"Do you want me to take those to the post office?" Silas asked. "I can go that way."

"No, thank you," Hope said. "I'll take them. It's a nice day so I'm planning to go for a walk along by the river and I need to call into the market for some more silks for my embroidery." An expert needlewoman, Hope produced the most exquisitely delicate stitchery. Before her marriage to Silas she had worked on commissions for the local drapery store as a way of making money. These days she only did it for pleasure or as personal gifts for her friends.

"As you wish," he said, finishing his coffee.

He gathered up his papers ready to leave when Hope heard knocking at the front door. A few minutes later Violet burst into the room. They both glanced up at the sudden intrusion.

"Violet!" Hope jumped up and ran to embrace her sister. "I'm so happy to see you." Violet's face was flushed and her breathing uneven as though she'd come up the stairs in a hurry. "Are you all right? Where on earth have you been?" she glanced around. "And where are the children?"

Violet kissed her cheek. She took a breath which seemed to calm her. "Good to see you too, sister," she said. "I'm sorry to have left so abruptly, but no doubt you've heard about Bert's latest attempt to ruin my life."

"I think we'd like some tea, Daisy," Hope said to the girl hovering at the door halfway between apologising for letting Violet push past her and wanting to stay to find out what all the fuss was about. "In the drawing room, I think."

She ushered Violet through into the front room overlooking the river. "I think we'll be more comfortable in here," she said.

Silas followed them.

In the drawing room Violet sank down into one of Hope's cream brocade covered armchairs. "The children are safe, somewhere Bert won't find them. I left them with a good friend."

Hope sat on the wide settee. Silas took the other chair. They exchanged glances. Hope nodded. "John told us about the note Bert left for you," she said. "I can see you saw it as some kind of a threat."

"Yes. A threat to take my children away from me." Violet's face crumpled at the thought. "That's why I took them away, but I can't live the rest of my life looking over my shoulder so I came back to find Bert and sort out this nonsense once and for all."

Daisy arrived with the tea. Hope thanked her and she withdrew.

"I need to find out what he really wants," Violet said. "I can't believe he actually intends to take Rose and William on and care for them as part of his family. It's ridiculous."

"Have you any news of him?" Silas asked bending forward in the chair, his eyes keen with interest.

"I went to his lodgings. The place we stayed at when I first went away with him." She had the grace to look shamefaced. "His landlady said she hadn't seen him for a couple of days. Said I should try the theatre. I went there, but they haven't seen him either. They said that since his wife left him he's been a bit of a nomad. Never staying in one place for long. They don't know how to get in touch with him. I wondered whether he'd been here to see you, or if you'd any news of his whereabouts."

"He did come here," Hope said. "It was the day after you left. He was looking for you."

"I threw him out," Silas said, taking the tea Hope handed him.

"I can't think of any reason he'd want the bothersome burden of two young children hanging around him," Violet said. "Not his style at all. Footloose and fancy free that's Bert." She took the tea Hope handed her. "He'll be after money. From what I hear he's down on his luck and he'll be using the threat of taking the children to refill his coffers." She sipped her tea.

Silence and apprehension hung in the air. Hope bit her lips unable to voice the thoughts running through her head.

Eventually Silas spoke. "There may be another reason," he said.

"Such as?"

He shrugged. "I don't know for sure, it's only the sort of talk you get around the rat pit from the gamblers there, but they're saying he's gone into a more disreputable business than even they aspire to."

Hope noticed the flash of steel beneath the soft veneer of his voice. She knew it was there but wondered if Violet had noticed it too.

Violet frowned. "What sort of disreputable business? I know he'd do anything for money, especially if he's as desperate as I've heard, with people chasing him to repay his debts, but…"

"The talk around the rat pits is that he's fallen in with a bad crowd." Silas looked as discomforted as Hope had ever seen him.

"What do you mean a bad crowd?"

He glanced at Hope as though wondering if he should say what he'd heard.

"Well?" Violet tapped her fingers impatiently.

"We all know there are men ready to do anything for money and men with money who will pay well to have their deviant fantasies indulged." He paused and took a deep breath before carrying on. "Often children are involved," he said.

The blood drained from Violet's face. Hope saw the inference taking root in Violet's mind. Everyone knew what went on but no one ever spoke of it. Violet's eyes widened as the realisation dawned. She shrieked, "No – not Bert. Bert wouldn't do that – not with his own children!"

"Children he didn't want," Hope reminded her. "They exploit the urchins and ragamuffins they pick up from the streets. Bert may think he'd get more for well-fed children from a good family."

Violet put her hands over her ears, shaking her head. Her whole body started to tremble. "No. No. I won't listen anymore. I won't believe it. Bert wouldn't sink that low. Sure he's a liar, swindler and crook who'd sell his own mother if there was money it – but his children – my children."

Silas tried to reassure her. "Like I said. We have no evidence. It's only rumour and gossip. But there's no smoke…"

"Bert wouldn't do that. Not the Bert I knew. If he's after the children it'll be for money. I'll go and see him. Find out exactly what it is he thinks he can get out of us and let him know once and for all that he's getting nowt." Violet turned on Hope. "How you can bear to live with a man who has such terrible ideas and so little regard for his fellow men I don't know." She glared at Silas. "Shame on you both for having such terrible thoughts." Then she jumped up and, with a rustle of skirts, stormed out.

"What was that all about?" a bewildered Silas asked.

"I haven't a clue," Hope said, but recalled that Violet storming out had been a regular feature of their years growing up together.

"Should I go after her?" he asked. His brow furrowed and concern filled his face.

"No. It's just Violet doing what she always does when she can't face things, but I'm worried about her. You don't think she still has feelings for Bert do you?"

Silas shrugged. "Hard to imagine after the way he treated her, but the ways of women have long been a mystery to me. Are you sure you don't want me to go after her. See she's all right?" He put his cup down and stood up.

Hope shook her head. "No. Once Violet gets an idea in her head it'll take a mountain of dynamite to shift it," she said. "She'll be back when she's calmed down." She frowned. "It must have come as a shock. What we said. A horrible shock."

Silas nodded. "It'd be a shock for anyone." He paused and looked at Hope, fear in his eyes. "Will you be all right? I mean if she comes back?"

"I'll be fine. I can handle Violet."

"But if Bert hears she's back in town looking for him?"

"You mean he may come here? Not if he remembers the last time he called." Hope smiled as a swell of love for this man she'd married washed over her. Ruthless in business and when it came to looking after his own family, but hopeless when it came to women.

"If you need me I'll be at the club," he said. "I'll leave Abel here with you. You may have need of him if Bert does decide to call." He pulled her into his arms, kissed and held her close for several minutes. "I wish I could stay and protect you," he said.

"Knowing you're my husband and you love me is all the protection I need," she said, but when he left part of her went with him.

Chapter Nine

Outside Violet felt sick. Tears welled up in her eyes. She knew about the trade in photographs, postcards and films that went on under the counter in small scruffy shops in the city and the men who frequented the bars and pubs where they could get hold of such abhorrent items and about men who wanted more than just to look. She'd never suspected Bert of any interest or involvement in such a repugnant trade. Still, if money was short –would he forget his moral duty, put aside his inhibitions and try it? She wasn't sure. He may have the face of an angel, but that impression was far from the truth. It had been a long time since she'd last seen him. Anything could have happened to him. Time and circumstances change people, she knew that.

Her heart hardened as she strode along hardly aware of where she was going. A sharp breeze from the river made her shiver in the afternoon sunshine. As she thought about what Silas had said her jaw clenched and her hands curled into fists. Bert had never shown any inclination to become involved in any sort of sordid trade. He was a performer who valued his reputation. If it ever got out that he'd even thought about what they were suggesting… No. They were wrong. Bert may be unscrupulous when it came to cards and con tricks, but he'd never enter into any arrangement that would soil his reputation or hint at his being anything more than a family entertainer. His life and his business depended upon it.

Having got that clear in her mind she stopped and glanced around. She'd been walking fast, with no particular destination in mind, simply trying to put as much distance as she could between herself and the cruel things Silas had been suggesting, but no matter how fast she walked the thoughts kept running through her mind. Now she'd stopped she was surprised to find that her footsteps were leading her towards the Hope and Anchor, the pub she'd grown up in and the only real home she'd ever known.

The bar bustled with activity when she walked in. Several men from the market stood at the bar and others sat at tables, reading the paper or sorting out their day's takings. Alice, behind the bar, saw her first. She looked up from serving a thickset, bulky man Violet recognised as the local fishmonger. The smell of fish permeated the air around him. He nodded to her as she passed.

"Violet," Alice cried. Her eyes lit up and her face cleared as though the sun had come out from behind a dark cloud. She lifted the hatch to let Violet through to the back of the bar. "Come through," she said. "John's in his office. He'll be glad to see you. I know he's been worried sick." She glanced around. "Have you brought the children home? Where are they? Are they alright?"

"I've come alone," Violet said. "I just wanted to sort things out with Bert. Find out what he's after. Has he been here? Have you seen him?"

Alice shook her head. "No. And I don't expect to. I'm sure he knows what John thinks of him and what would happen if he showed his face in here." She glanced around the bar at the group of men who'd gathered to watch Violet and see what was happening. She got the distinct impression that they'd be happy to pitch in and give Bert a good hiding if he was stupid enough to turn up.

She smiled. It was good to know the family had such support from their neighbours. Ever since she could remember, even as a child, she felt safe here and she knew her parents were well liked and respected by their customers. It was a good feeling to be home, if only it wasn't for the threat of Bert coming and spoiling everything, just as he always did.

John was just as pleased to see her as Hope had been. He rose from behind the desk where he'd been going over some paperwork and greeted her warmly. Then he stood back holding her at arm's length while his gaze wandered over her. She was wearing one of Nesta's old dresses under a tight-fitting brown corded jacket. The cream cambric skirt brushed the tops of her brown boots and the brim of her straw hat carried bunches of brown and cream roses. Although the style was dated it suited her.

"Well," John said, his eyes shining with approval. "You look a lot better than I expected. Still, you always were a survivor. How are Rose and William? I take it you haven't brought them with you?"

"No, I've left them with a friend."

"Can I get you anything?" Alice asked, hovering in the doorway. "Tea or something to eat? Elsie hasn't left yet."

Violet smiled. "A large gin would be good," she said.

Alice glanced at John to get his approval before she went to get it.

Violet noticed and said, "Believe me I need something after what I've just heard."

John nodded and Alice scurried out.

John pulled up a chair for Violet and Alice returned with a large gin which she placed on the desk in front of Violet before going back to the bar.

Violet took several sips, its sharp, bracing taste flowing through her like iced water on a hot summer day. Once she'd had time to compose herself and rearrange her thoughts, she told John about going to Bert's lodgings and then to the theatre, not finding him so going to see Hope and Silas in case they might know of his whereabouts.

"And did they?" John asked her.

She swallowed another gulp of the reviving drink. "Regrettably no," she said, although she felt sure John already knew the answer to the question. "But Silas did enlighten me about the most scurrilous accusations flying around among the nastiest of the alleged gentlemen who frequent that den of iniquity he calls a gentlemen's club."

John smothered a smile. It was clear he'd already heard the 'scurrilous accusations'. "Come now, Violet," he said. "You've changed your tune. There was a time you hankered after a job at that 'den of iniquity' and if my memory serves me the owner of the said establishment."

Violet blushed. Although accurate, John's remarks didn't quell her anger. "When I was young and foolish," she said. "Before I knew better."

John sat back. "Envy's a terrible thing," he said.

Violet jumped up and grabbed the glass off the desk, gulped down its contents and said, "I need another." She glared at John. "Don't worry I'll get it myself."

In the bar she forced a smile onto her lips for Alice as she helped herself to a large gin. She needed to pull herself together. John was right. It was no use blaming Silas; he was only trying to help. And it was true, she had envied Hope. Even as children growing up Hope had been the one who got everything right while she muddled through. She recalled Granny Daniels, when they were learning to sew saying, "Why can't you make your stitches beautiful and neat like Hope's." That was one of her earliest memories of being in Hope's shadow.

She never felt valued and appreciated in the way Hope so obviously was. It was only her singing and dancing that allowed her to shine. She had especially envied Hope her good fortune when Silas chose her to work in his club and eventually to become his wife, but not now. True, Hope had a handsome, wealthy husband, a nice house by the river, while Violet had to rely on John's support for her living. That had rankled, but since she'd had the twins everything had changed. From the moment they drew breath she knew she'd die before she'd let anyone harm them. Things she'd thought important, money, her singing, her career had paled into insignificance when she had them. They'd become her world and her reason for living and she wouldn't swop places with Hope for all the money in the universe.

A couple of sips of the strong spirit in the glass steadied her nerves and she felt able to return to talk to John.

She shouldn't have been surprised to hear that he'd heard of Silas's scurrilous suspicions. Of course John was the head of the family and, in the absence of a husband, responsible for her and her children. Silas would have spoken to him before even speaking to Hope, his wife. Such was the ways of men.

"And you believed him?" Violet asked. "Believed that about a man you know was the father of my children?"

"Well, I—"

"How could you? How could you even consider it?"

John looked uncomfortable. He shifted in his chair, looking like a gambler who's lost more than he can afford and doesn't know how to extricate himself from the game. "We have to consider it, Violet," he said, his voice rising as frustration twisted his face. "Don't tell me you think Bert wants to see his children so he can start supporting them and make them part of his family?"

Violet's anger was rising to match John's. "There's only one way to find out," she said, "and that's to go and ask him." She stood up. "That's what I'm going to do."

"But I thought you said you couldn't find him?"

"I know a few places he might be," she said, "and I'll not rest until I do find him. When I do I'll let him know in no uncertain terms what'll happen to him if he ever thinks he can come near me or the children again." With that she gulped back the rest of the gin, slammed the glass on the desk, gathered up her skirts and stormed out.

She boiled with rage. Why did nobody believe her? Why did they always think the worst? Then she remembered how Bert had treated her when she told him she was with child and how he behaved when the worse for drink and she realised she couldn't blame them.

Chapter Ten

Violet's heart was in turmoil. John was just as bad as Hope – blaming her for all that was wrong in her life. It had always been the same. Hope was the clever one, the smart one, the nurturing one who'd looked after young, crippled Alfie when he was growing up. It was always Hope they turned to in times of trouble or difficulty, never her.

Oh, she was pretty enough to stand behind the bar and smile at the customer at Christmas, when they hosted events for the local dignitaries, but it was Hope Silas Quirk had chosen to be his bride. She never could understand that. There was no accounting for the tastes of men – which brought her back to thinking about Bert.

All her life she'd craved excitement and she found it when she ran away with Bert, or thought she had, until the beatings began. Even then she could forgive him. He'd introduced her to a world she never knew existed. A world of glamour and thrills she'd never have known if she'd stayed in the run-down East End pub where she'd grown up. It was only when she became pregnant she learned of the fragility of that world and the ease with which people were thrown away when they had outlived their usefulness. She couldn't forgive him that.

It was late afternoon by the time she'd calmed down enough to think about what to do next. The day had been sultry and the warmth lingered in the narrow streets. It was still light enough for the street lamps not to be lit. It would an hour or two before dusk would descend and the streets become impenetrable.

She found a bench by the river and sat thinking about Bert. The river gave her a sense of space and gazing across it helped to focus her mind. She watched the waves lapping against the boats tethered to the shore and the birds flying overhead. A sickening dread welled up from the pit of her stomach. Could what Silas had said be true? She shuddered. Men made money out of other men's fantasies, she knew that. They made money out of that sickening trade too so, repellent as it was, she had to consider it. Could Bert have sunk so low?

She tried to remember places he'd go, people he knew. In her mind she went through all the theatre managers and other performers he may have stayed with. None came to mind as being likely to put him up when his popularity was fading. They were always on the move anyway, no one stayed in one place for very long.

Then she recalled Ruby Dyer, an ex-performer who'd had a soft spot for Bert. Ruby lived in a rundown terrace off one of the alleys in Clerkenwell. If anyone knew what Bert was up to it would be Ruby. She'd always make a fuss of him and he often stayed with her overnight, when they'd had a row or he was too drunk to find his way back to their lodgings. She remembered going to her house a couple of time. Times when she'd been thrown out of lodgings because the rent hadn't been paid. She didn't know her address but recalled the house had a red door. She remembered wondering why she didn't have a red light over the door, considering that was mostly her trade.

She managed to catch a hackney to Clerkenwell. The streets looked unfamiliar and dusk was falling. The last of the sun stained the sky with colour. The first shop she went into to ask brought no luck. "Ruby Dyer? No, sorry," the lady behind the counter said. The next wasn't much better but the street was becoming more familiar. Further along she went into a shop on the corner, bought a packet of biscuits and asked if they knew if Ruby Dyer still lived near.

"Old Ruby?" The shopkeeper smiled. "Aye, she's still about." He walked to the door and pointed to a turning across the street. "Across the road and round the corner," he said. "About halfway down. Can't miss it. It's got a red door."

Violet thanked him. Walking down the alleyway she had no trouble finding Ruby's house. It was just as she remembered. Three steps led up to the red front door. She went up and rang the bell. She glanced around as she stood on the doorstep. A man pushing a cart went by, but other than that the road was empty.

When Ruby opened the door Violet took in her dishevelled state, the colourful dressing gown she wore hung off one shoulder exposing more than Violet had any right to see. Her dyed red hair was awry and a lit cigarette dangled from her deeply rouged lips. Her eyes narrowed in the smoke as she surveyed Violet. Eventually she took a breath, removed the cigarette from her mouth, blew out a plume of smoke and said, "I know you don't I?"

"You do," Violet said. "The Cockney Songbird. Friend of Bert Shadwick. He used to come and stay here sometimes."

Ruby's face cleared. "Aye that's it. You're Bert's little tart. Although you don't look so little now." She glanced up and down the empty street as though expecting visitors who hadn't yet arrived. "Well I suppose you'd better come in."

The hall was just as grubby as Violet remembered. Entering it brought a flood of memories, none of them pleasant. A musty smell hung in the air and cobwebs brushed her hair as she walked past. She steeled herself. What happened next wouldn't be easy but she was doing it for her children. She had to remember that.

Inside Ruby poured herself a large gin from a bottle on the sideboard, stubbed out her cigarette and settled on the settee. She didn't offer Violet anything. Glancing around at the state of the room, the tattered curtains, the stained rug, the crumpled silk cloth thrown over the worn settee, she decided she'd refuse if she did.

"So, what can I do for you?" Ruby said, her glance running over Violet as though assessing her worth. "I don't suppose you've come to enquire about my health?"

Violet wasn't sure how to begin. She could hardly accuse Ruby of being involved in Bert's nefarious business. She shrugged. "I was looking for Bert. I know you and him…"

"Me an' 'im?" Ruby gave a raucous laugh. "There was no me an' 'im. 'E did me favours and I did 'im some. Weren't more to it than that. If you're after digging up old dirt that's been under the carpet for years you're a bit late, darlin'."

Violet felt on firmer ground now. Ruby was a lush, that much was obvious. Years ago she'd been quite something, a performer of note lauded by all the critics, loved by theatre managers and audiences, but nothing fades faster than starlight at dawn. Violet knew that now. "Just wondering if you'd seen him? If you knew where he was living these days."

Ruby eyed her speculatively. "Why? Why would you want to see 'im? What I heard was that 'e got you up the duff and sent you back to your family. If you're after some sort of child support," she laughed, "well, you're gonna be very unlucky."

"No," Violet said. "Just the opposite." Then she had another thought. "What's he up to nowadays anyway? Still doing the same old routine?" She glanced around making her question appear as casual as possible. "I heard he'd got in with a bad crowd. Trying his hand at mucky pictures, I heard."

Ruby looked shocked. "Mucky pictures? Who told you that?"

Violet shrugged. "Just gossip I heard around the place. I wanted to warn him. Let him know there's people looking for him who would like to see him come to a sticky end."

Ruby laughed and took a gulp of gin. "Well, they'd best join the queue then." She paused, swirling the rest of her drink around the glass. "Mucky pictures? Could be anybody. Men from all walks of life. You never know. I know of some who present themselves as pillars of the community, high ranking officials and that, who have dirty secrets they wouldn't want the world to know about. I can't see Bert getting involved. Too rich for 'is blood." She finished her drink, stood up and poured herself another. "Time was decent men would deal with perverts like that, take 'em off the streets, but not now. Too many men with power and influence involved in that sickening trade these days." She grimaced. "There's always them as wants more 'an just to look an' all. Disgusting I call it." She sunk back onto the sofa and took a swig of gin. Violet saw her mellow as the drink took effect.

"Poor old Bert," she said leaning back on the settee. "Never was as good as he thought he was. Always fell short if you know what I mean. Part of life's flotsam floating on a sea of disappointment and just about keeping 'is head above water."

Violet's lips twitched into a smile, which she quickly hid with a deep frown. She eased herself into the chair opposite Ruby. "So where is he now do you think?"

Ruby sighed and raised her glass. "Washed up on the shores of desperation I shouldn't wonder," she said and took another swig of gin.

Violet waited.

Ruby struggled to focus before she said, "He could be anywhere. Bert the Magnificent Merlin, Master of Magic, his favourite trick was disappearing. Usually before he paid the bill." She laughed. "We had some good times, me and Bert, but you never could rely on him. Bit of a chancer." She took another swig of gin. "He had family you know. A brother. Lived somewhere south of the river. Dead Man's Island, I think. One of the last remaining rookeries." She giggled. "Terrible place. Wouldn't go there after dark, but Bert was proud of knowing the villains who lived there. Gave him some sort of notoriety. Humph. Notoriety – Bert, who was soft as marshmallows and just as likely to be enjoyed by the ladies."

She finished her drink, lay back and closed her eyes, as though drifting off into some remembrances of the past. The glass fell from her hand and rolled across the threadbare carpet. Violet rose and let herself out, glad to be in the fresh air again, but Ruby's words kept repeating in her head.

Chapter Eleven

Walking back through the streets as darkness fell and street lights were being lit, Violet's mind was buzzing like a thousand bees circling the hive. Ruby was right. Bert could be anywhere. He had friends all over the country. Running away to Yarmouth may not have been such a good idea. He might remember the boarding house where they'd stayed when they were performing in the theatre on the pier, although in the inebriated state he was in for most of their stay it may have been obscured from memory.

He probably wouldn't remember Nesta, at least she hoped not. If he did it wouldn't be too difficult to work out where she'd gone. Her heart dropped to her boots as swirling doubt filled her body, making her want to retch. Had she done a terrible thing, leaving the children with Nesta? If he did turn up there and she was absent Nesta would have no recourse other than to let him take them. He was their father, and as Silas had said, he had rights. Nesta would be in no position to argue. Even if Bert wasn't interested in that sort of thing himself, acting for those who were was where the money was made.

She almost stumbled as the sick feeling in her stomach made her lurch forward towards the gutter. She held on to a lamp post and caught her breath. Her imagination was running away with her. She tried to convince herself she'd got it wrong. Bert would never think of that disastrous week in Yarmouth. His performance had been booed off stage. It was something he'd put out of his mind as he drank the memory into oblivion. That's when the beatings got worse. It was only Nesta made her life bearable then. Would Bert remember her kindness?

Thoughts of her children filled her mind and her nagging doubt turned to the physical pain of missing them and the helplessness of being so far away from them. How could she protect them if she wasn't there? Then there was Gabriel.

Ruby's words about men of power and influence, who appeared to be the most respectable, high-minded of gentlemen and their lust for excitements outside of the normal tastes of men flooded her brain. She replayed in her mind the way he'd pick them up in the street. Then she saw the vision of Gabriel scooping William up when he'd run towards the beach, William's little body wriggling and squirming in his grasp. Was that as innocent as it had appeared? Her stomach churned and her heart ached at the thought of it.

She must have been mad to leave them. She decided to go back as soon as she could, then she vowed she'd never let them out of her sight again.

Darkness enveloped her as she walked back towards the river. She couldn't face going back to Hope's where she'd intended to ask if she could stay. Perhaps she shouldn't have said that to Hope about her husband. They didn't know Bert the same way she did. They'd only seen the worst of him. And if it wasn't for Silas they'd all be worse off, she knew that. He'd been a tower of strength for the whole family and shown them nothing but kindness and generosity at a time when they'd lost everything. Since he'd married Hope he'd been a constant support to them all in all sorts of ways. It wasn't his fault that people were saying bad things about Bert.

She sighed. She should go back and apologise, but she couldn't, not now, not yet. She needed time to think about what she could say, think of something that would excuse such poor behaviour. She decided to get a room at Bert's old lodgings. It was near the station and the earliest she could get the train was in the morning.

The next morning she was at the station well before the train was due to depart. All the way back she worried, chiding herself for her stupidity in leaving them. She recalled her last conversation with Gabriel, when she told him she was going to London. He'd offered to go with her. "I can drive you," he said. "I have business in London anyway. I was going in a couple of weeks, after my holiday, but I could go earlier if it means travelling with you and the children."

"That's very kind of you," she'd said. "But I have to go alone. Family business. You know how it is."

"Of course. I didn't realise."

"I'm leaving the children with Nesta."

He'd looked relieved. She remembered that. "Good," he said. "You'll be sure to come back then."

"I'll be sure to come back," she'd said.

She'd taken it that he was anxious to continue their liaisons, but the relief could just have easily been for the fact she was leaving the children behind.

When she arrived in Yarmouth she was first off the train. She rushed out of the station into the sunshine and managed to get a cab to the Promenade. She hurried along the front to Nesta's lodging house.

"Hello, love," Nesta said. "I'm glad to see you back. Get things settled with Bert did you? He wasn't such a bad sort I don't suppose, as sorts go."

Violet smiled. She glanced around, expecting to see William and Rose coming to greet her. "Where are the children?" she asked.

"Oh. You're friend came this morning and took them out."

Violet's stomach turned over. "My friend? You mean Gabriel?"

"Aye, that's the one. Said you'd told 'im he could take 'em to a motor car rally or some such."

"What do you mean? I said he could take them?"

Alarm filled Nesta's face. "That's what 'e said. Showed me the leaflet an' all. It's up the coast a way." She shook her head and wrung her apron in her hands. "Did I do somat wrong. Oh I knew I shouldn't have let them go. He seemed so sure, and William was that excited..."

Violet remembered the car rally Gabriel had spoken about. She had promised the children could go. Had she got him all wrong? Was he taking them as a kindness? It was no use upsetting Nesta unnecessarily. "Oh, the motor car rally. Yes. I did say they could go. I'd forgotten the day. Please, don't look so worried, Nesta. I'm sure they'll be all right and home in time for their dinner, starving and full of chatter about the day."

Nesta relaxed. She wiped her hands on her apron. "Well, I'd best get dinner on then," she said and smiled.

Violet sighed. There was nothing to do but wait until the children returned. If they weren't back by dinner time, then she'd worry.

Dinner time came and Violet started to get anxious. She paced the room, keeping watch out of the window. Her heart swelled with relief when she saw William and Rose skipping along, and Gabriel following them. She'd forgotten how good looking he was and what a fine figure of a man he made as he strode along. The lift in her heart on seeing them wasn't entirely due to watching the children coming home. William was waving a Union Jack flag and Rose carried a bunch of flowers. They both had the remains of ice creams on their faces.

She ran to the door to greet them, taking them both in her arms and hugging them. William squirmed out of her grasp, anxious to tell her all about the day and show her the model motor car he'd been given, while Rose held out her the flowers and a small beaded bag Gabriel had bought for her.

"It looks as though you've all had a very good time," she said, smiling up at Gabriel, inwardly forgiving him for causing her so much anxiety. He really was handsome and she hadn't realised how much she missed his company. "You'd better come in and you can tell me all about it over dinner." She glanced at Gabriel. "That includes you, unless you have other plans."

He grinned. "No plans that don't include you," he said and took her arm to lead her in.

In the kitchen after dinner, Violet helped Nesta clear the plates before she headed off for her shift at the pub. "Nowt to worry about with that one then," Nesta said, handing Violet a clean plate to dry up.

Violet smiled. "No, nothing at all. My sister, Hope, always said I had too much imagination for my own good, and in this instance she was right."

"I thought you was more worried than you let on. Still, all's well that ends well."

Violet nodded. Talking about Hope reminded her of the spat they'd had and the things she said before she walked out. Now she needed Hope's help. It was the only place she could be sure the children would be safe. Hope was the one person she could depend on. She'd never turn her or the children away.

"Talking of my sister," she said. "I'll be taking the children back with me at the end of the week. You've been very kind letting us stay, but the season will start soon and you'll need the room for paying customers. We can stay with Hope for a few days. She'll be delighted to have the children while I look for Bert to sort things out," she said, "and staying with Hope will mean they'd also have Silas's protection. Bert wouldn't be stupid enough to go up against my brother-in-law, Silas Quirk."

"If you're sure," Nesta said. "It's been lovely having you, but I must admit, having the room back will be handy."

"That's fixed then."

Gabriel offered again to drive them, but Violet insisted on taking the train. "That's good of you," she said, "but it's too much to ask. We can take the train. There's no reason to cut your holiday short."

"I'll be in London myself in a week or two," he said. "Will I be permitted to call on you?"

Violet had been hoping he would. No one made her heart leap the way he did and she didn't want to admit how much she'd miss him. "I look forward to it," she said and she really did. She gave him Hope's address. "This is where I'll be staying," she said.

He took the note and put it in his wallet. The warmth of his smile raised Violet's hopes that it wouldn't be long before he'd use it to find her.

The journey back to London was uneventful, although the children were miserable at having their holiday cut short. "I don't see why we couldn't stay longer," William said, pouting. "It was fun. More fun than being at home."

"I know, but holidays don't last forever," Violet said. "You'd soon get tired of the sun and the beach and time on your hands all day."

"I wouldn't," William said. "When I grow up I'm always going to be on holiday."

Violet smiled. If only that were possible, she thought. "Anyway, we're going to stay with Aunty Hope so it'll still be like a holiday. Until you start school in September."

William pouted again and Violet's heart fluttered. The twins were five and due to start at the local school after the harvest holidays. She'd never be able to protect them there so she needed to sort things out with Bert before then.

Chapter Twelve

Hope glanced nervously out of the window, watching the cabs and carriages in the street below. She'd received Violet's telegram asking if she could put them up for a few days while she 'sorted things out with Bert'. She recalled Violet's earlier visit and how she'd stormed out in her usual fashion when she heard something she didn't like. But that was the thing with Violet. She'd blow up like a firework, spitting sparks of indignation and spite, but her anger would soon burn itself out and she'd be back, sweet as cherries once she'd calmed down.

Hope read the telegram again. Brief and to the point as she would expect, but it gave no sign of what Violet was expecting her to do or how long they were to stay. Typical Violet, she thought. Acts on impulse. Never thinks things through. In a way she resented her assumption that she and Silas would be free and available to put them up and look after William and Rose without notice, but then, she recalled Violet's sunny nature, her optimism and how things always turned out right for her and immediately forgave her as she always did.

A few minutes later a hansom cab drew up at the kerb and Hope saw Violet and the children alight. William ran up to knock on the door while Violet paid the cab. Hope smiled and hurried down the stairs to let him in, bumping into Daisy who'd heard the knocking and was on her way herself to answer the door. "I'll get it," she said. "It's my sister and her twins. Can you bring tea; I expect they'll want some refreshment after their journey."

Daisy nodded and turned back towards the kitchen.

Hope opened the door and swept a delighted William into her arms. Rose came next, Hope stooped to include her in the embrace. She glanced up to see Violet coming along the path. "Come in," she said, pushing the door wide for the children to run through. She didn't want any contretemps on the doorstep for all the neighbours to enjoy.

"I'm glad to see you looking so well," Hope said as she ushered them upstairs into the elegantly decorated drawing room. "Wherever you've been staying it certainly agrees with you."

"We've been at the seaside," William piped up. "It was fun and we didn't want to come to home." He glowered at Violet.

Daisy arrived with a tray of tea.

"I'm glad to be home," Rose said defiantly. "I want to see Amy again and show her my shiny purse and the shells I collected on the beach."

Hope laughed. "Well, if you go to the kitchen you can show Daisy and Mrs B might be able to find you some milk and biscuits." She glanced at Daisy who nodded and ushered the children out ahead of her.

"I'm sure Mrs B will find something for you," Daisy said with a grin.

Hope poured the tea. "Now perhaps you can tell me what's been going on," she said. "We've all been worried silly since you took the children away. Have you seen Bert? Have you sorted anything out with him?"

Violet took the tea Hope handed her. "No, but I've spoken to people who know him and they agree with me, it's most unlike Bert to get involved in anything that might damage his reputation. I've also realised that the children are safer here with family than anywhere else with strangers. I'm hoping you and Silas—"

"Of course we will. I'd love nothing better than to have them stay here, you know that."

Violet smiled and sipped her tea. "I've heard that Bert has family, a brother I think, living on Dead Man's Island. I intend to go there and find him."

"Dead Man's Island! Are you sure?" Hope's voice rose several octaves at the horror the place conjured up. Dead Man's Island, located in a gully south of the river near the docks, was notorious for being home to the most disreputable, thieving, murderous villains in London. It was also overcrowded, squalid and dangerous. Many Victorian rookeries and run-down lodging houses had been demolished, but that only meant the inhabitants moved on to the next one. Dead Man's Island would be the last to go.

"That's what I've been told."

"But you can't go there, Violet. It's a vile place, housing the worst criminals in the city. It's far too dangerous, even in daylight and it would be the height of stupidity to go there." She put her cup and saucer back on the tray and stood up. "I'll send a message to Silas. Let's ask him what he thinks."

Violet's face turned stony. She banged her cup and saucer down on the table. "Please don't bother," she said in a voice that stopped Hope in her tracks. Then she took a breath and seemed to regain control of herself. "I'm sorry. I didn't mean that to sound so ungrateful. Of course I appreciate your taking us in and looking after the children, but I'm old enough to make my own decisions. I don't need Silas's help or opinion. I can go alone."

Hope's heart sank. Violet was being her usual difficult, stubborn, wilful self. She returned to her seat and picked up her tea. She took a sip. Then put the cup down again. "I'm sorry," she said. "I know you're perfectly capable of sorting this out but I worry about you. It would be a favour to me if you would allow Silas to help." She took Violet's hand. "We're family," she said. "Families help each other out. You shouldn't have to face this alone."

Violet crumbled. The defiance in her eyes died. "I'm being an awkward cow, aren't I?" I shouldn't have got on my high horse. I don't deserve such good friends – family or not. Of course I'd value Silas's help." Hope had a sneaking suspicion that it was what she was angling for in the first place, but her fierce pride had prevented her for asking for it.

"Good. First thing tomorrow you and he can go to this Dead Man's Island place and if you find Bert having Silas with you may help focus his mind on leaving you and the children alone."

Violet nodded and Hope breathed a sigh of relief. Silas would ensure that Violet wouldn't do anything stupid when she saw Bert and he'd also be certain to arrange for some of his men to be in the vicinity should further persuasion be needed.

Once she'd finished her tea Violet went to unpack and settle the children into the room made ready for them.

Later, when Silas returned home Hope went to see him in his study. When she told him about Violet wanting to visit Dead Man's Island he was stunned. "Dead Man's Island?" he gasped. "Is she mad? That's extremely dangerous, even today."

Hope's heart beat faster. "I know. I did try to tell her."

"Is there no way we can persuade her not to go?"

"I'm afraid not. If you don't go with her she'll go alone."

Silas sighed. "That would be the height of folly." His brow puckered. "I'll take a couple of men," he said. "If she's insisting."

"She is."

Violet had brought a picture of Bert on one of the leaflets which Nesta had saved. He handed them out to advertise his performances. Hope showed it to Silas.

"I'll get some copies made," he said. "It may help. People don't always remember names, especially landlords, but they may remember his face. My men can start asking around tonight. With a bit of luck we may find him elsewhere than Dead Man's Island."

"Thank you," Hope said and once again reflected on how lucky she was to be married to Silas, a man who solved problems with hardly a ripple. That was something Violet must miss, she thought. She had John to rely on to look out for her but, even though he was her brother, Hope knew he wasn't half the man Silas was, nor did he have the manpower or resources that Silas could summon up when it came to solving a problem like Bert Shadwick.

Breakfast the next morning was a much more lively affair than Hope was used to. The children chattered and squabbled over the jam and William bounced with excitement when he told them about his holiday. "We went for a ride in a motor car," he said. "One day we went out and there were lots of motor cars and engines.

When I grow up I'm going to have a motor car. Brmm brmm"

"Really?" Silas said. "That must have been quite thrilling." He glanced at Hope. It was clear he was thinking the same as her. Violet had made no mention of going out in a motor when they talked last night and, knowing Violet, there was bound to be a man involved.

"That's enough chatter, William. Get on with your breakfast," Violet said, giving him a chastising stare.

"Can we go to the park and feed the ducks?" Rose asked. It was their usual treat when Hope took them out.

"Yes and I can sail my boat," William said.

"You have a boat?" Silas asked. "That's grand."

"Ma bought it for me on holiday, but I can't sail it in indoors." William pouted.

"Then you must certainly go to the park," Silas said, "if your mother agrees." He looked at Violet. "Abel can go too. He'd enjoy sailing boats and feeding ducks."

"Thank you," Violet said.

"We saw lots of boats on the Broads," William said. "When I grow up I'm going to have a boat, a big one, a proper one."

"The Broads eh?" Silas said and looked meaningfully at Hope. It was a clue to where they'd been staying.

Violet must have noticed it too. She sighed with exasperation. "William. I wish you'd stop this chatter and get on with your breakfast, or you won't be going out at all."

The rest of the breakfast was eaten in solemn silence.

Once breakfast was finished the children were sent out to play in the small garden at the back of the house. It wouldn't contain their exuberant high-spirits for long, but Hope, Violet and Silas retired to the drawing room to have coffee and plan the outing to Dead Man's Island.

"Are you sure you want to do this, Violet?" Silas said. "I could go alone, or with one of my men."

"No. It's my problem I need to go. I don't believe Bert is as bad as people make out. He wouldn't do anything to hurt his children."

Hope glanced at Silas, the memory of Violet's cuts and bruises when she came home, pregnant and unmarried, filled her mind. She wanted to remind Violet, but feared she'd only make her more determined. At least if Silas was with her she'd have some protection.

Violet finished her coffee and put her cup back on the saucer. "I'll go and get the children ready," she said. "I know they're looking forward to being spoilt by their Aunty Hope."

Hope laughed. "Am I so obvious?" she said.

Violet laughed. "Yes," she replied.

"I'm not sure Violet knows what she's letting herself in for," Hope said when she was alone with Silas. "There are some places it's not safe to go even if you have company."

"Don't worry, I'm going to ask one of my men to come with us. If it becomes too hairy I'll send Violet back. It would be best if she didn't come, but I don't suppose it's any use telling her that."

"No use at all," Hope said.

Silas stood to go.

"Please take care of yourself," Hope said rising from her seat. "Don't go playing the hero. I couldn't bear it if anything happened to you."

He took her in his arms. "It's you who should take care. You'll be with the children Bert is after and with a chatterbox like William going with you their whereabouts won't stay secret for long. I'm the one's going to be worrying about you."

"So that's why Abel's coming along?"

"Yes. He'll want to come with me but I'd rather he was with you. Not sure how he'll take to boats and duck-feeding though."

Hope laughed. Her heart swelled with love for this man she'd married who would give her the world just for being herself. How could she envy Violet her children or anything else when she had Silas by her side? No indeed, she was the lucky one.

"The sooner this thing with Bert's sorted out the better," Silas said. "I worry about those children as much as you do and want them to stay safe with their mother. I can't think that Bert getting hold of them would be anything but a nightmare for us all."

"That's one thing we all agree on," Hope said.

Silas grinned and kissed her. A thrill ran through her body as it always did when his lips met hers. She felt the warmth of his body, the strength of his arms and wished she could stay forever in his embrace. She'd rather she was going with him, not Violet. Every moment spent with him was like a precious gift to be treasured. She'd never dreamed she could love so intensely and so passionately. They'd been married for five years and her want of him hadn't dwindled.

"I'm the luckiest man alive," he said, his intense blue eyes staring into hers. "I'll never do anything to risk our happiness." He kissed her again and made his way out to wait for Violet.

Chapter Thirteen

Violet was on her way down from the second floor bedroom where she'd been gathering her things ready to go out when she heard a noise in the hall below. Peering over the banisters she saw a thick-set man talking to Silas and gesticulating in an excited fashion. He had a heavy boned face, a dark shadow of hair covered his skull. She recognised him as being one of the men who worked at Silas's club.

Sensing her presence Silas looked up. He grinned. "One of my men has had reports of Bert being seen in Mile End," he said. "I suggest we go there first. It may save us a lot of trouble."

"Mile End? Are you sure it's him?" Violet frowned and dashed down the stairs.

Silas introduced the man as 'Knuckles', "due to his penchant for pigs' trotters," Silas said, although Violet thought it could equally well have been for the huge fists jutting out from the sleeves of his green jacket.

Knuckles held out Bert's picture. "A lot older, heavier jowled, rougher, like he's seen hard times, but definitely him."

Violet tried to think who Bert might know in Mile End. "There are a couple of theatres where he used to perform, but his act wasn't particularly well received, if I remember right. I can't think he'd go there unless he was desperate."

"We showed his picture. A magic shop in Mile End and a boarding house in Hoxton. Both said he'd been there recently," Knuckles said.

"Oh yes, the magic shop. I remember that. It's where he used to get his tricks."

"That settles it," Silas said. "Mile End first, then Hoxton and if we don't find anything we'll try south of the river tomorrow. If he's staying with his brother as you suspect an extra day won't make any difference, but if he's not..."

"Fine," Violet said putting on her coat and hat in front of the mirror in the hall and adjusting her hat to show her curls to best advantage. "The sooner we find him the better."

"Wait up, little lady," Knuckles said. "I didn't reckon on taking no female. Best you wait 'ere, love."

Violet fumed. She glared at Knuckles. He wasn't as tall as Silas, nor as broad across the shoulders, but muscles bulged under the taut material of his dark green jacket. "No. I have to see him. Find out what this is all about. There may be a good reason..." Her voice faded at the improbability of what she was saying.

"And what're you gonna do when we do find 'im?" Knuckles asked.

"You forget, I know all his dirty little secrets. They won't stay secrets for long if he doesn't leave us alone."

"Oh I see, blackmail is it? Hmm. Might work I suppose. Still think you'd be better staying here." Knuckles's mouth twisted into a look of disapproval.

"I can handle Bert," she said.

Silas's eyebrows rose. She could see that he was thinking; 'like you did before?'

"I know better now and I'm stronger, plus it's my children he's talking about."

Knuckles looked at Silas who shrugged. "If we go without her she'll only follow on her own and put herself into even more danger."

Knuckles sighed. "If you say so, guvnor, but it don't feel right taking no woman. Not right at all." Despite his reluctance Knuckles took out a bunch of papers. "It'll be one of the cheaper lodging houses," he said. "I've got one or two addresses."

"Lead the way, Knuckles," Silas said and Violet realised he'd adeptly managed to include the doorman in the search. Still, the more the merrier, she thought.

Outside the weather was still fine, the early morning sun dappled through trees as they passed. They managed to catch a hansom to take them north to Mile End. No one spoke as they rattled through the congested streets, each keeping their thoughts to themselves. Any other time Violet would have enjoyed the journey leaving the wharves and warehouses behind to travel through busy shopping streets and past rows of terraced houses, but today anticipation curled in her stomach at what lay ahead.

The first place they tried was the magic shop. As soon as Violet saw it the memories came flooding back. She'd been there with Bert. The bell on the door tinkled as they walked in. The man behind the counter, a weedy looking young man in a tweed suit, was packing away some boxes of playing cards. Violet recalled the tricks Bert used to do with them. She recognised the shop assistant too, he'd often served Bert when the owner of the shop was busy.

"Good morning," the assistant said. "How may I help you today? Some party tricks, or something more professional?"

"We're not here to buy," Violet said. She got out Bert's picture. "I wondered if you'd seen Bert Shadwick lately. I know he used to shop here."

"Old Bert? What a coincidence. He did come in a couple of days ago. Well, could have been a week. I hadn't seen him for ages, then, there he was. I didn't know he was still working. Looked very... um... sort of... out of sorts if you know what I mean. Didn't buy anything. Said he was looking to 'upgrade' the act." He chuckled. "Looked like he could do with a bit of upgrading 'iself."

"You wouldn't know where he's staying would you? I mean, for an old friend." Silas produced a gold sovereign and placed it on the counter, holding it down with his finger.

The assistant paused, sucked his lips, and glanced from one to the other of them, taking in Silas and Knuckles' bulk. Eventually his gaze rested on Violet. "Got you up the spout 'as he. Bad luck, dearie. Should 'ave kept your legs together." He chuckled.

Violet was shocked by his crudeness. Her temper flared, but before she could react Silas stepped forward, reached across the counter and grabbed the man by the lapels of his coat, almost lifting him off his feet. "That's no way to speak to a lady," he said. "She asked a civil question and expected a civil answer. Do you know where he is?"

The assistant's eyes almost popped out of his head. He struggled to answer but managed to utter, "Sorry. No. Didn't mean no 'arm."

Silas let him go, throwing him back against the shelves behind him. "You're lucky I'm in a hurry," he said, "or I'd stay and teach you some manners." He pocketed the sovereign and walked out. The others followed.

Outside Violet was still shaking. She knew of Silas's reputation as being someone who could take care of himself but witnessing it was quite different. Knuckles, on the other hand, seemed to be quite used to it. "No joy here. Let's try the lodgings next," he said and again led the way.

"We'll never get a cab this far north," Silas said. "Best we can hope for is a hackney."

As it turned out they ended up walking the three miles. It took them more than an hour. They stopped at a coffee stall for some refreshment and Violet showed the stall holder Bert's picture. He shook his head. "I ain't seen nobody. Never sees nobody, just gives 'em hot drinks."

When they got close to Hoxton they asked the newspaper boy on the corner, several of the women standing on the doorsteps and the men lounging in the pub doorways, but no one admitted to having seen him. A tobacconist thought he might have seen him, but couldn't say for sure.

Everywhere they went the men were treated with grudging respect but that respect didn't extend to Violet. The gawking stares she received ranged from the obscenely lecherous to looking as though they'd seen something they'd scrape off their shoe.

"Looks like we're on a wild goose chase," she said after a while.

"No, it's just the people," Silas said. "They don't want to get involved in what looks like trouble. Doesn't mean he hasn't been here."

By the time they reached the first lodging house on Knuckles's list without success Violet was quite dispirited. Her feet ached from walking and she was hungry, but determined not to give up. Knuckles must have noticed her distress. "Not far now," he said. "I've got a feeling in me bones that we'll strike lucky soon." He nodded towards Silas who'd strode on ahead, moving with the intensity and power that comes to men who work hard and take care of themselves. "You've got 'im on your side and 'es the luckiest blighter I ever come across. Can't go wrong if you stick with 'im."

"Thanks," Violet said, but somehow she didn't feel the same.

A bit further on a man stood by the side of the road with a barrel organ playing and a monkey dancing around. A small crowd had gathered to watch. Silas dropped a shilling into the monkey's cup and showed the organ grinder Bert's picture.

"Aye. I seen 'im," he said. "Tight arsed bugger. Stood here twenty minutes and never give me a farthing."

"How long ago?"

"Couple of days I reckon, but it's not a face I'll forget."

"Thanks," Violet said, her spirits lifting. At least they were on the right track and Bert was most likely still in London and staying in the vicinity.

The next lodging house they came to the landlord was standing in the doorway. Thin faced and badly dressed, his shoes were scuffed and his jacket stained and creased. He was chewing tobacco. Silas showed him Bert's picture. "This man been staying here?" he asked.

The man spat out the tobacco which landed on the cobbles, leaving a stain. "Nah. Sorry can't 'elp you," he said.

Violet got the impression he wouldn't if he could.

"There might be something in it for you," Silas said.

Sudden interest lit up the man's face. He took another look at the picture then handed it back. "Try round the corner, first door on the right. Can't miss it, it's painted blue." He pointed to a turning further down the road. "'E sometimes takes people in. Best I can do."

Silas thanked him and gave him half-a-crown.

The next place they stopped at they had better luck. "Aye, been and gone. Left owing me rent an' all. If you sees 'im tell 'im he owes me, or better still, tell me where 'e is and I'll tell 'im."

"When did he go?"

"Couple of days. Owes me for the week though." He looked Silas and Knuckles up and down. "I 'opes as 'ow you finds him and gives him a walloping. If you do, give 'im one for me." The disgruntled landlord turned and shut the door on them.

Chapter Fourteen

Silas put his arm around Violet's shoulders. "Don't worry," he said. "There's another day tomorrow. We'll cross the river and try Dead Man's Island."

"There's one more place we could try," Knuckles said. "A bit of slum land the other side of the river. Under the arches at Waterloo Bridge. The sort of place people go when they've nowhere else. Full of dossers and down-and-outs. No place for a lady." He glared at Violet.

Violet had felt his disapproval hanging over her like a dark cloud all day. "I'll be fine," she said. "And I'm coming whether you like it or not."

Knuckles looked at Silas. He shrugged. "Keep a close eye on her," he said. "If it gets too bad we'll all go back and I'll come again tomorrow with more men."

"Whatever you say," Knuckles said, clearly unhappy at Silas's decision.

They started walking south towards the river. Violet's feet were aching and, despite the warmth of the day, cold. Most of the time they were walking in the shadow of tall buildings along roads where the sun never ventured. She shivered in the chill breeze. She wished she could go home, but her desire to prove to them that she was as good as they were prevented her. Luckily they managed to catch a hackney passing through Smithfield which saved them some shoe leather. The hackney dropped them at Waterloo Bridge. The driver refused to go south of the river, so they walked across the bridge.

Violet could see why Knuckles was so concerned. She smelled the stench before they reached the first of the filthy hovels that covered the area. As they walked on she saw rows of dilapidated buildings, the windows broken or stuck together with paper, the holes filled with rags. Through open doors she saw walls thick with grime. The women and children lounging in the doorways were ragged, unwashed and unkempt. Children rolled in the gutter oblivious to the rotting detritus and corpses of rats. Seeing the state of the children she immediately wanted to lift them out of the gutter and take them away to a better place. How could anyone who loved their children allow them to live in such a hellish place, she thought. Still, she reasoned, they wouldn't be here if they could afford anything better. This is where the dregs of society ended up. It was a salutary lesson.

As they moved away from the river the disgusting odour seemed even worse. It filled Violet's nostrils. She wrinkled her nose trying to dislodge it to no avail. A rat ran across in front of her, making her jump. She curled her hands into fists to stop them shaking. Perhaps Silas was right. This wasn't such a good idea. Further into the slum the road got narrower, the roofs of the houses arched closer, almost touching over the path cutting out any light that might be bold enough to try to enter this terrible place. Although only late afternoon the darkness enveloped them like a cloak. Silas was a little way ahead of her, Knuckles walking by her side.

Silas approached one or two of the men, showing Bert's picture, only to get, at best, a shake of the head, at worst a projection of spittle that narrowly missed his boots. Still Violet had the feeling of hostile eyes upon her, watching her, waiting. They came to a part where the path narrowed. Alleyways led off from either side of the road. She was glad of Silas's protection as he walked ahead of her. Knuckles dropped behind, his head turning from side to side watching.

An eerie silence hung in the air. Violet's stomach clenched with fear. She had the feeling that if she were to call out no one would hear, or if they did her cries would be unheeded. She shivered and was about to stop Silas going any further. She'd had enough and wanted to go home. Coming here now seemed the worst idea in the world. She couldn't imagine Bert coming here anyway. The Bert she remembered had been a gentleman. He may have fallen on hard times, but he'd been fussy about his dress and he'd turned his nose up at the dingy houses they stayed in. He always let her know they were only temporary, a question of needs must, and he was used to better things. He wouldn't be seen dead in a place like this.

Before she could open her mouth to speak all hell broke loose. Suddenly the path was filled with men jumping out of the alleyway alongside them, shouting and waving weapons in front of them. One of them carried a heavy chain which he swung in the direction of Silas's head, catching him a blow that sent him sprawling on the filthy cobbles. Violet's scream was stifled by a hand over her mouth and a vice like grip around her waist. Her nostrils filled with the scent of ether. Her head jerked backwards. She could hardly breathe. She felt herself being dragged along, despite trying to gain some purchase against it with her shoes. Heart pumping and burning with rage and fright she struggled to free herself. She saw Knuckles, who'd moved towards her, set upon by two other men. A face pressed against her ear, stubble grazed her face, hot smelly breath warmed her cheek. She saw Silas try to rise. Another blow struck him, sending him sprawling again. Knuckles tried to get free to get to her, he was felled with one blow and then everything went black.

Chapter Fifteen

The morning was bright and sunny for the outing to the park. Abel carried the picnic basket , Rose held Hope's hand while William carried his boat. They managed to catch a hansom cab and were soon in the park enjoying the sunshine. It being early there were not too many people about. The people who were there were walking their dogs or throwing sticks for them.

There were a few rowing boats out on the lake as they walked past the boathouse. Further on they found a bench under the trees where Hope and Rose could sit while William and Abel set about sailing William's boat. Ducks and geese flocked to where they stood as though looking for food.

"Can we feed the ducks?" Rose asked. "I like the ducks."

Hope took out a bag of breadcrumbs Mrs B had put in and passed it to Rose, who giggled with delight as she threw some into the water for the ducks.

William jumped about with excitement. "Where can I sail my boat," he asked.

Abel took him along a little way away from the ducks. He studied the breeze and the flow of the water, assessing the best place to start. Once he was satisfied that the boat would sail William set it on the water. Watching them together made Hope smile. William and Abel got on so well she was glad Abel had come. William could be a bit of handful, but he was so in awe of the older boy he did everything Abel told him without a murmur.

When all the breadcrumbs were gone Rose sat on the bench with Hope. She'd brought along her doll.

"What's your doll called?" Hope asked her.

"She's called Dolly."

"That's nice," Hope said. "What a lot of clothes she has."

"Yes. Ma made them."

Hope could see that. The materials were glittery and colourful. So very like Violet, she thought.

Rose sat happily chatting as she changed her doll's outfits, first for tea, then for a rainy day and then a night out at the theatre. Hope noticed Violet's influence. Sitting in the warm sunshine Hope wished she'd persuaded Violet to come with them instead of going with Silas and Knuckles.

"I'm sure Silas will be every bit as persuasive as you," she'd said. "He knows Bert. Knows how to talk to him man to man." But Violet had insisted upon going along.

"It's my problem, they're my children and I'm responsible for them," she said. "I'm going whether you approve or not."

Violet had never let anyone's approval or disapproval stop her from doing what she wanted in any case, so Hope was at least glad that she'd agreed to let Silas and Knuckles go with her.

"She once had feelings for Bert," Hope said to Silas before they left. "I'm afraid those feelings may not have changed, despite her experience. She wants to see him again and I'm not sure that's such a good idea. He did have a certain charm in the old days, even I admit to that."

"There's no accounting for love," Silas said. "I love you deeply, more than life itself. No matter what you do, however your treat me, I'll always love you, my feelings will never change. Why should Violet's be any different?"

Hope tried to imagine treating Silas badly but she never could, her love for him was as deep as his for her. And he was right, nothing would ever change that. She could only hope that Violet's love for her children would eclipse any feelings she had for Bert and that her love for him was as shallow as he was.

At lunchtime they moved away from the side of the lake which had become more crowded to enjoy their picnic in a shady spot nearer to the bandstand. Both William and Abel had removed their shoes and socks to wade into the water to collect the boat when it drifted too far out of reach. Hope gave them a towel to dry themselves.

The music from a brass band drifted across on the breeze. Over a feast of buns, ham and cheese, pork pies, cake and biscuits with orange juice for the children and a thermos of tea for Hope and Abel, the discussion centred around a detailed analysis of the best way to sail a boat on the lake to ensure not losing it or having to wade in a fetch it when it hit a tree branch, or went in further than was wise.

After the picnic they walked to Rotten Row to watch the horses and carriages where ladies took their usual constitutional. Then Hope took them to the ice cream parlour, which William declared was his favourite place in all the world. "When I grow up I'm going to eat ice cream every day," he said.

By the time they left the park dusk was falling. All day Hope had worried about Silas and Violet, pushing thoughts to the back of her mind to put on a happy front for the children. She didn't want them to worry or be upset. To them it was just a day out with their aunt and Abel while Ma had some business with Uncle Silas. That's how Hope wanted it to remain.

There were no cabs waiting at the edge of the park so Abel went to find one. He returned within a few minutes and they were soon on their way home.

When they arrived Hope was surprised to find that Violet had not returned. She'd expected her back in time for tea with the children. Silas and Knuckles weren't there, but Hope thought they may have gone directly to the club. But not Violet. Surely she'd come straight home?

"Perhaps she gone to see Masser John," Abel said.

Hope shrugged. "Maybe," she said, but she wasn't convinced.

"Should I go see?" Abel asked.

"No," Hope said. "No need. I'm sure she'll be here soon. She'll want to see the children and let us know how she got on. Meanwhile, the children will want their tea."

It was dark and the children had gone to bed when Hope heard the wheels of a carriage draw up outside. She rushed to the window to look out. By the light of the street lamp she saw Knuckles alight first, then she watched him reach inside to help Silas. He draped Silas's arm around his shoulders and supported him as they made their way up the path. Hope gasped and rushed downstairs to open the door.

"What on earth—?" Hope stared wide-eyed at the men. Knuckles also had blood on his face and a bruise darkening under a swollen eye. A tear in his jacket stretched from shoulder to hem. Hope noticed bloodied grazes on his knuckles.

Silas pulled himself up when he saw Hope. "It's all right," he said. "Just a scratch, I'm fine now." He wasn't.

"Broken ribs I reckon," Knuckles said. "And a sore head. He'll have trouble breathing for a while but 'e'll mend, in time." He helped Silas into the downstairs parlour and placed him gently on the couch. Hope put the light on and saw the gash on Silas's head. Blood matted his hair, one trouser leg was ripped and stained with blood.

The commotion brought Daisy out from the kitchen.

"Get some water and some bandages," Hope said. "Quickly. I want to see how bad it is and if I need to call Doctor Matthews or take these two to the hospital."

"No need," Silas said. "Please, don't make a fuss. We got into a fight. Did Violet come home?"

"Violet? No. She's not here. I thought she was with you?"

Silas and Knuckles looked at each other. Silence stretched between them and filled the room. All Hope could hear was the beating of her heart and the pulse throbbing in her ears. Her jaw dropped open. A ferocious storm of fear stole her breath. "Oh my Lord," she said. "Where's Violet?"

Chapter Sixteen

"I've called Doctor Matthews," Daisy said when she returned with a bowl of water, carbolic, cloths and bandages together with what looked like the entire contents of Hope's medicine cabinet. "Sent a lad with a note. Told 'im it's urgent." Her disapproving look wasn't lost on Hope.

Abel helped Knuckles remove Silas's jacket and torn trousers, while he protested loudly that he was fine.

Doctor Matthews arrived shortly after. A dapper man in his early fifties he quickly took charge of the situation. "Definite cracked ribs and lucky not to have a fractured skull," he said. "You may have some concussion. You should stay in bed at least overnight." He bathed and dressed Silas's wounds while Silas protested loudly that he was fine. "Fine are you?" he said. "Well, if that's fine I'd like to see you on a bad day then." Silas grunted. "I'll give you something for the pain and to help you sleep," Dr Matthews said. "You'll feel a good deal better after a night's rest."

"I'll keep an eye on him," Hope said. "If he gets any worse I'll call you myself."

Doctor Matthews gave Hope some tablets, then turned to Knuckles. "I'll give you something for the bruises too," he said. "Though from the look of you I suspect you're used to a few of them."

Knuckles managed a grin.

Anxiety churned Hope's stomach. If the gang could do this to men like Silas and Knuckles, what chance would Violet have against them?

"Any idea what happened to Violet?" Hope asked.

Knuckles shook his head. "It all happened so quick. No warning. First I saw was your man there being felled wi' a chain. I tried to help and got coshed for me trouble. Didn't see what happened to Violet. She may have run off..." Hope sensed he was voicing something he doubted but felt bad about.

"Or gone for help?" Hope said.

"Well if she did none came. By the time I come round all I saw was Mr Silas on the cobbles."

"We were taken by surprise," Silas said. "I blame myself. We shouldn't have gone in unarmed."

"No, it were my fault," Knuckles said. "I was the one suggested going there in the first place." The distraught look on his face said more than words could. "Shouldn't 'ave taken a woman though."

"I'll go back with you and look for her," Abel said to Knuckles. "If you think you're up to it?"

"Oh aye, I'm up to it." Knuckles brightened at the prospect of getting his own back on the gang. "This time we'll be ready for 'em."

"We should be calling the police," Hope said, but even she knew they'd do nothing. The street gangs that operated near the river and in the slums of the East End were notorious and they'd ventured into an area even the police never went if they knew what was good for them. "I don't like the idea of Abel going. He's only a child..."

"No I'm not," Abel said. "I can look after meself, same as govnor. I should've bin with 'im." The sorrow in his voice and the look on his face persuaded Hope that he felt as bad about Silas's wounds as anyone. It was no use trying to stop him going. He felt responsible for Silas's safety, and he hadn't been there when Silas needed him most.

It took half-an-hour of Hope's threatening and cajoling to convince Silas to let Abel and Knuckles go without him.

"We'll call in at the Hope and Anchor first in case Miss Violet's managed to get home," Abel said. "Then, if not we may still be able to find out something about what happened to her. Another day it will be lost, people forgotten, everything changed."

"Take Eddie and Jo with you," Silas said, once he'd seen that he'd be more of a hindrance than a help if they did meet any resistance in the dark alleyways of the slum. "And make sure you're armed."

Knuckles grinned. "Oh we'll be armed all right," he said. "Should've thought of that afore. Going in like we did was simple minded, but I thought we was looking for a soft bellied theatre performer, not a desperado."

Hope went with them out into the hall. "You will be careful, won't you," she said to Abel. "I couldn't bear it if anything happened to you." His wide grin and the light in his dark eyes showed her he was determined to be the man Silas needed him to be.

"Are you sure you're all right?" she said to Knuckles, eyeing up his bruised face and grazed knuckles.

"Aye. I'm used to it," he said. "Your man, there," he nodded to the parlour door, "'e put up a good fight but 'e was no match for a heavy chain and men with hate in their hearts."

Hope could see there was no way she could persuade them not to go, despite the lateness of the hour. "Take care," she said, holding Abel's arm. "If you're not back by midnight I'll have the whole of the Metropolitan Police Force out after you."

He grinned and they went on their way.

Once Silas's head and leg were cleaned and bandaged, arnica rubbed on his bruises and his ribs bound, Doctor Matthews and Hope helped him up to bed. The doctor prepared a sleeping draught which he promised Hope would put him out until morning and ensure a good night's rest.

Hope returned to the drawing room where she'd have a good view of the road. The conversation of the evening played over in her mind. Perhaps Violet had managed to get away. Where would she go? The nearest place from Waterloo Bridge would be Hope's home, but there was a chance she may have gone to the pub, or to a local boarding house for help.

It was after midnight when Abel and Knuckles returned. Eddie and Jo had gone back to the club. Hope had been pacing the floor. She poured them each a brandy. They both had the weary look of someone who had pushed themselves to the limit.

"We tried all the alleyways around the place they were attacked," Abel said. "Boarding house, lodgings, even tried the old fishmonger's shed. No one had seen her, or if they had they were keeping quiet about it." He swigged back the warming, restorative drink and Hope poured him another. "At least we know she's not lying injured in a gutter somewhere, or we'd have found her. She may have gone somewhere for help. If she's been taken in we may have better luck in the morning."

"Taking a woman like that. Ain't right," Knuckles said and Hope guessed he still felt he was to blame.

"You've done all you can tonight," Hope said, "and I'm grateful. Let's hope things look better in the morning."

A dispirited Knuckles left and Hope watched him, his footsteps dragging along the path. Abel stood next to her.

"I should've gone with them," he said, a bitterness she'd never heard before in his voice. "Masser Silas and Knuckles. I should have gone."

"It wasn't your fault," Hope said. "You did as Mr Silas wanted." But she couldn't help agreeing. This would never have happened if Violet had gone to the park with her and left Silas to go with Knuckles to look for Bert.

Chapter Seventeen

Violet awoke with what felt like cannonballs crashing around in her head. She shivered in the cold. She lay still for a while, eyes closed trying to focus her mind. She couldn't remember going to bed or how she got there. The first thing she noticed was the dank smell of sweat and something worse coming from the mattress she was lying on. She sniffed and opened her eyes but darkness filled the room. It took a few moments for her eyes to become accustomed to the gloom. Slivers of pale moonlight came through the gaps in planks that roughly boarded up the room's only window. She put her hand to her head. Something dark and sticky matted her hair. When she took her hand away she saw it was blood. A rough, worn, grey blanket covered her body; beneath it she wore only her chemise, stockings and petticoat. No wonder she was cold.

As she stirred a sharp pain knifed through her head and she closed her eyes again. Her limbs felt heavy and her whole body ached. Where was she and how did she get here? She remembered nothing. A rising swell of panic turned to nausea. Pushing her discomfort to one side she pulled herself up, turned and planted her stockinged feet onto the rough floorboards. She looked around at dark walls, the wallpaper hanging in strips to reveal patches of damp mildew. She could just make out a chest of drawers stood next to a small wardrobe against the wall furthest from the foot of the bed. A jug and bowl on the top promised water. Her throat was sandpaper dry, her lips cracked and swollen. How long had she been there? She had no idea. Her only thought was to get out and go home. A great swell of misery engulfed her. She tried to call out but the thin sound echoed around the dismal room. She felt bereft of strength.

She edged her way along to the end of the bed, then rose up and grabbing onto the chest of drawers for support, she reached for the jug. Her spirits lifted. There was water in it. She poured some into the bowl, cupping her hand to catch enough to sip, then splashed it over her face before a fresh wave of exhaustion engulfed her. She made her way back to the bed, wrapped the blanket around her body and fell into a fitful sleep, where the nightmare of the attack played over and over in her brain. It was all her fault. She knew that. Everything was her fault. It always was.

Chapter Eighteen

Doctor Matthews called early the next morning. "How's the patient?" he asked Hope, handing her his hat as he made his way up the stairs to the bedroom.

"He slept well, I think," Hope said, following the doctor. "He's anxious to be up. I'm afraid there's no keeping him in bed today."

"Any news of your sister?"

"No. I'm afraid not. That's added to his anxiety. He feels it's all his fault and no amount of persuading will make him think otherwise."

"That's the trouble with patients," the doctor said. "They tend to have no patience."

Hope smiled. "I'll arrange for some tea," she said and left the doctor to deal with Silas. Downstairs she popped into the kitchen and asked Daisy to take a fresh pot of tea up for Silas and the doctor. She was half-way through sorting out the children's breakfast when Knuckles, Eddie and Jo arrived. Hope showed them into the downstairs parlour.

"Any news?" Knuckles asked.

Hope shook her head.

"How's your man?" Knuckles asked nodding to the upstairs.

"Doctor Matthews is with him now. I doubt he'll be able to persuade him to stay indoors today."

A few minutes later Doctor Matthews appeared. "How is he?" she asked.

"A lot better. Thankfully he's a generally fit man, in his prime, so to speak." He patted Hope's hand. "No need to worry, my dear. He just needs to take it easy for the next couple of days and he'll be right as ninepence."

"Thank you," Hope said, although Silas taking the doctor's advice was as likely as her flying to the moon. She went to show him out when Silas appeared. His breathing appeared shallow and Hope saw the pain etched on his face, but knew he'd never give in to it.

"Don't forget, nothing strenuous," the doctor said, wagging his finger at Silas. "You've had a nasty blow to the head. Take it very easy."

"Yes, Doctor. Of course," Silas said and stepped aside so Hope could show him out.

"Have you three eaten?" she asked when she returned.

"Aw don't worry about us," Knuckles said. "We're fine."

"Well, you're welcome to join us for breakfast," she said. "The least I can do is to make sure you go out with something in your bellies."

Hope had arranged for Rose and William to have breakfast in the kitchen with Daisy and Mrs B. She didn't want them getting upset seeing Silas's injuries. "It'll be a treat," she said, "and you can help Mrs B make some cakes for tea."

Rose clapped her hands in delight, but William pulled a face. "Can't we go over to the park again? I enjoyed going to the park."

"Perhaps later," Hope said, "and if the cakes turn out all right we can take them with us."

Over breakfast with Silas, Knuckles, Eddie and Jo, Hope tried to persuade him not to go out with the others. "Knuckles knows where to go and Abel, Eddie and Jo'll go with him. You're in no fit state."

"They'll not get the better of us again," he said. "This time we'll be prepared."

"You told John that violence solves nothing. Surely you haven't changed your mind?"

"I haven't, but we may have to defend ourselves." He touched Hope's cheek. The warmth of his hand sent a thrill through her, as it always did. "What sort of man would I be if I didn't go? Anything may have happened to Violet. I'll not rest until I find her. Please don't ask me to."

A wave of the deepest love washed over Hope. She recalled how often he'd come to her rescue and how much she depended on him to keep her safe. He'd risk his life for me, she thought. How can I not expect him to do the same for Violet?

With a heavy heart Hope showed them out and wished them well. Silas kissed her goodbye and told her not to worry, as if that were possible, she thought.

"I'll worry until you come home safe," she said.

"I know," he said and kissed her again.

Once they were gone Hope put on a brave face for the children. No sense letting them get upset too. They spent the morning making the promised cakes which turned out passably well.

At lunchtime John arrived from the pub. Hope showed him up to the drawing room. "Sorry I couldn't come sooner," he said, "but I had to wait for Alice's ma to come to look after Amy. Alice is watching the bar. Any news of Violet?"

"No. Silas and Abel are out again looking with the others."

"They didn't get a chance to tell me much when they called in last night. What has happened exactly?"

Hope told him as much as she knew herself.

"Street gangs?" he said. "Shouldn't we be calling the police? It's not something we can deal with ourselves."

"That's what I said, but Silas is right. They'd only go around asking questions and have a snowball in hell's chance of getting the truth. Silas knows Violet and I trust him to do his best to find her, no matter what it takes."

John sank down onto a chair, deflated. "I wish there was something I could do," he said. "I feel so helpless, like I should be out looking too."

"You wouldn't know where to look. Silas does. Anyway, you have your own family to worry about."

"Violet is family," John said. "I never thought I'd say this, but I miss her. Miss having her around. I miss her perpetually sunny outlook and how she looked after Amy. Alice and Amy miss her too."

Hope smiled. She remembered living with Violet before she married Silas. She was the most irritating creature, but you couldn't help admiring her spirit, eternal optimism and resilience. "I'll let you know as soon as I hear anything," she said, showing John out. "Now I have to keep the children amused for the afternoon and hope she comes home in time to put them to bed."

Hope worried all afternoon. She wished she could have gone with them, but she'd only slow them down and anyway, Violet going was a mistake she was now paying for. At least with the children she'd have something to keep her busy.

The afternoon stretched into evening. The children were in bed before Silas returned. Hope ran to open the door when she saw him coming up the path.

Standing in the doorway in the lamplight she saw his face drained of colour. He shook his head. "We'll try again tomorrow," he said, but Hope knew they'd only be going over old ground.

Where was Violet? What on earth could have happened to her?

Chapter Nineteen

A noise outside the door woke Violet. She heard heavy footsteps followed by the sound of the door being unlocked. Immediately alert she opened her eyes. Shafts of daylight came in through the gaps between the planks across the window. She took a breath. Her head throbbed and her heart ached. She pulled herself up to a sitting position and swung her legs round to sit on the edge of the bed. The door opened and a heavy-set man in boots and a workman's coat came into the room. He carried a large, cracked mug and a hunk of bread in his massive fists.

"So you're in the land of the living?" he said, his voice rough, his face rougher. He gave off an air of depravity like a bad smell.

"Who are you? Where am I? Why have you brought me here?"

"Name's Jackson. Jackson Mullins. But you can call me Jake," he said. "I hear you bin asking about my brother Bert."

Realisation hit Violet like a slap. "You're Bert's brother?"

"Half-brother. Same mother different father. My pa was Ma's pimp. Ended up in prison. Bert's pa was a toff. Well off an' all. I got thrown out when Bert came along. Apple of 'is mother's eye was Bert." He paused as though reflecting on his lot in life. "Mind you, they got turned out when 'is pa died. Poetic justice I call it. He handed Violet the coffee and bread. "Get that down you, you'll feel a lot better. Don't want you complaining I didn't look after you."

Violet took the mug of coffee and hunk of bread. "What are you going to do with me? Can't keep me here forever and where's Bert? I want to see Bert."

"Oh yes, Bert. Good ol' Bert. Bin doing magic tricks since he was three y'know. That's how he kept Ma off the streets. Soft though, Bert. Always too soft, but good for the odd handout when things were going well."

The coffee was hot and strong and revived Violet's spirits. She glanced at the door, assessing whether she could reach it before Jake stopped her.

"Don't even think about it," he said, noticing her glance. "There's men downstairs who'll treat you a lot less kindly than I will."

"What do you want with me? You've no right to keep me here."

Jake laughed. "No right? That's rich coming from you."

"What do you mean? Do you know who I am?"

Jake laughed again. "Course I know who you are. You're Bert's little trollop who give 'im two kids and won't let 'im see 'em. Talk about rights."

Suddenly Violet understood. "You mean Bert put you up to this. Kidnapping me to get them? You're mad. He's mad." She thought for a minute. "What did he promise you? Whatever it was I'll double it if you let me go."

Jake shook his head a wide grin on his face. "I must say you're a caution. Bert always said you was a one off. He sure knows how to pick 'em I'll say that for 'im."

A torrent of fury rose up in Violet at this vile man who claimed to be related to Bert. At least Bert had been a gentleman in his day, this man was an uncouth monster who bore no resemblance to Bert. "I can't imagine that Bert has the wherewithal to pay you anything at all, if what I've heard is right. He's on his uppers, I doubt he's got a brass farthing to his name."

Jake turned and strode towards the door. "You're right. He was skint. I told 'im I could get well paid for 'is kids. Kids 'e never wanted in the first place. Give 'em a good life an' 'all selling 'em to some rich couple who can't 'ave their own. I made 'im write that note. When 'e found out there weren't no rich family an' I wanted 'em for somat quite different, he backed out – after I paid 'im an' all."

Violet gasped in horror. "Something different? What exactly?"

Jake sniggered. "I runs a good business catering to the tastes of men who can afford to indulge their various, shall we say, commonly frowned upon pleasures. Trouble is young uns are hard to come by these days, 'less they're skin and bone and half dead. Takes the pleasure out that does." He shook his head. "That's what Bert couldn't understand. Can't 'ave that can I? 'Ad to sort 'im out, didn't I?"

"Sort him out? How?"

He raised his eyebrows. "Usual way. Won't get no more trouble from Bert. You should be pleased he's brown bread an' feeding the fishes."

"Brown bread? Dead? You mean you killed him? Killed your own brother?"

"Half-brother," Jake said. "Worst half an' all."

"Now you're going to kill me? And will I be 'feeding the fishes' as you put it?"

"Kill you? Nah. You're worth more to me alive. Just tell me where them kids are and you can go – or I may kill you – just for the fun of it." He sniffed. "Don't worry, I'll find 'em. Won't take me long." He went out, banging the door behind him. She heard the key turning in the lock.

For only the second time in her life Violet prayed. Her mind went over what Silas had said. He was right, the children were in danger, but it wasn't Bert they needed to be afraid of. If Jake killed Bert he'd have no hesitation in killing anyone who came after him. She sat there shaking while Jake's words spun round in her head. Bert was dead. Her Bert. The man she fell in love with when she was sixteen was dead. She hadn't expected that. She saw his face, the curl of blonde hair that fell across his forehead, his sparkling blue eyes and wide, warm smile that oozed effortless charm. Oh he was a charmer and now he was gone. She felt as though a light had gone from the world and it would never shine again. Tears rose to her eyes. A shiver ran down her spine.

Dear Bert, he wasn't all bad. She took a deep breath and gazed around. She had no idea where she was but the man who'd brought her here had killed Bert and she could be next. Nausea rose up to her throat, she tried to stand but her legs had turned to jelly. She just made it to the bowl on the chest of drawers before she was violently sick. She staggered back to the bed. The room spun. She crawled back into bed and once again sunk into to oblivion.

Chapter Twenty

The next afternoon Hope had thought to take the children out for a breath of fresh air but a shower of rain made her change her mind. She glanced out at the storm clouds gathering in the sky.

"Are we going to the park again?" William asked. "Can I take my boat?"

"No lovely, I'm afraid we'll have to put off our outing. Perhaps tomorrow."

He looked so downcast she almost changed her mind. A little rain shouldn't put them off doing what they enjoyed, she thought. She glanced out of the window and her brow creased. A man stood under the lamp post opposite, in the rain. Roughly dressed and wearing a battered trilby, he appeared to be watching the house, oblivious to the rivulets of water running over the dark stubble of his cheeks. She noticed his shoes were scuffed, his jacket ripped and his demeanour menacing. A shudder went through her. Perhaps keeping the children indoors wasn't such a bad idea. At least in the house they'd be safe.

"Let's go to the kitchen and make some hot chocolate and we can have some of Mrs B's latest batch of biscuits. How about that?"

"Yes," chorused William and Rose in unison.

Hope breathed a sigh of relief. She'd tell Silas about the man across the street when he came home. It was something else to worry about. She was still in the kitchen with the children at five o'clock helping to make cakes for their tea, when she heard a knock at the door.

Her heart jumped into her mouth. Had something happened to Silas? She dropped the bowl she was holding onto the table. "I'll go," she said to Daisy who had risen herself to answer the door. "It may be Silas forgotten his key."

She hurried to the front door. What would she do if it was the man across the road intent upon snatching the children for Bert? She pulled the kitchen door closed behind her. She'd never felt so defenceless in her life. If only Abel had stayed with them. Where was Silas?

She took a deep breath before she opened the door. She almost fainted with relief when she saw Inspector Penhalligan of the Metropolitan Police standing on her doorstep. Then a thousand worries rushed into the brain. Was it Silas? Had something happened to him?

Inspector Penhalligan raised his hat. "Good afternoon," he said. "May I come in?"

Hope's heart sank. He had a serious expression on his face. She'd known Oakley Penhalligan since before she married Silas. He'd become a friend. Whenever she saw him she was impressed with his manner, the intelligence in his face, his quiet confidence. Now the serious look had her even more worried.

"Of course," she said moving aside for him then leading him upstairs to the first floor drawing room. All the while her heart was pounding.

Penhalligan glanced around the room. "Is your husband in?" he asked.

So it wasn't bad news about Silas, Hope thought. Her whole body relaxed. "No, not just now. Can I help?"

"Are you expecting him back soon or should I try the club?" Inspector Penhalligan, although not a member of Silas's gentlemen's club The Grenadier, it being too rich for his means, he often called in there and knew Silas's routines and when he could usually find him there.

"I'm expecting him home for tea," she said. "If you'd care to wait. I can have tea brought up." She'd feel a lot safer with the police inspector's presence. She glanced out of the window. A police wagon stood in the road outside the house. The man across the road had gone. The sky had darkened and rain spattered the window.

"Very good of you," he said, settling himself into a well upholstered chair. "If you think he'll be home soon."

"I'm sure he will," Hope said, ringing the bell for Daisy. Inspector Penhalligan was a man she trusted and could talk to. Here at last was a chance to tell him what had been going on. Perhaps he could help them find Violet.

They were halfway though their tea, having exchanged pleasantries and talked about the weather, when she heard Silas arrive home.

"Ah, there he is," she said and went downstairs to greet him. He'd removed his coat but raindrops sparkled in his raven hair and the bottoms of his trouser legs were spattered with mud. He shook his head at the questioning look on Hope's face.

"Inspector Penhalligan has come to see you," she said.

"So I see," Silas said, nodding to the police wagon still standing at the kerb. "Has he said anything about Violet?"

Hope shook her head. "He's not said anything much. He was waiting to talk to you."

Silas sighed. He looked even more worn out and weary than the previous day. Hope feared Penhalligan would tire him further. She followed him upstairs. In the drawing room he strode over to the table where the tea tray sat.

"I'll get Daisy to make a fresh pot," she said and rang the bell. The air prickled with rising tension. Nothing of any consequence would be said until Daisy had brought more tea and then departed.

"Thank you," Hope said as Daisy left, having set a fresh tray of tea with three cups on the table.

"I hear you've been looking for Bert Shadwick," Inspector Penhalligan said. "Asking a lot of questions."

"It's a personal matter. Family business," Silas said. "Nothing to worry the police about."

"Really?" His eyebrows rose as he looked at Silas, obviously noting the healing gash on his head and his stiffness of movement. "From what I've heard you've been in a fight, and taken a bit of a beating from the look of it. Care to tell me about it?"

Silas shot Hope a warning glance, rapidly dismissing any intention she had of persuading Penhalligan to help them search for Violet. He took a seat opposite the inspector. She stood to pour the tea, handing the men each a cup.

"Like I said, family business." Silas shifted uncomfortably in his chair.

Penhalligan took a sip of tea, put the cup back on the saucer and placed them on the table beside him. "I have some news for you then," he said glancing at each of them as though waiting to gauge their reaction.

"Bert Shadwick's body washed up in the Thames last night. We think he went in around Waterloo Bridge."

Hope gasped. Shock tightened her chest and stole her breath. She gazed at Silas. His face showed no emotion. "You mean he's dead?" she said, her cup rattling on its saucer as her hand shook. She sank onto the settee glad to be able to sit down.

"I'm sorry," Penhalligan said. "One of the constables who found the body recognised him. Said he'd seen him doing his magic tricks at the Alhambra a couple of years ago." He sipped his tea, keeping a watchful eye on her. "This has obviously come as a shock to you," he glanced at Silas, "if not to your husband."

Silas sat upright in his chair, his fist curled. "I can assure you I had nothing to do with anything that may have happened to Bert Shadwick. As you rightly say, I was looking for him. Regrettably I failed to find him."

"I have only your word for that," Penhalligan said, a hard edge to his usual soft Cornish burr.

The tension between the two men deepened. Hope recalled Penhalligan's long standing animosity towards Silas. He'd accept his hospitality at the club, or at social functions, probably for the sake of proprietary, but always there was an undercurrent of enmity. He'd tried to get Silas's club closed down, blaming him for all that was wrong in society. Envying his wealth and success. It was the not so pleasant side of Oakley Penhalligan that people chose to ignore at their peril.

"Mine and the men who were with me. You can ask them."

"Men in your employ, paid to do your bidding and keep your confidences."

"What are you suggesting?" Hope said. A swirl of hot rage boiled inside her ready to explode like a raging volcano.

"I'm suggesting that your husband knows more about this murder than he's prepared to tell. Why were you looking for him, for instance? Some sort of grievance between you that couldn't be settled peaceably?"

Hope's anger erupted. "If you must know Silas and his man Knuckles were attacked in the street by a gang of thieves and my sister Violet is missing. They're the ones you should be looking for," she blurted out.

Penhalligan's interest perked up. "Attacked in the street? And Violet was with them?" He looked thoughtful for a moment and Hope remembered how, at one time, she'd thought him keen on Violet. "I'd like to speak to her too. She had reason to hate her former lover. Perhaps that hatred got out of hand."

"Like I said, she's not here. We don't know where she is. She may be in danger. If you spent more time rounding up the street gangs and less time harassing law abiding folk like my husband and myself then maybe none of this would have happened." She paused for breath.

A shadow scudded across Penhalligan's face. "You think she was taken against her will?"

"Of course she was. She may be irresponsible and impetuous, but she'd never leave her children. She just wouldn't." Hope's frustration threatened to bring on a thunderstorm of tears. She turned to Silas.

"She was with us when we were attacked. By the time I came round she was gone," Silas said. The deep misery of it reflected in his face. Hope's heart went out to him. Such an admission would be deeply humiliating for a man like Silas.

"When was this? The attack?"

"A few days ago," Silas said. "In the alleyways by Waterloo Bridge."

"The pathologist reckons the body probably went into the river by there a couple of days ago, so it all ties up. And you're still saying you didn't find him?"

"We didn't find him," Silas said, his jaw hardening.

"And Violet's disappeared? Bit of a coincidence, especially as she's the one I'd most like to talk to."

Fury mixed with deep disgust raged inside Hope. "She's probably been taken by the men who killed Bert," she said. "There was a man watching the house this morning. I was going to take Violet's children out, but the rain stopped me. He was watching for us. I'm sure he was."

Penhalligan raised his head to glance out of the window. "Did anyone else see him?" he asked. "Or did you tell anyone?"

Hope's fury knew no bounds. "So you won't take MY word now?" she said, her voice raised in anger. "You think I'm making it up?" She couldn't believe he could doubt her word or Silas's. "If our word isn't good enough you're no longer welcome in my house," she said. "Thank you for telling us about Bert. Now, please go."

"I'll go when I'm ready," he said, but it seemed he had little more to say. He stood and picked up his hat. "This isn't the last you'll hear on the matter. I'll be back."

Hope closed the door behind him, but turmoil churned inside her. Bert was dead and her old friend,

Inspector Penhalligan, was blaming Silas and Violet for it.

Chapter Twenty One

Once Inspector Penhalligan had gone his words kept reverberating in Hope's head. "I can't believe he really thinks you had anything to do with killing Bert," she said. "He knows you, or at least I thought he did. And blaming Violet is ridiculous."

"She had good reason to want him dead," Silas said, "and she's not here to defend herself, but you're right, Violet would never kill anyone." He poured them each a brandy. "I'm more convinced than ever that whoever attacked us took Violet, and they knew who she was. I've been going over what happened, or my memory of it. We were directed into that alleyway by someone who knew Bert, and we were being watched, I'm sure of it and Knuckles said the same. It wasn't a random attack. It was planned."

"Oh my Lord," Hope said. "Why would anyone want to kidnap Violet? She's never done anyone any harm in her whole life. She's a single mother with two children. It doesn't make sense." Tears of rage and helplessness welled up, but Hope blinked them back. Her voice shook as she said, "You don't think they're going to kill her too, do you? I mean, if they killed Bert…"

Silas put his arms around her and gently pulled her close. She heard the rasp in his breath and guessed his ribs still pained him. "No," he said. "They won't kill her unless they have to. She's worth more to them alive than dead. That's one thing we have to be thankful for."

"Of course," Hope said, sudden realisation emerging like a stranded ship when the tide goes out. "They're going to ask for money to let her go."

"Exactly my thoughts," Silas said.

"And we'll pay it?"

"Yes, whatever they ask."

Hope considered the alternatives. "Supposing they take the money and kill her anyway? They may even kill you. This is something the police should be dealing with, not accusing you of murder." The horrifying thought made the tears she'd been holding back brim her eyes again. "I couldn't bear it if anything happened to you," she said.

Silas smiled and kissed her hair as she rested her head on his broad shoulder. "I won't let anything happen to me," he said. "Nor to Violet."

"There was a man watching the house earlier," Hope said. "Roughly dressed and standing in the rain. The police wagon must have scared him away. Do you think he had anything to do with Violet's kidnapping?"

"Could just have been a coincidence," Silas said. "A down and out looking for a handout, but I'll leave Abel and Eddie with you tomorrow, to be on the safe side." I wouldn't want anything to happen to you either."

He kissed her again and Hope found comfort in his arms.

The next morning Silas said he was going with Knuckles to retrace their steps through Mile End and Hoxton visiting the boarding houses where Bert had stayed. "Bert was alive then and we may not have been the only ones looking for him. That's the most likely place we picked up the tail. Now that Bert's dead the people who knew him may be more forthcoming. No one wants to be mixed up in murder."

"Please be careful," Hope said.

"And you. And if that man comes back send a message to Penhalligan. Let him deal with it."

When Silas had gone Hope decided to go and see Inspector Penhalligan herself. She wanted to know more about Bert's death and Oakley Penhalligan had been a good friend in the past. She'd helped him investigate her father's murder and he knew more about her family than she'd care to think about. She didn't believe he really thought Violet could have killed Bert and she wanted to find out what evidence he had against Silas for herself.

She left the children with Daisy, Abel and Silas's man Eddie. Eddie was a porter at the club and she knew him well. He'd been a bare-knuckle fighter when he was younger and could still hold his own in the ring against much younger men. "Don't worry, Mrs Quirk," he said. "I've children of me own. I'd give everything I've got to protect them an' all."

"I don't want them out on the street until this thing's over and Violet is safely back with us," she said. "They're only to go in the garden at the back until this thing's settled, or at least until I've spoken to the police. I need to be sure they're safe before letting them go out."

"Understood," Eddie said.

She put on her summer coat and straw hat. The sun was still shining and, if she hadn't been so worried about the visit and what she might discover, she'd have enjoyed the walk to the police station. She nodded to people she knew on the way, but didn't stop to chat.

She was a woman on a mission and didn't want to be distracted from it.

The police station felt familiar. A deluge of memories flooded her mind, but she didn't have the time or patience to indulge them. She was worried about Violet. How would she feel being held against her will, away from her children not knowing whether they missed her, or whether anyone was out looking for her?

A surly looking sergeant sat at the desk. She'd not seen him before. "Good morning," she said. "I've come to see Inspector Penhalligan. Is he in?"

The sergeant's gaze travelled slowly over her before he spoke. "Is he expecting you?" he asked.

"No. But I'm sure he will want to see me."

"What's it about?"

She pondered her answer. She didn't want to say it was a private matter, that would be inappropriate, but on the other hand she didn't want this man to question her further. She could hardly give the real reason: that she wanted to know why Penhalligan was accusing Silas of murder.

"Please tell him that Mrs Silas Quirk would like to see him and that I have some information for him about a matter I believe he is working on. At least that was my impression when he visited yesterday."

Mentioning Silas's name and the visit had the desired effect. "Thank you. If you'd care to wait, Madam, I'll see if he's free."

Hope sat staring at the wood panelled walls. She recalled previous visits to the station when the outcomes had not always been as she desired. She hoped today would prove more fruitful. She remembered the inspector's reluctance to talk about his cases without a good reason, and then only if it benefitted the case. A good ten minutes passed before Inspector Penhalligan appeared. "Mrs Quirk," he said. "Always a pleasure."

He showed her into his office. It hadn't changed a bit in the years since she'd last sat here, opposite him at the desk he occupied. The same solid mahogany desk, the same pictures and certificates on the wall, the same filing cabinets piled high with papers. "What can I do for you?" He knocked his pipe out in the large ashtray on the desk, avoiding Hope's gaze.

"You seem to be under the ridiculous impression that Silas had something to do with Bert Shadwick's murder. I'm here to tell you that it's insane. He'd no more kill Bert than you would. I think you know that."

Penhalligan leaned back in his chair. "Really? You sure of that? It wouldn't be the first time."

"Not the first time? What do you mean?"

"I mean it wouldn't be the first time he's killed a man. He's done it before."

"No," Hope said. "Silas wouldn't." Her heart raced. Was the inspector right? There was a lot she didn't know about Silas's past but even so...

Penhalligan leaned forward, resting his arms on his desk. "As I believe I've told you in the past, Hope, when we investigate a murder we find out more than you imagine about the people involved. Silas Quirk has a history of violet assault."

Hope stared at the inspector willing him to be wrong. True, Silas had a reputation for being ruthless in business, but not violent. Never violent.

"I don't believe you," she said. "You're mistaken, although why you should want to blacken Silas's name mystifies me. I don't know what you hope to gain by it, but I'm going to prove you wrong."

"Ask him," Penhalligan said. He rose and made to show her out. "If there's nothing else."

Hope's mind whirled, the wildest of thoughts buzzed through her head. She'd seen Silas deal with the most aggressive, violent and often drunk customers at the club in a calm efficient way, never resorting to violence. What was Penhalligan trying to say? She had to get to the bottom of it.

"As a matter of fact there is," she said. "It's Violet. She's missing and I fear for her safety. I… we… think she may have been kidnapped, unless of course you think Silas killed her too." The tears of frustration building up inside Hope threatened to overflow. Why did men have to be so stupid?

Penhalligan sat down again, a look of deep concern filled his thin, intelligent face. "I'm sorry, Hope," he said, his gaze softening. "Of course I don't think Silas killed Bert intentionally. But he's been in a fight and as I said before, it's not the first time his temper has got the better of him. I'm afraid there's more to your husband than you know. It could have been an accident, but disposing of the body in the river – that's unforgiveable. Every man, even a blaggard like Bert Shadwick, deserves a Christian burial."

"Like I said, Silas didn't do it. He was looking for Bert when he was attacked by a street gang. He fought with them, not with Bert. He never found him. They knocked him out. When he came round Violet had disappeared. She's been taken by someone who knew her. Someone who was waiting for them. What are you going to do about that?"

139

Several minutes passed before he spoke. "What draws you to that conclusion?" he asked. "It wouldn't be the first time she's left without warning or telling you where she was going."

"No, but she wouldn't have gone willingly without her children."

Penhalligan nodded. He couldn't dispute what Hope said. He'd known Violet since before the twins were born, celebrated with them at their birth, and knew how much they meant to Violet.

"Silas is out now looking for her. He thinks who ever took her knew who she was and hoped to gain by it. Can't you do anything to help?" She wanted to add 'instead of wasting time accusing innocent people of murder', but didn't.

"Do you have a picture?"

Hope reached into her bag and took out a photo of Violet. She'd had it taken shortly after the children were born. John used it on the posters advertising the Saturday Night Musical Evenings in the pub.

"I'll get this circulated and get the foot patrols to look out for her. We'll treat it as a missing person until we learn different," he said.

"Thank you," Hope said. Inspector Penhalligan showed her out.

Outside the station she paused, relieved at being believed about Violet, but Penhalligan's words about Silas were lodged so firmly in her head a sledgehammer wouldn't shift them.

Chapter Twenty Two

Violet calculated that three days had passed while she'd been in the room. Difficult to work out as the days appeared hardly lighter than the nights, the only difference being the cold draught coming in through the broken window. In daytime a heavy stench of rotting vegetables and the carcasses of rats came up from the alleyway below. Today she felt a little stronger. Jake brought soup and bread every day, not enough to stave off the constant hunger gnawing at her stomach, but enough to keep her alive.

She'd asked him for her clothes. He'd laughed and said, "You won't be needing 'em so I sold 'em. Quality goods they were. Got a good price an' all."

He'd laughed again.

"So I'm to die of pneumonia then?" she said, so he brought her another blanket, so worn she wondered how it had managed to escape the dustbin, or maybe that's where it came from. She held it up and what little light there was shone through the worn bits. "If I had some scissors and a needle and thread, perhaps I could darn some of the holes," she said.

He grunted. "Best be grateful," he said. "You're getting nowt else."

Wrapping it around her body didn't give her much warmth, but at least it covered her up. She walked over to the boarded up window and peered out through the gaps where the haphazardly nailed planks didn't meet. Beyond the planks shards of broken glass remained in the frame. She tried to reach them, but her fingers weren't long enough. She glanced around the room looking for anything that might help. The chest of drawers revealed nothing of interest, but a wooden pole for hangers stretched across the inside of the wardrobe made her pause. She pulled at it. It gave a fraction. A harder tug and one end came away. She braced herself, pushing her foot against the side of the empty cupboard and heaved at the other end with all her strength.

When it gave way she fell backwards and landed with a heavy thud on the bare floorboards, gasping for breath, the pole in her hands. She lay breathless for a moment, then she heard the heavy tread of Jake's footsteps coming up the stairs.

As quick as she could she shoved the pole into the wardrobe, shut the doors and sprang onto the bed, pulling the blankets over herself.

Jake came in. He glanced around. "I thought I heard somat," he said. "What you bin up to?"

Violet feigned sleep.

Satisfied that nothing had been disturbed Jake retreated, closed and locked the door. She heard his descending footsteps.

With a sigh of relief she got out of bed, retrieved the pole from the wardrobe and went over to the window. A light spattering of rain pattered against the glass. At first she tried loosening the broken shards of glass with the pole. When they didn't budge she gave a hearty shove and one fell out, taking it out of reach. It tinkled as it landed in the alley below. Violet cursed in frustration. With a shard of glass she'd at least have a sort of weapon to defend herself.

She ran her hand over the lowest plank of wood. It looked as though it had been there for a long while. Her fingers curled behind it. It felt damp. Some fragments of rotting wood came away at her touch. If the wood was rotten enough…

Raising the pole into position to lever the plank from the window, she pulled hard. The plank moved a little. Heartened she tried again. It moved a bit more. She took hold of the plank and, wriggling it back and forth, managed to wrestle it from the window frame. Holding it firmly in her hands she tried swinging it from side to side. Although rotten it it still felt fairly heavy. Heavy enough, she thought, to use as a weapon.

About an hour later she heard Jake's footsteps coming up the stairs. He'd be bringing her supper. He'd have his hands full and be off guard. The perfect time to pounce.

She waited behind the door until it opened and he stepped into the room. Then she sprang out and swung the plank putting all her weight behind it. It hit Jake square on the side of the head. He stumbled sideways. She swung the plank again, hitting him on the back of the head and he fell, the bowl of soup he'd been carrying hit the floor first, spraying its contents across the boards.

Violet stepped beside him as an uncontrollable rage engulfed her. Shaking and sobbing she battered him around the head and shoulders, wielding the plank with all the pent up fury inside her hitting him again and again until, with a loud crack, the rotten plank broke in half.

Jake lay still, his head bruised and bloody. Violet didn't care. He'd killed Bert, the father of her children, his own half-brother, who didn't deserve it.

She'd go to the police and tell them. And she'd tell them about the gang that attacked Silas and Knuckles and abducted her. Oh yes. She had plenty she wanted to tell, but all she could do was collapse in a heap and cry.

The crying didn't last long. Jake groaned and his hand moved.

Heart pumping with fear and fright, Violet threw the remains of the plank at his head, leapt over him and darted out onto the landing.

He'd said there were other people in the house. She stopped for a fraction of a second and listened. She couldn't hear anything from downstairs. Trembling and hardly able to breathe, she hurried on tiptoe down the stairs. No one appeared from any of the rooms. Jake's coat hung on a hook by the front door. She grabbed it and slipped into it before opening the door. The street outside looked empty, steady rain splashed the cobbles. Without further thought she dashed out and sprinted as fast as she could along the road. When she came to a junction she glanced from side to side, not knowing which way to turn. The narrow streets appeared dark and empty. Houses crammed along either side leaned into the roadway. She dodged into a doorway stopping to catch her breath. At last she was free, but where on earth was she?

She walked further along, glancing behind to make sure she wasn't being followed. If she could find a shop or a pub she could ask directions. The path she followed narrowed, alleyways turning off offered no hint of a safe place to stop. She turned down narrow twisting lanes, but saw only closed doorways. Even the windows showed no lights, as though the whole place was deserted. The rain seeped through her stockings and soaked the hem of her petticoat, making walking more difficult. The cold slithered into her bones. Tired, cold, wet and hungry exhaustion overcame her. Darkness filled the streets and she was lost. There appeared to be no way out of this warren. Perhaps she'd have been better off staying where she was, at least with Jake she was dry and fed. Here she'd probably die of pneumonia or something worse. She sank down into a doorway and sobbed.

Later, as the rain eased off a rotund woman wearing a heavy cloak and carrying an umbrella appeared, walking along the road. She stopped in front of Violet. Violet glanced up.

"Hello, ducks. You alright?" the woman asked. "You look like you could do wi' a bit of 'elp."

"Oh yes. Please. Can you tell me where I am? I need to find the nearest police station. I want to report—"

The woman laughed. "Polis station? You won't find one of them round 'ere." She looked Violet over. "I can offer you a place to dry off and have a bite to eat if you want."

Overcome with gratitude Violet thanked her, stood up and followed her. She stopped at a door a few yards further along the road, opened it and showed Violet in.

"It ain't much to look at," the woman said, "but it's better 'an being on the streets."

The woman took Violet through to the kitchen where a stove heated the room. It was warm and cosy. A table stood by the wall, three chairs grouped around it. A tall glass-fronted cupboard held plates and various items of crockery. Several pans stood on another cupboard by the stove. The woman lit the gas light and pushed a large pot onto the stove. She turned to Violet. "Give me your things and I'll dry 'em by the fire." She reached up and pulled a pair of woollen stockings and a heavy wool skirt from an airier above the table by the wall. "'Ere, put these on while yours dry."

Violet peeled off her wet things and handed them to the woman. "I don't know how to thank you," she said. "But when I get home I'll see you're well rewarded."

The woman opened the front of the stove and hung Violet's things on the back of chairs in front of it. "The way I sees it goodness has its own rewards," she said. "You must call me Sadie. Everyone does."

"Well, thank you, Sadie. I'm truly grateful," Violet said. "Now, perhaps you can tell me exactly where we are."

Sadie stared at her. "Why, you're on Dead Man's Island," she said.

Chapter Twenty Three

When Hope left the police station what Inspector Penhalligan had said about Silas's past played on her mind. How could he have failed to mention something so important as killing a man? She thought back over all she knew about Silas. She knew he'd spent time in America but that part of his life was a closed book. He never spoke of it. Was that the reason?

The fact that Inspector Penhalligan, a man she regarded as an old friend, knew about it and appeared to be using it to wage some sort of vendetta against Silas, bothered her. What was Penhalligan trying to prove? That Silas killed Bert? No. She'd never believe that.

Silas said they couldn't find Bert, hadn't seen him. Why would he lie? If they'd found him and there'd been a fight as Penhalligan suggested, Silas would have told her. He wouldn't toss the body into the Thames to cover it up, he just wouldn't. But why hadn't he told her of his past?

The worry gnawed at her heart. Did he not trust her? Did he think she'd think less of him? No. Impossible. Her love for him was deeper than that, nothing would ever change it. And she trusted him. No man alive was as principled, honest and honourable as Silas.

She hastened her step. She'd ask him. He'd clear it up in an instant.

As she approached the house she saw a hansom cab parked outside. She gasped as she watched Esmé Malone, Silas's sister, alight. Only Silas ever called her Esmé, her given name. Everyone else called her by the nickname, Dexi, which she'd earned while working at The Grenadier due to her dexterity with cards. The memory of Dexi's letter flashed across her brain. Immersed in Violet's problems the visit had completely slipped Hope's mind.

She rushed forward to greet her sister-in-law. Dexi, wearing a deep crimson suit and the most outrageous hat, hugged her and kissed her on both cheeks. Suddenly the street seemed to be filled with the heady perfume of tuberoses and endless possibilities. Hope's heart lifted. With Dexi around life was always easier and brighter. Difficulties melted away. She had a way of putting things into perspective.

Dexi visited every August. She said Paris, where she'd opened her own gambling club and casino, held little to entertain one at that time of year. Anyone who was anyone went south for the summer, spending it in Cannes or on the Riviera. Very little money could be made in Paris in August, so Dexi took the opportunity to visit family and friends in London. Her arrival usually heralded a mad social whirl for Hope and Silas. Invitations arrived for visits to house-parties, balls and race meetings around the country. There'd be afternoon teas and shopping expeditions to the luxury stores on Oxford and Regent Street and, of course, to Dexi's dressmaker for a new wardrobe. There were bridge and poker parties where Hope still marvelled at her skill with cards.

The coachman, overseen by Hortense, Dexi's maid, unloaded two trunks onto the pavement and a carpet bag. Hope greeted Hortense warmly. She'd come to respect her down-to-earth good sense when she worked for Dexi in the club helping Hope dress every evening.

The commotion on the pavement brought Abel to the door of the house. When he saw them he rushed out. Dexi embraced him, then, holding him at arm's length looked him up and down.

"I swear you've grown taller since I last saw you," she said. "And broader." She squeezed the muscles on his arm.

Abel beamed. He turned to Hortense.

Deep love and pride shone in Hortense's eyes as she appraised her younger brother. "Well," she said. "Don't just stand there like Colossus, put them muscles to work. Take the luggage up."

Grinning widely Abel stepped towards the largest trunk, picked it up, swung it onto his shoulder and marched along the path into the house. The noisy reunion had alerted Eddie too, and he came and picked up the second trunk. Hortense picked up the carpet bag and followed Abel into the house.

Dexi paid the cabby and went with Hope into the house. "Is it the usual room?" she asked, watching her luggage being taken up the stairs.

"Yes. Of course," Hope said. Whenever Dexi stayed she had the room on the second floor at the front opposite Hope and Silas's room. It was the second best room in the house. Violet had a room at the back with the children, as Hope had thought it would be quieter.

William and Rose were hovering in the hall with Daisy. Dexi looked surprised to see them. She crouched down in front of them. "Hello," she said. "Have you come for a visit?"

William nodded. "We're staying with Aunty Hope and Uncle Silas. They're looking after us while Ma's away, but she'll be back soon," he said.

"I see." Dexi smiled her beguiling smile. "The last time I saw you two you were babies. My how you've grown."

"I'm not a baby," said an indignant William. "I'm big now."

"So I see," Dexi said. "And you, Rose? How are you?"

Rose giggled.

Dexi reached into her bag and took out two paper wrappers. "It's a good job I remembered these," she said. "Although I don't suppose you like fudge."

"I like fudge very much," William said.

"Then you shall have some," Dexi said and handed them each one of the wraps. "Now, how about I have tea with Aunty Hope and come and see you both later? Will that suit?"

The children agreed that it would and Dexi and Hope went up to the drawing room.

"So, where's Violet?" Dexi said.

"We don't know," Hope said. Then she told her about the note from Bert, Violet's fear of losing the children, and how she'd set out with Silas to find him and reason with him, or, more likely, Hope thought, to pay him off. "Now we've heard that Bert's dead and the police think Silas killed him."

Relating the story brought a fresh swell of despair over Hope. If it hadn't been for Daisy appearing with a tray of tea and some sandwiches and cake Mrs B had thoughtfully added, she would have collapsed in a heap of tears.

Pouring the tea and handing out the sandwiches provided a welcome distraction. Then Silas arrived and Daisy brought in another cup, saucer and plate.

When Silas greeted Dexi, or Esmé, as he called her, Hope saw the deep, unconditional affection between them. She envied it. True she had her family, John, Violet and Alfie, and knew they'd do anything for her, but it wasn't the same deep fondness she saw between Silas and his sister. She saw again how they enjoyed each other's company. She knew Silas to be a passionate man, passionate about his family, passion that extended to her family too. She wondered if Dexi resented that or if she was the only one who felt that burden. He'd been generosity itself, both to her and her family since even before they married, and they were all better off because of it. Now impulsive, irrepressible, irresponsible Violet was putting it to the test again.

She watched as he embraced his sister with care. He'd brightened considerably at her presence. He glanced at the table and picked up a couple of sandwiches, putting them on a plate. "How was your journey?" he asked. "Not too discomforting I hope."

"Stuffy and hot as Hades on the train," Dexi said, helping herself to a piece of cake. "The Channel crossing could have been calmer. But I'm here now and glad to see you."

"And I you," Silas said and tenderly brushed a tendril of Dexi's black as night hair, a perfect match to his, back into place from where it had fallen across her forehead. "And are you well? I expect every day to hear how you've met someone and fallen madly in love."

Dexi laughed. "No one would ever match up to my expectations," she said. "I'd need a man as strong, passionate and caring as you."

Dexi stood back and looked at Silas's face. She touched the bruise on his cheek and the healing gash across his forehead. "Hope told me about Violet's disappearance and your being involved in a fight, but seeing the reality…" she shook her head. "Is it something I need to worry about?"

Silas grinned. "No, my dear. Just a little skirmish in one of the slums. I'm fine now and my search for Violet continues. Did Hope mention that that charlatan who fathered her children is dead and Penhalligan believes I did it?"

"Yes, she did mention it," Dexi said. "Why on earth would Penhalligan think you killed him? It's beyond me."

"He said Silas had killed a man before, so he thought he wouldn't be above doing it again," Hope said.

Silas looked shocked. "He told you that?"

"Yes. He seemed to think it gave him the right to paint you as a vicious killer," Hope said.

"Oh stuff and nonsense." Dexi almost exploded with rage. "Silas saved my life that day. If it wasn't for him, I wouldn't be here. How can he say such a ridiculous thing?" She put her hand on Silas's arm.

Silas shrugged. "I did come home battered and bruised. He would assume I'd been in a fight. But kill someone and throw them in the river. How can he believe that?" A look of pure incredulity crossed his face.

"I for one don't believe it," Hope said. "Whatever happened in the past I know you'd never do such a thing."

Dexi glanced at Silas. Seeing his reluctance to explain what had happened before they came to

England, she decided she'd better. "It was, what, ten years ago? In America," she said. "I was married then to Jack Malone, a riverboat gambler." She paused as though lost in reverie. "Happy exciting days on the Mississippi. The boats were the most glamorous things you've ever seen. The salons all painted white and gold with crystal chandeliers hanging from the ceilings. Music played, drinks were served and high-stakes poker games were the order of the day."

She seemed to be getting into her stride. "This particular day Jack had heard that Beau Hetherington was on the boat, looking for a game. He'd come straight from the California gold mines, with money in his pocket and Jack wanted some. Oh you wouldn't believe what went on then, on the boats. People who'd been shut up in the mines for months coming into town with their gold. Mines worth half a million dollars would change hands on the turn of a card. It was out of this world and unbelievable." She shook her head at the memory.

She sipped her tea and continued. "Jack heard this guy was on the boat and persuaded him to play at our table. Ten players sat down at the beginning of the evening. Jack, me, a guy named Rafferty, another called Coles, Beau Hetherington and a four others whose names I can't recall... Silas was dealer." She put out her hand and touched his arm again.

"Every round the stakes were getting higher. Several of the others dropped out and as the evening wore on it was clear that animosity was building between Jack and Hetherington. Jack was the big winner, Hetherington consistently losing. It was gone midnight when it came down to Jack and Hetherington. Rafferty and Coles were still at the table but both had folded, as had I. Jack kept raising the ante, pushing Hetherington. Hetherington was raising back, betting with his gold, pushing Jack. Jack outbid him. The pot was several thousand dollars huge. Hetherington wouldn't let it go. He must have raised Jack ten times. He put the deeds to his mine in the pot." She closed her eyes at the memory. She shuddered. "The tension in the room that night," she said. "Unbelievable. Once in a lifetime you see a game like that."

Hope found herself holding her breath. She could almost feel the tension. "What happened?" she said.

Dexi smiled. "Hetherington called. He laid down three Aces and two Kings. Full House, Aces over Kings. Normally that'd be unbeatable, but Jack had a Royal Flush." She stared at Hope. "Do you know the odds of that happening? More than a million to one."

"So Jack won."

"Hetherington accused him of cheating. Jumped up and pulled out a gun. He shot Jack and pointed the gun at me. Silas jumped up and punched him, an uppercut to the jaw, if I remember right. His head flew back and he fell against a stone pillar. The next shot went high and brought the chandelier crashing down onto the table. It started a fire. Silas grabbed me, threw me over his shoulder and carried me out to safety. He saved my life." She smiled fondly at Silas.

"So what happened next?" Hope was enthralled.

"Jack won that pot fair and square. There were witnesses. I'd lost a husband but gained a gold mine. I sold it. We moved back to England and opened The Grenadier." She gazed at Silas again. "Best thing I ever did," she said.

"Whew," Hope said. "Well that explains it. What happened in America ten years ago has nothing to do with Bert or his death."

"No," Silas said. "And I'm sure Inspector Penhalligan knows that full well." He took Hope's hand. "I fear he was trying to put a wedge between us. Though, heaven knows why."

"He'll never do that," Hope said. "Not in a million years." Dexi's story did go a long way to explain the deep affection between brother and sister. They had the sort of trust and closeness that only comes with shared experience.

Chapter Twenty Four

Sadie ladled some soup from the pot on the stove into a bowl and put it on the table with a spoon for Violet. "Get some o' this inside you," she said. "You'll feel all the better for it."

Violet picked up the spoon. The soup was even more unappealing than the stuff Jake served up every evening. Beige in colour with what appeared to be vegetables floating in it, along with a slick of grease. Sadie cut a chunk of bread from the loaf on a side table and handed that to Violet. Violet smiled her thanks. Hunger gnawed at her stomach and the bread and soup, however unappetising, would at least warm her and fill her up.

She took a spoonful. It tasted better than it looked. Violet's hunger made it palatable and she soon finished the bowlful while Sadie watched her.

"Good," she said, when Violet had finished. "Now rest a while then we'll think about what to do next."

Reassured, Violet leaned back in the chair, the events of the last few hours had exhausted her. How lucky, she thought, that Sadie came along when she did. I could have been left to die in the street if she hadn't come along, she thought.

The warmth of the fire and the cosy familiarity of the kitchen, with its stove, cupboards of crockery and oak table, lulled Violet into a doze. Her eyelids felt heavy, every bone in her body ached. She felt herself drifting off. Sadie's voice seemed to be coming from a great distance. She became aware of another person in the room. A man. She heard Sadie telling her that things would look brighter in the morning, then oblivion, sweet and comforting as a lover's arms, embraced her.

The next morning she awoke and glanced around, trying to make sense of her surroundings. A rough sheet and a red and gold bedspread covered her almost naked body. The four-poster double bed she'd obviously slept in had matching drapes and a pulled back curtain around it. A jug of water and a glass stood on a nightstand next to the bed. She eyed it suspiciously. Her head thumped and her throat ached from dryness, but the water looked too tempting. She sat up, poured a glass and sniffed it. It smelled all right. She took a sip. Just one, no more. She tried to swallow to ease her throat as she gazed around. A large jug and bowl stood on a washstand next to a wooden wardrobe. A dressing table and mirror graced the far wall next to a fireplace that showed evidence of a fire recently extinguished. The dressing table held brushes, combs, powder and an array of bottles. Curtains covered the window.

She eased her legs over the side of the bed and went to the door. It was locked. She rattled the handle, called out, banged on the door, but nobody came. She tiptoed over to the window and drew back the curtains. Gazing out between the iron bars that ran, prison-like from top to bottom, she saw clouds scudding across a summer blue sky over the rooftops of the buildings on the opposite side of the alley.

This wasn't so bad, she thought as she made her way back to sit on the bed. More comfortable than the prison Jake had kept her in. Gazing around at the incongruously ornate decorations and the pictures on the walls that wouldn't be given space in a respectable house, she realised she'd woken up in a tart's boudoir and that kind, caring, totally convincing Sadie ran a brothel.

Just because she was in a brothel didn't mean she had to sit here in her underwear. She pulled the bedspread off the bed to wrap around her. The material was very thin and torn at the edge. She pulled at the tear and it ripped further. She continued to rip it until she pulled off a strip wide enough to cover her from armpits to knees. Once she'd wrapped it around herself she looked in the mirror. It wasn't the most fetching of outfits but it did provide a modicum of modesty.

She walked around the room again, looking for anything that might be of use but found nothing. Sighing she sat on the bed and pulled her knees up to her chest. She'd wait. Someone was bound to come for her. Then all she had to do was persuade them that she'd see they were paid more for taking her home than they'd earn in a year selling her services.

All she had to do was wait.

Chapter Twenty Five

The next morning Hope, Silas and Dexi were in the dining room having breakfast when a parcel arrived for Silas. Daisy brought it up and gave it to Silas to open. "Ah, good," he said. "I hoped these would arrive today."

He opened the parcel and showed Hope the flyers he'd had printed. Hope took one and read:

£500 Reward for safe return. Then there was a picture of Violet and the address of The Grenadier.

She gasped. Five hundred pounds!" she said. "That's a fortune."

"Yes. Enough I hope to ensure that those involved in her abduction question their loyalty. If she's being held against her will, as I'm sure is the case, then someone must know where she is."

Hope handed the leaflet to Dexi for her perusal.

"What about the police?" she said. "Shouldn't you speak to Inspector Penhalligan? I'm not sure what he'll make of your offering such a substantial reward."

"Penhalligan is concerned to catch Bert's killer. I'm only concerned with Violet's safe return. If offering a reward makes that possible it will be worthwhile."

Hope put her hand on Silas's arm. "You're too generous. We already owe you more than we can ever repay."

Silas frowned. "I fear that I must bear some responsibility for Violet's disappearance. If I hadn't allowed her to come with us and if I wasn't in a position to pay for her release, then perhaps she may never have been taken in the first place."

"It's not your fault," Hope said, appalled that Silas should be made to feel responsible. "If it's anyone's fault it's Violet's." She couldn't say what was in her heart, that she loved Violet more than words could say, but why did she have to be so infuriatingly impulsive and reckless?

Dexi handed the flyer back to Silas. "That should do the trick," she said. "I doubt the men who attacked you are getting one tenth of that amount for their trouble. They must know where she was taken. It's a start."

"Good. As long as I have your approval I'll get these handed out around Waterloo today. Then my men and I will wait at The Grenadier for news."

Hope wasn't convinced, but it was no use arguing with Silas when he was doing everything in his power to find her sister. And, perhaps he was right. Perhaps he was the real target all along. Men with money so often were.

After breakfast Hope went downstairs to have her coffee with the children. The children had breakfast in the kitchen with Daisy, Abel and Mrs B, an arrangement that suited them all. She enjoyed seeing them and planning their day. Silas went to his office to look over some paperwork Dexi had brought for him to read through on her behalf. She announced that she was 'off to the dressmaker'. "I may be some time," she said with a broad smile. Hope knew that meant she'd be ordering several dresses and she'd want Hope's opinion on them when they were delivered.

"Are you sure you don't want to come with me?" she asked Hope, eyeing her serviceable blue morning dress.

Hope laughed. "No. I plan to spend the day with the children," she said. "They're missing their mother. It's the least I can do."

When she arrived downstairs an exuberant William greeted her. "Can we go over the park," he said, enthusiasm shining in his little face. "Can I sail my boat again? Can I?"

Hope glanced out of the window. The sun was high in the sky promising a fine day. But she still worried about the scruffy man she'd seen across the street the day before, watching the house. "Maybe later," she said. "First of all you can help Mrs B make some scones for this afternoon's tea."

After making the scones the children were itching to go out. So Hope suggested a game of croquet in the garden. "I hear that Abel is a crack hand at croquet," she said. "I think we should challenge him and Rose to a game. Show them how it's done, eh, William? There's just time for a game before lunch."

"Croquet?" William screwed up his nose. "That's a girls' game."

"On the contrary," Hope said. "It's a game of skill. I bet you couldn't even beat Rose, that's why you don't want to play."

"I do want to play," William said, suddenly changing his mind. "I can beat everyone."

"Well, we'll have to see about that then, won't we?" Hope said.

Daisy got out the half-sized croquet set Hope had bought them and they ran to get their outdoor shoes on. It was decided that Hope would partner Rose and at William's insistence, Abel would partner him.

They were in the hall when someone knocked on the front door. "I'll go," Hope said, being the nearest, but she hesitated. Suppose it was the man who'd been watching the house the day before?

Abel pushed past her. "Best let me," he said. He opened the door. The man standing on the doorstep looked entirely presentable.

He raised his grey top hat. "Good morning," he said. "Is this the residence of Mrs Violet Daniels? I do hope I've come to the right place."

Hope and Abel exchanged glances. Hope stepped forward. "I'm Mrs Silas Quirk. Whom may I be addressing?"

"Oh. Sorry." He reached into the inside pocket of his smart grey suit and brought out a card which he handed to Hope. "Gabriel Stone," he said. "I'm looking for Mrs Daniels. This is the address she gave me. I do hope I haven't been misled."

Hearing voices William's curiosity got the better of him and he came into the hall to see what was going on. Seeing Gabriel he whooped with delight and rushed forward, a wide smile lighting up his face. "It's Ma's friend Uncle Gabriel," he cried. "He's got a motor car. Have you come to stay? Will you play with us? Can we go for a ride in your motor car?"

Hope and Abel exchanged glances. If William knew him he must be telling the truth. He'd come looking for Violet.

"You'd better come in," Hope said, stepping aside to allow him to enter. "This way. My husband's upstairs. Have you come far? Can I offer you some refreshment?"

"Thank you. I've come from Norfolk. A lovely county. I met Mrs Daniels when she was staying there."

Abel ushered William out into the garden, reminding him that they had a challenge to meet on the lawn. "You can see Masser Stone tomorrow, if your aunt agrees."

"Daisy can join you while we have our coffee," Hope said. Reluctantly William followed Abel out.

Showing Mr Stone upstairs to the drawing room Hope recalled William talking about going for a ride in a motor car while they were on holiday. She smiled as she realised this must be the gentleman involved. Why had Violet never mentioned him?

She showed Gabriel into the upstairs front drawing room. Silas joined them. Once coffee had been served, Gabriel told Hope and Silas about the time he'd spent with Violet in Yarmouth. "She told me she'd be staying here. I said I would call. I looked forward to seeing her again. I'm sorry to have missed her."

Hope guessed from his demeanour that he had a more than casual interest in Violet. The way he spoke of her told her more than the actual words ever could. He seemed like a pleasant young man too. She judged him to be in his late twenties, successful and well mannered, if a little overly familiar. He appeared to have little time for formality and she admired his openness.

"You're not the only one looking for my sister," Hope said.

Silas told him about Violet's fear of the children's father taking them away from her. "That's why she took the children away," he said. "But then decided to come home and face him. Regrettably we never found him and now the police inform us that the man is dead."

Gabriel's eyes widened. "I hope dear Violet isn't in any trouble. Now you're telling me she's missing?"

Silas told him about the attack and coming round to find Violet gone. Hope watched the blood drain from Gabriel's face. Puzzlement filled his eyes.

"I don't think Inspector Penhalligan believes we were attacked," Silas said. "He thinks we found Bert Shadwick, the children's father, and set upon him, killed him and tossed his body into the Thames. He probably thinks Violet's gone into hiding because she's involved."

"But that's crazy," Gabriel said. "Violet would never do anything like that." His hand was shaking. Silas brought out the whisky and poured them each a glass.

"I'm sorry. All this must have come as a terrible shock," he said. "I have been out every day with my men looking for Violet. I don't believe she killed Bert. Violet would never kill anyone, but someone did. And if they killed him, they may have taken Violet and plan to kill her, or get what they can from us by way of a ransom. Whatever happens none of us will rest until she's home and safe with us and her children." The determination in Silas's voice cheered Hope. A fresh swell of love washed over her. Silas showed Gabriel one of the flyers he'd had printed.

Gabriel sat for a while lost in thought, as though trying to make sense of what he'd heard. It wouldn't be easy to digest, the carefree girl he'd met on holiday being embroiled in such abominable circumstances. A heavy silence filled the room, the only sound the ticking of the clock and the quiet clink when Silas refilled their glasses.

Eventually Gabriel finished his drink and set his glass back on the table. "I know a few people in London," he said. "I have contacts. I'll make enquiries." He took a small notepad and pencil from his inside pocket and wrote an address. "I'm staying at this hotel. Please let me know if you hear anything more. I'll do whatever I can to help. I just want to see Violet again."

Hope took the note. He was staying at a well-known hotel just off the Strand. Hope was impressed.

"I do hope you'll join us for dinner this evening," she said. After all he was a friend of Violet's and she was dying to know more about him, how they met and a million other things Violet had omitted to mention. "If you have no other engagements."

"Thank you. That's very kind of you. I'd be delighted," he said.

"Well, what do you think of that?" Hope asked Silas once Gabriel had gone.

"Seems a nice enough chap," Silas said. "Although I don't know why Violet never mentioned him."

"No. Not like Violet at all," Hope said, knowing how Violet usually talked about her conquests in the most gushing terms. "Still, the mystery of William's ride in a motor car is solved."

Silas chuckled. "Yes, what would we do without William's constant chatter? We wouldn't know anything at all."

Chapter Twenty Six

Back in the hotel Gabriel tried to make sense of what he'd been told. Apparently the girl he'd met on holiday had been kidnapped. But why? She didn't appear to him to be in any position to pay off a ransom, on the contrary, she'd talked of her struggle to make a living and to support her two children. It looked as though her brother-in-law was well enough off, but if you wanted a ransom, why kidnap the sister-in-law? Why not the wife?

None of it made any sense. He began to wonder what sort of set up he'd walked into.

He ran a bath and sunk into it to go over the events of the last few hours. He thought back to the first time he saw Violet standing at the station with her children, looking so lost and vulnerable. She was strikingly beautiful and it had been difficult to move his gaze away from her. He'd wanted to know more about her. He thought about his sister who also had two children, although the thoughts running through his head weren't exactly brotherly. He'd hoped that if ever she was stuck at a railway station without transport someone would come to her aid. So, being a gentleman, he'd offered to help.

The boy, William, reminded him of himself at that age, so eager to try everything with no thought for anything other than the pleasure to come. When had he lost that innocent, wide-eyed eagerness? He sighed and slid further under the water.

Violet intrigued him. He'd come to Yarmouth, as he'd told her, looking for furniture, but not as he'd said as a salesman. His father, a successful businessman, owned a string of hotels across the country and Gabriel was looking for suitable furnishings for his latest acquisition, a luxury hotel in Yarmouth. Gabriel hoped to find locally crafted pieces and small treasures that would turn a bland, impersonal hotel room into a cosy, welcoming place that people wanted to return to. If he succeeded he could prove to his father that he'd earned a place on the company board and had sufficient business acumen to take on a more responsible role within the company. Then he'd met Violet.

He had to admit that spending time with her had brought him more joy than he thought possible. He admired the way she looked after her children, taking a job in one of the seafront bars to pay her way, not expecting anything of him, other than to enjoy his company, as he enjoyed hers. She graciously accepted all he offered, again with no expectation. He'd never met anyone so spontaneous and optimistic and no one he felt so at home with. She brought colour and light into an otherwise grey world.

She'd said she was widowed, but it didn't take him long to uncover the truth. Impossible to keep any secrets with a chatterbox like William along. He'd learned all about their living in a pub with Uncle John and Aunt Alice and Amy and Violet's singing in the pub on a Saturday night. He guessed from Nesta's lodging house that Violet had a theatrical past. The Sea View Guest House wasn't grand enough to attract the wealthy summer visitors and he'd soon realised it was where performers from the Winter Gardens and the End of the Pier Show stayed for the season. So, Violet was a pub/Music Hall singer. His mother, an American socialite, would be appalled. The idea made him smile which only increased his attraction to Violet.

He thought about his mother. She'd often worried about him being twenty-nine and not yet showing any signs of wanting to get married and settle down. She kept introducing him to 'suitable young ladies' who'd 'be a good match' or even would be 'a great catch', but, although he enjoyed their company for a time, he hadn't been enamoured enough to want to make it permanent.

He'd thought the same about Violet at first, thinking it was a fleeting summer romance, a brief encounter he'd look back on in the years to come and remember as a pleasant interlude in his life, no more than that. But since Violet's return to London he'd found himself thinking of her almost every minute of every day. Every morning the day ahead seemed empty of purpose if he wasn't seeing her. Places that had been full of life now appeared bereft of warmth, the laughter he remembered gone. Flashes of memory played in his mind – the children on the beach and their delight in it. The look in her green eyes and the way they lit up, sparkling like a faceted gem, when she saw him. Her gentle features and the warmth and radiance of her smile… She'd unlocked a longing in his heart that he'd never imagined he could feel.

He sighed again, pulled the plug and let the water run out of the bath. It had gone cold anyway. He rubbed himself dry with a towel and put on the robe the hotel provided, one of his suggestions his father had baulked at, but which turned out to be well received by guests.

The afternoon sun was high in the sky and he pulled down the window blinds in the sitting room. He still couldn't get Violet out of his head.

He'd come looking for her only to find a tangle of events he found hard to fathom. If it hadn't been for the children he'd have thought he'd come to the wrong place. He tried to recall what Violet had told him of her sister and brother-in-law. She'd said her sister had 'married well' and he'd noticed the touch of envy when she said it.

"She adores the children but has none of her own," she'd said. Seeing Hope Quirk with the children that had been obvious.

The story of the children's father shocked him. Violet's wish to protect them rang true. Just like the Violet he'd come to know, he thought. He looked again at the leaflet Silas had given him. He had no reason to doubt his sincerity when he said he'd do anything to get her back. He obviously felt some degree of responsibility for Violet, which was natural and as it should be. He also had the means to pay well for her safe return. It also became clear to him that Violet hadn't mentioned him to them. Why not?

Had he meant so little to her that she'd forgotten him? No, that wasn't it. He couldn't believe that. They'd become so close and never seeing her again would be more than he could bear. It was no passing interest either. The deep affection he felt for her had been intensified by her plight. The thought that she was in grave danger aroused in him a determination to find and protect her, no matter what it took or what sacrifices he had to make. Whatever the reason she hadn't mentioned him to her family, he'd find out when he saw her again, supposing he did.

He moved to the writing desk, pulled out a piece of paper and began to write. He tugged the bell rope and within minutes a page boy appeared at the door.

"Ask Harry to come up," he said and sent the boy on his way.

Harry, the concierge, appeared a few minutes later. Gabriel knew him well. The Addison Hotel, off the Strand, had been his father's first hotel and Harry his most reliable employee. Nothing went on in London that Harry didn't know about. He'd been chosen for his knowledge of the area but also for his discretion, tact and diplomacy. Gabriel knew him to be trustworthy. "I want you to find out all you can about these people," he said, handing him the paper. The list he handed Harry contained the names: Silas Quirk, Violet Daniels and Bert Shadwick.

Harry smiled and tapped the side of his nose. "It will be done," he said with a grin.

Satisfied, Gabriel got dressed and made his way out of the hotel. He had time to call on a couple of old friends before he made his way back to Violet's sister's house for dinner.

Chapter Twenty Seven

As the day wore on Violet became restless. She got off the bed and paced the room. Every now and again she pounded on the door, yelling for someone to come and let her out. She got no response. She heard footsteps going up and down the stairs, men's footsteps. They passed her door and disappeared into one of the rooms on the same floor. Then she'd hear young girls calling out, sometime laughing. When she banged on the door the laughing grew louder. There was no doubt in her mind what was going on in those other rooms. How long before she would be expected to perform the same services as these other girls? Why didn't Sadie come and see her? Then she'd offer her more money than she'd ever dreamed of to let her go. What was she waiting for?

She splashed her face with the water in the water jug and dried herself on a towel left beside it. She pulled the drawers of the chest open; they were empty save the paper drawer linings, put in to stop the colour of the rough wood seeping into anything in the drawer. Opening the wardrobe revealed two red and black gaudy gowns, slashed to the waist and slit down the skirt to allow easy access to the body beneath. Articles of underwear that would have no place in any respectable woman's wardrobe hung alongside the dresses. She closed the doors with a shudder.

Next she ventured over to the dressing table, picked up one of the combs and ran it through her hair. She looked at the brushes, but decided against using them. She examined each pot on the table in turn, opening it, sniffing it and closing it. She wrinkled her nose at the unpleasant odour of cheap scent.

The powder and paints reminded her of the theatre and the heavy stage make-up she used to wear. A huge puff sat in a box of chalky white powder, pots of rouge and dark powdered mascara scattered around the table, there was even a black pencil for outlining the eyes or covering spots or moles. She guessed anyone using it would want to cover as many spots or blemishes as they could, or at least enough to convince any man the worse for drink that he was getting the beauty he'd paid for. She shuddered as she recalled how often the print of Bert's hand on her cheek had been covered by powder and rouge.

She opened all the drawers to see if there was anything that could be of any use to her, but there wasn't.

Exasperated by her inability to raise any response from continually banging her fist against the wood of the door, she moved to the window. The bars were sturdy and well fixed. Beyond them a casement window, its catches covered with paint and immoveable, gave a view over the alley beyond. Outside, below the window, a group of small boys sat on the cobbles tossing stones into a circle as though playing marbles. She banged the window to attract their attention. No response.

She noticed that one of the quarter panes of glass in the window had a crack running from corner to corner, top to bottom. She picked up one of the hairbrushes and jabbed it between the bars. At first nothing happened, so she tried again and again, hitting harder each time, eventually the ancient glass gave way and fell from the frame to shatter with a crash on the ground below. The boys glanced up. She called out to them. Quick as they could they gathered up their stones and ran off. Damn, she thought.

Gingerly she cleared the rest of the glass from the frame, throwing it out. She could put her hand through. When she glanced out again she saw a boy, older than the others standing, staring up at the window.

"Hello," she called. "Can you help me? I'm locked in." She was going to ask him to fetch someone, but that someone would probably be Sadie, so she thought better of it.

"You broke the window," the boy called up to her.

"Yes. I wanted to talk to you. I'm locked in and I want you to help me."

The boy stared.

She had another thought. "Do you want to earn sixpence?" she said. "Or a shilling?"

"A shilling," the boy said, suddenly interested. "How?"

"Can you take a message to a friend for me?" He looked like one of the street boys who'd run messages for tuppence, let alone a shilling. "Wait there," she said.

Quick as she could she pulled out a sheet of drawer lining and with the kohl pencil wrote:

'I'm being held on Dead Man's Island. The boy knows where. Violet.' Then she folded the paper into four and wrote Hope's name and address on the outside.

"Take this to my sister," she said and she'll give you a shilling, or more even, if you're quick." She put her hand out of the window and dropped the paper, watching it float to the path below. The boy stooped and picked it up. He read the address and put the paper

173

in his pocket, then laughing, he ran off. Violet felt crushed. There was no guarantee the boy would do anything other than join his friends and all have a jolly good laugh. Perhaps she should have offered more, even a sovereign. A swell of desolation washed over her. She'd pinned all her hopes on a small boy, a street urchin, bought with the promise of a shilling. Was that the best she could do?

Outside the world was going about its normal business. Blue sky and sunshine peeked over the opposite rooftops. Why would anyone bother to come and find her? A knot of despair filled her stomach. She could think of nothing to do other than crawl back into the bed and hope that small boy would do as she said. She'd just have to wait until somebody came.

Her frail hope was dashed later that evening. She heard the door being unlocked. Immediately alert she jumped up. Sadie came in carrying a bowl of soup. A man appeared behind her, his bulk almost filling the door frame. The floorboards shook under his weight as he stepped forward, a dark scowl on his face.

Violet gasped. Alarm surged through her. A prickle of panic ran up her spine. Had he come to claim her services? She'd be no match for him. She swallowed back the nausea rising to her throat.

He strode up to Violet, raised his arm and swung a backhand slap across her face. The power of it sent her sprawling back on the bed. The ring he wore gashed her cheek. She put her hand to her face and felt warm blood seeping through her fingers.

"What's the meaning o' this, Bitch?" he raged, flicking a piece of paper onto her prostrate body. Violet glanced at it and saw it was the note she'd dropped out of the window.

"Try that again and you'll be fish food," he said.

Sadie tutted. "You really are a silly girl," she said. "After all we've done for you, being so kind an' all." She left the bowl of soup. Violet heard the key turn in the lock.

The next morning the window was boarded over.

Chapter Twenty Eight

At breakfast Hope saw the relentless, churning agony of despair on Silas's face. Another day without any news of Violet and she knew he blamed himself. "It wasn't your fault," she said to reassure him again.

"No, but I should have been able to protect her," he said. "I'll never forgive myself for that."

"No one could do any more than you've done," Hope reminded him. "I'm sure Violet, wherever she is, understands that."

"I just wish I could do more." He sighed. "I have some work to do at the club, so that's where I'll be if anyone comes forward with any news."

"I'll let you know if I hear anything and I'm going to see John and Alice this morning. They may have heard something." She smiled. "I can tell them about Mr Stone's visit and see if Violet mentioned him to them."

He nodded and took her into his arms to kiss her before he left. Dexi had already gone to see her dressmaker and Hope expected her to be away for some time. She found some colouring books and crayons for the children and left them with Abel and Daisy. She was leaving the house on her way to see John and Alice at the pub, when a small boy dressed in a tattered shirt and short trousers with no shoes stopped her. He couldn't have been more than about seven or eight, a couple of years older than William, she thought, and yet so much scrawnier. He looked like a beggar. Her heart went out to him. His dark sorrowful eyes, in a face pale as paper, reflected the misery of a life on the streets that she wouldn't wish on anyone.

She put her hand into her purse to find something for him.

"Are you Hope Quirk?" he asked.

Stunned that he should know her name Hope replied, "Yes. How did you know?"

"Violet sent a message," the boy said.

Hope gasped as breath left her body. She grabbed the boy. "Violet? You've seen Violet? Where?"

The boy squirmed from her grasp. "She said you'd give me half-a-crown," he said.

"Yes, yes, of course. You shall have half-a-crown when you tell me where she is."

"The man gave me a shilling to forget, but I might remember for half-a-crown."

"Man? What man?"

The boy shrugged.

Hope put her hand into her bag and brought out a shiny half-crown. She held it in front of him. "You shall have this when you tell me where you saw my sister, Violet."

"'*I'm being held on Dead Man's Island. The boy knows where,*' that's what the note said and I remembered the address."

Dead Man's Island? She recalled hearing something about Bert having a brother there, could it be him? "Well, that's certainly worth half-a-crown," she said handing the coin to the boy. "But I will give you a lot more if you are telling the truth and can show me where you saw her." She pulled one of Silas's flyers out of her purse. "Is this the girl?"

The boy's eyes widened when he saw the leaflet. "Five hundred pounds?" he said as if unable to believe what he was seeing.

"Yes and it's yours if you can take me and my husband to where she is." Her heart pounded at the thought of finding Violet.

The boy grinned. "Half now and the rest when we find her," he said.

Hope laughed. "Oh no. Let's find her first and then you shall have the reward, but here's something to show good faith." She handed him a gold sovereign. "There's more if you're telling me the truth."

The boy took it. He turned it over and over in his hand. Hope guessed he'd never seen one before.

"It's a sovereign," she said. "Worth eight half-crowns."

A wide grin lit up his face as he put it in his pocket. "All right, lady. I trust you," he said with a confidence that belied his years.

"First I'll take you to see my husband who's offering the reward," she said. "Then, if you can take us to where the lady is being held you shall have it."

He nodded and walked along with her to The Grenadier to tell Silas what he'd told her. On the way Hope bought them each a pie. The boy wolfed his down. She wished she could find him some shoes and a decent coat.

She asked about his family and learned he was an orphan who looked after himself on the street rather than enter the workhouse. "I do odd jobs," he said. "And I can read and write. Pastor Brown taught me."

So someone cared for him, she thought and was glad. "What's your name?" she said. "I can't keep calling you 'boy'."

"Don't have a name," the boy said. "Lost it with me ma and pa."

Hope's heart lurched. She recalled that children put into the workhouse were given a number. They lost their identity along with everything else. "What do they call you then?" she asked, thinking he'd probably earned a nickname of some sort at the pastor's school.

"The boys at school call me Oik," he said.

"Well, I'll not be calling you Oik. Your parents must have given you a name."

"Peter. My given name's Peter. Ma used to call me Peter Pumpkin." Hope caught the catch in his voice and saw the fleeting tenderness in his eyes. A wistful look filled his face, as though a longing for something gone had passed over him.

"Do you mind if I call you Peter?"

The boy's jaw set. "Just you then, not the others."

Hope smiled as her heart began to melt.

When they arrived at The Grenadier she found Silas talking to Dexi and Gabriel who'd come to the club to offer his help looking for Violet. Hope noticed he'd changed out of his smart grey suit into working men's clothes. Silas and Knuckles were also dressed to be able to pass through the slums without raising eyebrows.

"Are you sure the boy's telling the truth?" Gabriel asked when they heard what the boy had to say. "And not just making it up to get money out of us?"

The boy looked indignant. "She gave me a note. I swear."

"So, where's the note now?"

The boy's face reddened. "A man gave me a shilling for it and told me to forget all about it, but I remembered what it said and who I was to take it to."

"That's right," Hope said. "How else would he know to come to me?"

"He could have heard the gossip on the street, or even seen the leaflet."

"And made up such a convincing story?"

"Dead Man's Island is the other side of the river. How did you get here?" Silas said.

"I walked, didn't I? Through the tunnel."

"Where the trains run through?" Hope said. "Isn't that dangerous?"

The boy shrugged. "It ain't 'ard if you knows where to get in and out. We do it all the time."

"Well, I for one believe him," Hope said. "Why would he lie? He'd soon be found out."

"There's only one way to see if he's telling the truth," Silas said, gripping the boy by the shoulder. "Are you willing to take us there and show us the place you saw the lady being held?"

"Yes, sir, I am."

"Good, then let's not waste any more time." Silas rounded up his men and made sure they were armed. "If we're set upon again I want to be sure we're ready," he said.

"Shouldn't we inform the police?" Gabriel suggested.

The boy shook his head, alarm lighting up his eyes. "No polis. I ain't a grass."

"Let's make sure it's her before we bring them in," Silas said. He turned to Hope. "I'd be happier if you stayed here with Dexi. It could turn very rough."

"She's my sister," Hope said. "Of course I'm coming."

Silas was about to argue, but seeing the look in Hope's eyes relented. "Well, stay at the back and Eddie can keep an eye on you."

They had to cross the river to get to Dead Man's Island. It took about half an hour to walk to Wapping steps and on the way Hope bought the boy a hot chocolate drink, although the day was mild. She couldn't help admiring his self-assurance, despite his circumstances. In her mind she saw how different this boy's life could be with love and a bit of money.

Chapter Twenty Nine

By the time they managed to get a ferry and cross to the gully and Dead Man's Island it was mid-afternoon. When they reached somewhere they could land Gabriel went ahead of them. Nothing in his life had prepared him for the sights, sounds and smells that assailed him as he walked through the streets of the slum.

The first thing he noticed was the smell. An all pervading stink of rotting wood and the carcasses of dead animals filled his nostrils. Then there were the live rats and other vermin that caught his eye as they ran into their holes as the men passed. Derelict buildings either side of the path gave an air of a place abandoned. He felt danger lurking in the narrow, twisting lanes and dark alleyway. They passed smoke blackened tenements, the path thick with assorted refuse and animal droppings. Scavenging dogs and fighting tomcats added to his unease. It was a long way away from the sunny beaches of Yarmouth. Walking along he found it as menacing by day as it would be by night. He shuddered at the thought of Violet, who he'd come to admire so fervently, even knowing about a place like this, let alone being kept in it.

The boy led the way. Silas and his men strung out behind, keeping in the shadow of the run-down buildings. Gabriel trudged along with them, his gaze flicking from side to side. The path was narrow, and got narrower until they walked single file. The boy stopped at the entrance to a dim alleyway. "Down there," he said. "The house with the red light and the boarded up window."

"Wait here," Gabriel heard Silas say to Hope, "and keep hold of the boy. I want to make sure he hasn't led us on a wild goose chase."

"It's a brothel," Gabriel said, seeing the red lamp in the window. "And open for business from the look of it."

Gabriel and Silas edged up to the building. A door stood half-open, as though inviting people in. A red lamp in the window next to it shone light onto the street. Through the window they saw men lounging on couches with scantily dressed young girls, none more than fourteen from the look of them. While they were watching one of the men stood up, pulling the girl sitting with him to her feet. They made their way out and their footsteps could be heard going upstairs. Nausea rose up to Gabriel's throat at the thought of what they'd be doing next. He shuddered. An abyss of horror opened up before him. What on earth was Violet doing in a place like this?

They waited a few minutes. He felt Silas behind him, so close his breath warmed his neck. Now they were here he found his courage faltering. He floundered. Once again he pondered how he'd ever got himself into this position. Then he thought of Violet and it became clear.

He swallowed and squared his shoulders. He suppressed the fear, sharp as a knife, that gripped his ribs, caused his gut to twist and burned through to heat his skin. The greatest fear was the fear of letting everyone down by not matching up to the moment. If Violet was here he wanted to be the one to get her out. How he envied Silas who suffered not a moment of self-doubt.

"I'll go in and check," he whispered to Silas. "I'll find out if they're holding Violet in there."

Silas signalled to his men to wait. Excitement, paired with nervous anxiety churned in Gabriel's stomach as he pushed on the half-open door and went in.

The woman sitting behind a wooden counter looked up as Gabriel entered. His heart was pounding so hard he wondered if she could hear it. Her eyebrows rose. "Good evening," Gabriel said, taking a small pouch from his pocket and placing it on the counter. It clinked as he set it down. "I'm looking for something a bit special," he said, raising his voice to keep the tremor out of it. "I hear that you have such a delight just waiting for the right offer to come along."

The woman's eyes lit up as she clocked the leather pouch on the counter. "And where did you hear such a thing?" she said. Gabriel tapped the side of his nose. "Word gets around to those with a taste for something with, shall we say, a bit more class than usual." He hoped he was pitching it right. Procuring women for sex wasn't something he was familiar with, although he knew a number of men who would be more comfortable and accomplished at the task than he. His pulse still pounded in his ears.

"Would five pounds secure a few minutes to view the prospect?" He picked up the pouch and tipped five gold sovereigns onto the counter.

"No 'arm in looking I suppose," the woman said, picking up the gold sovereigns and pushing them down her bodice between her ample breasts. "Foller me."

Gabriel followed her up the stairs. Out of the corner of his eye he saw Silas in the shadow by the now open door. When they reached the top landing

184

Gabriel glanced back to ensure he wasn't being followed by one of the men from downstairs. The hall was empty.

When they reached the first door the woman lifted a bunch of keys hanging from a belt round her waist and unlocked the door. As soon as the key turned in the lock Gabriel pushed her aside and barged past her into the room to be confronted by a quaking Violet, swaddled in what looked like a bedspread, holding the broken leg of a chair. She stood ready to pounce.

"Violet, it's me, Gabriel," he called out.

Violet's jaw dropped, along with the chair leg she was holding. Surprise filled her face. He stepped forward and swept her into his arms, holding her close. Once he had her he turned to face the woman who who'd recovered her feet and was standing between him and Violet and the way out. Before he could move towards her footsteps thundered up the stairs and Silas appeared behind the woman. He grabbed her around the neck and waist and, grimacing in pain, pulled her back and held her against the wall. Gabriel picked Violet up and, pushing past them, carried her down the stairs and out into the alley, where Silas's men were waiting.

Gabriel didn't stop. Fear gave him fleetness of foot as he ran carrying Violet back to where Hope was waiting with the boy at the end of the alley. Together they hurried to where the boat had been told to wait to take them back. Hope lifted her skirts and ran alongside him with the boy. When they got to the boat Gabriel put Violet down. He took off his jacket and wrapped it around her before Hope helped her into the boat. Then Hope helped the boy. Gabriel called another boat to wait for Silas and his men who would follow behind when they'd made sure no one from the brothel was tailing them. Once Gabriel, Violet, Hope and boy were all in the boat the ferryman took them back across the river. The boy sat next to Hope. "I was right wasn't I?" he said. "She was the girl on the poster."

"Yes, you were quite correct."

"So I can have the reward? All of it?" the boy's eyes shone.

"Indeed you can," Hope said. Gabriel noticed her putting her arm around him and pulling him close beside her. "But I think you may need some help and guidance in ensuring you make the best use of it."

"I know what I want to do with it," the boy said. "I want to buy a proper headstone for Ma and Pa. With the reward I can afford it, can't I?"

Hope looked quite taken aback, as though it was the last thing she'd expected the boy to say. "Then that's what we shall do," she said.

The rest of the crossing they sat in silence, the slapping of the water against the boat and the creak of the oars the only sound. Gabriel noticed the cut on Violet's cheek, still red with blood. He gritted his teeth and wanted to punch the man who'd done it. He vowed then that they'd be made to pay, whatever it took.

From Wapping steps they took a hansom. "The nearest hospital," Gabriel called to the driver. He gazed at Violet. "The doctors can check you over, make sure you're well enough to go home."

"No," Violet said. "I'm fine. Please take me home. I want to see my children." She paused and glanced down at her attire. "And have a bath and get properly dressed."

"I'll call Doctor Matthews," Hope said to reassure Gabriel. "He'll see she's well taken care of."

186

"Thank you," Violet said. She glanced at Gabriel as though realising for the first time who it was who'd rescued her. "I didn't expect to see you again," she said. "But I'm so very glad I have."

Gabriel had never been so relieved and happy in his entire life.

Chapter Thirty

As the hansom drew up at the kerb outside the house Abel and Dexi came running out. Dexi helped Violet out of the cab and up the path. Gabriel and Hope followed with the boy.

"Where's Masser?" Abel said.

"Don't worry, he's coming behind us," Hope said. "In the meantime please take care of this boy. See he's well fed and given whatever he wants. He's saved Miss Violet by his courage and we owe him a debt of gratitude."

"And the reward," the boy said.

"Yes. And the reward." Hope smiled. This small boy with his courage and optimism had touched her heart more than she cared to admit. Inside, Hope told Daisy to send for Doctor Matthews while Violet embraced her children. Abel took Peter to the kitchen to feed him.

"Poo. You're very smelly, Ma," William said. "And why are you wearing that jacket and that funny dress? Did you fall in the river?"

Violet laughed. "No, but I might as well have. I'm going to have a bath and get dressed, but I wanted to see you both first."

"To see if we've been behaving ourselves? Well, we have, haven't we, Rose?"

Rose nodded and hugged Violet. "I'm glad you're home, Ma, even if you do smell a bit," she said.

"I'll go and ask Hortense to run the bath and sort out some clothes for you," Dexi said. She leaned over and brushed her cheek against Violet's. "It's good to see you home."

"Thank you," Violet said.

"Daisy can make us all some tea and I hope you'll join us for dinner, Mr Stone. Silas will be back soon," Hope said.

"Thank you," Gabriel said. "I was hoping to stay until Violet had been seen by the doctor and I could be reassured of her good health. Then perhaps we should inform the police of her kidnap and let them deal with the kidnappers."

"There's plenty of time for that," Hope said. "Let's get ourselves sorted out first." The thought of calling Inspector Penhalligan, who'd more or less accused Silas, or failing him Violet, of murdering Bert was something she'd leave for the future. She thought of Oakley Penhalligan as a friend, but he was still a policeman, honour bound to do his duty as he saw it.

By the time the bath was ready Silas and his men had returned and Violet was glad to leave the noisy confusion of their arrival behind. Hope accompanied her upstairs.

In the bathroom Violet sank down onto a wicker chair next to the bath. Sudden exhaustion overtook her. Her hands shook. The speed of the rescue, the jumble of thoughts going through her mind, the surprise at seeing Gabriel again and wondering how he'd become involved and how much he knew about her circumstances had driven thoughts of everything but seeing her children again from her mind. But once she was alone in the bathroom with Hope the memories of being taken and held prisoner by Jake returned.

"Bert's dead," she said. "And I know who killed him. It was his brother Jake Mullins. He's the one who kidnapped me. I want to see Inspector Penhalligan and tell him."

Hope gasped. "Bert's brother killed him? Penhalligan thinks you did. You or Silas."

"Why would he think that?" Violet asked, but then realised that, given that they'd been looking for him, it was a reasonable conclusion to make. But she'd never wanted to kill him. Not Bert. She'd never have wanted that. She shivered and pulled Gabriel's jacket closer around her.

"He didn't believe you'd been taken. He thought you'd run off because of what you'd done. When Silas came home it was obvious he'd been in a fight. Penhalligan believed you'd found Bert and one of you had killed him."

"Well, now I'm free I can tell him the truth of it. Bert wouldn't go along with his brother's plans for the children and it got him killed. I knew Bert would never countenance anything like that. Not with his own children!"

"Still, he went along with it didn't he?" Hope said. "Sent you the note that started all this."

"Yes. Probably just wanted to get back at me for some reason. But Bert was never like his brother. You can believe me when I say that."

"Yes, I do. I remember him as being a bit of a conman, but never that bad. What Ma would've called a flimflam man. Dodgy but basically harmless."

Violet smiled at the memory of her mother. "Yes. Ma always did call a spade a digging implement didn't she? Couldn't abide pretentiousness."

Hope's glance ran over her. "Well, you can't go anywhere like that."

190

Violet glanced down at her disarray and pulled a face. The thought of Gabriel seeing her like this discomforted her, although he'd seemed to take it in his stride. Still, you never could tell with men. Who knew what they were thinking?

"As soon as you're ready we'll let Penhalligan know what happened and what you found out, but until then I think it best to concentrate on getting you well for the sake of your children. They've missed you more than they'll say."

"I've missed them too," Violet said. "And thought about them every minute."

"Good. Then perhaps you can tell me about this chap Gabriel and how come the children seem to know him so well."

Violet brightened. Meeting Gabriel was the one good thing to have come out of this whole thing and to see him here in London was more than she could ever have hoped for. "I'll be glad to once I'm properly dressed and fit to appear in company. Then I'll tell you all everything."

Hope helped her undress and bathed the wound on her cheek with carbolic. Hortense brought in some fresh clothes for her and some clean towels.

"Talking about Gabriel," Violet said, "when did he appear and what brought him here? How much does he know about me and Bert and everything?"

Hope laughed. "He turned up out of the blue. I was going to send him away, but William recognised him, so we invited him for dinner. He was most perturbed when he heard you were missing. I think there's more to that young man than he's told you about. I have a feeling that he has some secrets too."

"Really? Do you think so? So if I told him a few small untruths…" Violet distinctly recalled telling him she was widowed.

"Then I believe that makes you even," Hope said.

Hope left Hortense to help Violet with her bath and dressing. She'd also style her hair and make sure Violet looked as beautiful as she deserved.

While Violet was having her bath Hope took Peter to see Silas and make arrangement for him to receive the promised reward. They went into Silas's office, leaving Dexi to entertain Gabriel.

Silas pulled a chair round to the front of his desk, while Hope and Peter stood. He asked about his circumstances. "He lives on the street," Hope said. "I fear that if we give him the reward it would soon be taken from him by the other beggars, thieves and ruffians who live in the same area. It's a lot of money and needs to be properly managed to give him the best of life's opportunities. I think it wise if he stay with us for a while, until we can sort out some schooling and a proper place to live."

Silas stroked his chin while he gazed at the boy. "What do you think, boy?" he asked.

Peter's lips twitched into a half-smile. He gazed up at Hope, eyes shining. He looked so innocent, so fragile and so heartbreakingly vulnerable that she wished she could hug him to make everything better.

"I think the lady's right," he said. "I can do odd jobs and make meself useful. You won't be sorry you let me stay."

Silas smothered a chuckle with a cough. "Good, that's settled then. I will arrange for the reward money to be put into a bank account which you will be able to

192

draw on. Mrs Quirk will stand as Trustee." He picked up a pen and began to write. "I will make a small advance so you may buy clothes and shoes. In the meantime I'm sure Mrs Quirk can find you something that will suit." He wrote something on a piece of paper which he handed to Hope. "Mrs Quirk will take you to the bank tomorrow and then to the shops. Is that agreeable?"

Peter stared at him. "I want to buy a headstone for Ma and Pa," he said. "Will there be enough for that?"

Silas was stunned. He glanced at Hope who nodded. He wrote out another cheque. "I'll make sure there is," he said.

Hope took Peter to the kitchen where Daisy was preparing the dinner. "Master Peter is staying for a while," she said. "Please see that he is properly washed and dressed for dinner. You should be able to find something to fit passably well in the trunk in the storeroom. All Alfie's old clothes are stored there, but tomorrow I'll be taking him out to buy new."

"I've already had a wash today," Peter said, his thin voice anxious. "I washed under the pump this morning. Don't need another wash."

Hope smiled. "I'm sure you did," she said. "But Daisy will give you a bath in warm water. Won't that be good?"

Peter grimaced. The light in his dark eyes dimmed. "Don't need another wash," he said.

Hope sighed. "I'll leave it to you to sort him out," she said to Daisy. "Perhaps this time just a strip wash and a bath tomorrow."

"Where will he be sleeping?" Daisy said. "I'll need to make up a bed for him."

"He'll sleep in Alfie's room for now. I want to keep him close for the time being." Alfie won't be back until Christmas. I'm sure he wouldn't mind." Memories of Alfie when he was that age ran through Hope's mind. This boy reminded her so much of him. The same intelligent face, although rather more pinched and dirty than Alfie's, but the same eagerness in his eyes, although it could have been the thought of the reward that made his eyes shine so.

She smiled at Peter. "Go with Daisy, she'll look after you. I'm happy you're staying with us and I hope you will be happy here too."

Peter grinned. "I'm sure I will," he said. "Still don't need a wash."

Chapter Thirty One

Hope returned to see Silas in his office where he was finishing some paperwork. "Is he settled?" he asked.

"Yes. He's to sleep in Alfie's room. It'll be good to see it used. I do miss Alfie when he's away."

Silas looked at her. "I know you do," he said. Then he took her hands in his. "I fear you have grown attached to this boy. We know nothing of him. He may have family or people who care for him."

"His parents are dead, we know that. He has no family. The local Pastor takes cares of him when he's not living on the street. We are in a position to help him and I feel it is our obligation to do so."

"He may not be all he seems," Silas said. "His stay will be temporary and because of it your soft heart may be broken."

Hope pulled her hands away. "Better a broken heart than a cold one," she said. She remembered Dexi telling her once that love was a choice you make and a risk you take. In Peter's case the decision was already made and the risk ready to be taken.

Silas sat back in his chair and gazed at her. "He's a bright boy, but there's an air of independence about him. He'll not be easily melded to your will."

"All the better," Hope said. "That's what I find so intriguing about him. His self-assurance combined with a strange vulnerability."

Silas smiled. "You want to mother him."

Hope went quiet. It was an accusation she couldn't refute. With no children of her own she had harboured in her heart the possibility of making the boy's stay permanent. "Offering him our protection after all he's done for us is the least we can do," she said.

"I suppose it wouldn't hurt to make enquires," he said.

She smiled, leant forward and kissed him.

A few minutes later she was once again reminded how different the boy was and the difficulties she'd face looking after him. She went to check on him in the kitchen, where he was talking to William and Rose. They were tucking into some of Mrs B's scones while Daisy went to get Alfie's room ready.

"What's it like, living on the street?" she heard Williams ask Peter. "I don't think I'd like it," he said. "Don't you get cold at night?"

"There's places that'll take you in if you want," Peter said, "Or you can go and see Pastor Brown, he'll al'as give us somat. You can do what you like most of the time. I get hungry sometimes and have to filch somat to eat but that's not 'ard if you knows where to go."

"What do you mean 'filch'? What's that?" William asked.

"You know, take stuff."

"Without paying you mean," Rose said. "That's stealing and it's wrong. You get sent to prison for that."

"Yes," Hope said, walking into the room. "It's something you may have to do when you live on the streets in order to survive, but it's not something that Peter will be doing in the future, is it, Peter?"

Peter shrugged and Hope had to be satisfied with that. "You can all go out into the garden and play until dinner's ready," she said. As they went out she heard William say, "Have you ever been in prison?"

It was clear William wasn't going to let the matter rest. He was an inquisitive child and Peter was like a new toy. To be played with until something else came along.

Sighing with exasperation Hope went back upstairs and waited with Silas and Gabriel for Violet to join them after her bath.

When Doctor Matthews arrived Violet was ready to meet him. He listened to her heart and checked her pulse and looked down her throat.

"You seem very well recovered," he said. "I don't think I'm needed here any longer." He left her a sleeping draught in case she found it difficult to sleep after her ordeal. "If you have any adverse after-effects please don't hesitate to call me," he said.

"Thank you, Doctor Matthews. I'm sure I'll be fine now that I'm home among friends."

Downstairs in the drawing room Silas and Gabriel were having drinks with Dexi and Hope, talking about the rescue when she walked in. Gabriel stood up to greet her. "You look beautiful," he said with a wide grin on his face. "So much better than the last time I saw you."

Violet's heart beat a little faster. "And you, sir, are quite undressed." She handed him his jacket with a smile.

"Thank you," he said. Silas poured her a gin and handed it to her.

"I'm so glad to be home," she said. "I can't thank you both enough for such a daring rescue. It happened so fast I can hardly believe it. You are both truly wonderful." She raised her glass to them then swigged back the gin which revived and warmed her. Silas poured her another.

Both men were obviously elated at their daring. "You should have seen Gabriel, Violet," Silas said. "He went into that brothel as though to the manner born. It was as if he'd been frequenting brothels all his life."

"I was nervous as a kitten," Gabriel said with a grin. "I assure you it's not something I've ever done before, nor am I likely to do so again."

"Violet tells me that the man who kidnapped her was Bert's half-brother, his name is Jake Mullins and he killed Bert," Hope said.

"Phew," Silas said. "So we've all been under suspicion when it was his brother all the time?"

"Yes. I gather Bert didn't want to go along with the notion of using his children in his brother's sordid business and it got him killed," Violet said.

"Well, we'll have to make sure Inspector Penhalligan gets to hear about that," Silas said.

"I'm sure Violet will be able to tell us all the gory details over dinner," Hope said. "For now she needs to rest and spend some time with her children."

"Of course," Silas said.

Once Gabriel was sure Violet was all right he left to go to his hotel to change his clothes. "I'll call in at the police station and let Inspector Penhalligan know that you're back home and reasonably well," he said. "I'll tell him you'll call round tomorrow to speak to him, but I will let him know that Bert's brother, Jake Mullins, was the kidnapper and that he killed Bert Shadwick. That's the least I can do."

Violet agreed and thanked him. "I can never repay you for rescuing me so valiantly," she said. "I'll be forever in your debt."

Gabriel smiled. "That's something we can talk about when you're fully recovered," he said.

Violet didn't miss the twinkle in his eye as he said it either.

Hope watched Violet saying goodbye to Gabriel. Seeing her affection for him she hoped she would treat him well. She fell in love so easily and gave her heart so readily. She'd had so many admirers over the years and left a string of broken hearts behind her, but seeing her with Gabriel Hope guessed this would be different. She couldn't help but smile. Violet had fallen deeply in love, only she didn't know it yet. She hoped she wouldn't get hurt.

Back at the hotel Gabriel called for the concierge. He'd more or less made up his own mind about Violet and her family, but hearing the local gossip was usually enlightening. He hoped with all his heart that he wouldn't hear anything bad about her, anything that would prevent him deepening their relationship. He wanted more than a summer romance. But he had to be careful. His heart had been bruised before by women who turned out to be other than they appeared to be and he didn't want to make a mistake this time. He'd invested too many hopes and dreams in pursuit of Violet. The depth of his feeling for her surprised him. He'd fallen hard, he knew, and he couldn't bear to be disappointed. Whatever Harry told him he'd still feel the same about her. Nothing he said would make any difference, but he had to hear it.

"So, what can you tell me about the names I gave you?" he asked when Harry appeared.

"Well, sir, I can tell you that Mr Albert Shadwick's a gonner. Seems 'is body washed up in Wapping a few nights ago. Maybe a week. 'E was a stage performer with a reputation for the ladies, sir. Can't tell you more'n that." He sniffed as though a bad smell had assaulted his nostrils.

"Thanks but I already know that, Harry. Carry on. The others?"

"Silas Quirk owns a gambling and gaming club, The Grenadier. It does have a fearsome reputation, sir. Dog fights, bare-knuckle boxing and ratting too. And Silas Quirk is either the Devil Incarnate, or a Saint, depends who you speak to. A good friend to have and a bad enemy they say."

"Hmm. Just as I thought. What about Violet Daniels?"

"Ah. I see. Sir has a partic'lar interest in the lady. She's the younger daughter of a respectable family who ran the Hope and Anchor Public House. Parents both dead. Left 'ome to take up a career on the stage. 'Ad a notion to be a singer I believe. Came 'ome in trouble as so many stage-struck young girls do, sir, with a bun in the oven and no ring on her finger. Fell in wi' a bad lot, so I hear, and come 'ome in a terrible state. I'd say she got a raw deal and is trying to make the best of it. No reason to think else. Hard worker and a good mother they say. Twins, sir. No sign of a husband. Works in the pub to pay their keep."

"Good, that more or less confirms my own opinion. Thank you, Harry, I can't be too careful in my position. You've put my mind at rest." He put his hand in his pocket and pulled out a white five pound note which he pressed into Harry's hand.

"Thank you, sir. God bless." Harry touched the brim of his hat with courtesy and left the room.

Gabriel breathed a sigh of relief. She was a woman fallen on hard times. He could cope with that and she wasn't to blame for her predicament now. The future looked very interesting. Very interesting indeed.

Chapter Thirty Two

Gabriel arrived at Hope's house in time for a later than usual dinner and told them about his visit to the police station. "Inspector Penhalligan wasn't at the station so I left a note," he said. "I would have liked to talk to him, but I told him about Mr Shadwick's brother, the kidnap and Jake Mullins killing him. I fear he will want all the gory details." He turned to Violet. "I'll be happy to accompany you tomorrow. It may be quite an ordeal."

Violet's heart warmed to this handsome man she'd had the best good fortune to meet. She felt more cherished with him than she ever had in her life before.

The children were brought into the dining room to have dinner. Peter, dressed in one of Alfie's old suits, shirt and shoes, which were all too big, sat between William and Hope. His face was clean and his dark hair had been brushed to one side. It gleamed as though still wet. Wariness filled his eyes and he kept pulling at the unaccustomed collar of his shirt. He didn't say much, but kept a watchful eye on the other children, copying their actions and how they used their spoons and forks. He also ate a surprising amount and Violet wondered when he'd last sat at a table to eat, if ever.

William appeared pleased to have another boy to play with. "Will Peter be staying with us for long?" he asked.

Hope smiled. "Until we can sort out a permanent arrangement for him," she said.

William beamed. "He can play with my boat and my soldiers," he said, "and Abel can teach him how to play croquet so we can beat the girls. We'll have lots of fun."

"That's very generous of you, William," Violet said, delighted that the boy who'd saved her from the brothel had been accepted into the family so quickly.

Over dinner Violet and Gabriel talked about their meeting and the time they spent in Yarmouth. Violet didn't want to talk about the kidnap in front of the children so the conversation was pleasant.

"Is Uncle Gabriel going to stay in London now?" William asked. "And can we go for a ride in his motor car?"

Gabriel chuckled. "I think I told you it wasn't my car, but one I'd hired from the local garage. I suppose one could hire a motor vehicle in London, but the congestion on the streets would make it difficult to manoeuvre around. I think you'd miss the thrill of the open road and the beautiful English countryside."

"Why don't you buy a motor car, Uncle Silas," William continued. "Then we could all go for a ride."

"Hmm," Silas said. "I think Gabriel is right. The traffic in London would mar any enjoyment from the experience. Personally I've always found a hansom cab to be the most convenient form of transport in town."

"You won't go away again will you, Ma?" Rose said, toying with the food on her plate. "Aunty Hope has looked after us but I miss my dolls and Amy."

"We'll be going home as soon as I've settled my business," Violet said. She'd thought that Bert's death, regretful though it was, would mean the end of her problems, but now she realised that as long as Jake was around they'd still be in danger. The sooner he was locked up the better. She'd talk to Penhalligan in the morning.

The rest of the dinner was filled with reminiscences of the children's stay in Yarmouth, memories of Nesta, the beach and the fun they'd had.

After dinner Violet kissed William and Rose goodnight.

"Will you come and see us in the morning?" Rose asked.

Violet smiled. "Yes, of course I will. If it's a nice day we can go visit John, Alice and Amy and you can collect some of your dolls.

Rose grinned and snuggled down in the bed. Violet's heart filled with love for her children. What on earth would she do without them?

Hope insisted on taking Peter to the bed in Alfie's room herself and seeing that he had everything he needed. Violet guessed he'd be getting the same treatment. A bedtime story, a hot drink and a goodnight kiss. Hope had obviously grown fond of the child. Violet wasn't sure that was such a good idea and she hoped it wouldn't all end in tears.

Coffee and port were served in the drawing room. Gabriel sat next to Violet on the settee. Then the conversation turned to Violet's ordeal at the hands of Bert's brother.

"The last thing I remember is the terrible smell of a cloth over my mouth and not being able to breathe. When I woke up I was locked in a horrid, dank, dark room. It smelled worse than a cesspit. Jake Mullins came in and told me who he was and that he'd killed Bert because he refused to let our children be used for his nefarious trade. I knew Bert would never agree to that," she said, pleased that at least the faith she'd had in Bert had been justified.

"But it wasn't at Jake Mullins's that we found you," Gabriel said. "It was in a brothel. How did you come to be there?"

Violet shuddered at the memory of Jake lying on the floor, blood oozing from a wound on his head. "I managed to get out when he wasn't looking, she said, but didn't know where I was and couldn't find my way. It was raining and so cold I thought I'd die of pneumonia. A woman helped me, or at least I thought she was helping. Turns out she took me to work in the brothel."

She looked at Gabriel. "Luckily you found me before there was any chance of my being forced to participate in their trade."

"That's thanks to you and Peter," Gabriel said. "A braver little boy you'd be hard to find. I think we all owe him a debt of gratitude."

"Yes, and the reward," Silas said. "Peter will be staying with us until arrangements have been made for an account to be set up for him. As he's a minor it will be administered by Hope."

Violet smiled. "Here's to Peter," she said and they all raised their glasses.

It wasn't long after that that Daisy showed a disgruntled Inspector Penhalligan into the room. "Good evening," he said. "I'm sorry for the lateness of my call but I got a note to say that Violet had been recovered and had information regarding the murder of Bert Shadwick. Naturally I wanted to see for myself."

"Of course, Inspector," Silas said. "As you can see your information is correct. Violet is here and we are all very thankful for her safe return."

Inspector Penhalligan pulled one of Silas's leaflets out of his pocket. "And would this have anything to do with her, as you put it, safe return?" He handed the paper to Silas. "If you were thinking of offering a reward you should have cleared it with me first. These offers usually result in a lot of false information and people making things up in the hope of duping the person offering the reward into paying out for useless information."

Silas smiled and handed the paper back. "Which wasn't the case in this instance," he said.

Penhalligan still appeared far from happy. "So, how did she come to return so conveniently with information about the killer of a man she was known to have been looking for?"

Silas and Gabriel exchanged glances.

"Take a seat, Inspector," Silas said. "May I offer you a drink? I have a particularly fine brandy."

The inspector sat. Silas poured him a brandy. Violet was thankful for the time to think about the story she intended to tell. She wasn't sure how much information she wanted Penhalligan to have. None of it reflected well on her.

"I'll need all of you to make full statements of all the circumstances at the station in the morning, but in the meantime, I need the full name and address of the man you say killed Bert Shadwick." Penhalligan took out his notebook and pencil.

Violet stepped forward. "His name is Jackson Mullins. He's known as Jake. He is, or was, Bert's half-brother. They had a falling out and he admitted to me that he killed him and tossed his body into the river. He abducted me and kept me prisoner in a house on Dead Man's Island. I don't know exactly where. Is that sufficient for you?"

Inspector Penhalligan looked pensive, but wrote what she'd said in his book. "When was this?" he asked.

Violet glanced at the others for support. "I can't recall," she said. "I think I was drugged. I don't know how long I was there. It could have been days, or even a week."

"So how exactly did you escape and how come you arrived home accompanied by Silas and his men?"

Violet sank onto the sofa beside Gabriel. "It's all a bit of a blur," she said. "I can't rightly remember."

Gabriel stood up as if offering to help the inspector out. "If it's any help to you I will happily take you to the place where Miss Daniels was held tomorrow, but I think she has suffered enough for today, as indeed we all have."

"Oh yes, of course." Penhalligan picked up his glass and swallowed the warming, golden liquid. "It must have been a terrible ordeal for you all," he said. He stood to leave.

Gabriel put his arm around him ushering him towards the door. "Here is my card. I'll be happy to bring Miss Daniels to the station in the morning."

The inspector took the card and his manner became conciliatory. "That will be fine, Mr Stone. Thank you. I'm sorry to have intruded on what must be the end of a difficult day." He nodded to Hope, Silas and Violet. "Until tomorrow," he said as Gabriel showed him out.

Everyone heaved a sigh of relief when he'd gone. "Phew," Hope said. "I thought he'd never go."

"It's only a respite," Silas said. "Tomorrow he'll want the full story."

"Then we must decide exactly how much we want him to know," Hope said. "I'd prefer it if he didn't hear about Peter's part in it. If word gets back to the brothel-keeper that Peter came to us – well, I dread to think what might happen to him."

"Yes," Silas said. "I think an anonymous tip-off, or an overheard conversation might be a more convenient explanation."

"I'm happy to say I heard some men bragging about a tasty new addition to the goods on offer at the brothel and deciding to check it out for myself," Gabriel said.

"Penhalligan will never believe that Silas went to a brothel to partake of its services," Hope said. "He knows he just wouldn't."

"No. Gabriel needs to have heard enough detail to suspect it might be Violet," Silas said.

"Perhaps they saw her picture which reminded them of the description of the fresh goods on offer?" Gabriel suggested.

"So we decided to take a look?" Silas said. His forehead creased into a frown. "It'll be a hard sell, but if we stick to the story he'll not be able to dispute it."

"What about the reward?" Hope said. "He'll want to know if it's been claimed."

"None of his business," Silas said. "A private matter between me and my conscience."

So they went over the story again and again with Violet filling in small details that might add veracity to the tale until they were all clear on what they would say at the station.

"I've agreed to take Inspector Penhalligan and some of his men to the place we found you," Gabriel

208

said. "We'll be going at first light. It shouldn't take too long."

"I promised to take the children to the Hope and Anchor," Violet said. "It's Amy's birthday. Alice's sure to be throwing a party for her."

"Good," Gabriel said. "Give me the address and I'll meet you there."

Violet wrote it down and then showed him out. "I can't thank you enough for what you did today," she said. "I'll never forget it."

He grinned. "I'm counting on that," he said.

She felt a tug in her heart as he walked away.

Later, sleeping in the room Violet shared with her children, she couldn't believe how lucky she was to have such a supportive family and friends. She slept well for the first time since leaving Yarmouth, which felt like a lifetime ago.

Chapter Thirty Three

The early morning light through the window woke Violet. She'd spent so many hours in small dark rooms lately it came as a welcome surprise. The children were still sleeping.

She climbed quietly out of bed and tiptoed over to watch them for a while. She marvelled at William's quiet serenity. Still for once, his cheeks were pink with childhood innocence. She brushed his blonde hair smooth. Rose too looked like an angel sleeping, her long lashes brushed her cheek. She touch them each and hoped they knew how loved they were.

She shuddered at the thought of what Jake had planned for them. He was evil and the sooner the police picked him up the better. She hoped they'd hang him for Bert's murder. It was what he deserved. She found a wrap and went downstairs to the kitchen where Daisy already had the kettle on.

"Good morning, Miss Violet," Daisy said. "I'm glad to see you home. The children missed you so. Will they be coming down soon?"

"I left them sleeping," Violet said. "They had a late night yesterday. I just thought I'd take a cup of tea up."

Daisy smiled. "One cup of tea coming up," she said.

Violet took the tea and went back to the bedroom. She wanted to think about the day ahead. The visit to the police station loomed large in her mind. She wasn't looking forward to it. She now realised how foolish she'd been insisting on going to the most dangerous, disreputable part of London with Silas to look for Bert.

If she'd stayed at home with the children she wouldn't have been kidnapped and none of their difficulties would have arisen. She'd put not only her own life at risk, but also the lives of Silas and his men. It was not something she relished telling Inspector Penhalligan about.

Then there was her escape from Jake. She'd have difficulty explaining that without admitting what she'd done. True she'd battered him in self-defence and in an almighty rage, but even so, it was still something she'd find it hard to own up to. She dreaded what Penhalligan would think of her and, strangely enough, she found his opinion mattered. She recalled his help and support when her parents died. She'd thought of him as a friend, now he appeared to be an enemy.

Later, over breakfast with the children they talked about Amy's birthday party at the Hope and Anchor that afternoon. The children knew all about it.

"I'll take them to the Hope before I go to the police station," Violet said to Hope. "They can spend the morning playing with Amy."

"Will there be jelly?" William asked. "And ice cream. I like ice cream."

"I want to see Amy again," Rose said. "Do you think she's missed me? I've missed her."

"I expect there will be, William, and I'm sure she has, Rose," Violet said. "And we mustn't forget to take the presents."

"I like presents," William said. "Do you think Amy will like hers?"

Hope had taken the children to the toyshop in Regent's Street to each choose a toy for Amy. William had wanted to get her a toy train. "I'm sure she'll like it," he said, but Hope put her foot down and in the end

William chose a spinning top and Rose a tea set. Hope bought her a doll she could dress up.

"Of course she will," Violet said. "Now get on and finish your breakfast or we'll never get there."

"Is Peter coming?" William asked. "He's never been to a party before, have you, Peter?"

Peter glanced at Hope.

"I'm taking Peter into town this morning for some new clothes," she said. "But if he wants to go to the party this afternoon I'm sure he'll be most welcome." She glanced at Peter.

"A party? I ain't never bin to a party afore. Not a proper one," he said.

"That's settled then," Hope said.

Hope's eyes shone with a fondness Violet had only ever seen when she talked about her husband. Seeing Hope's affection for the boy she felt a stab of guilt. She was responsible for bringing him into their lives. How would Hope feel if it all went wrong and he was taken away? Another burden she'd have to bear. Why did life have to be so difficult?

Silas insisted that Abel go with Violet and the children. "It's not safe for you to go alone," he said. "If Abel is with you it will put Hope's mind at rest."

Violet couldn't argue. She'd put them all through so much, taking Abel was a small price to pay. Anyway, William at least was delighted with the idea.

When they reached the pub John left the barman Thomas in charge of the bar and greeted her warmly. "I've been so worried," he said. "Silas kept us informed of progress in the search for you, but seeing you here, fit and well, is a great relief." He welcomed the children too. "I think Elsie may have some sweets in the kitchen and this morning she mentioned making fudge for the party this afternoon."

William didn't need second telling. His eyes lit up as he dragged Rose to the kitchen with him. Abel went too.

"So, are you going to tell me what happened on Dead Man's Island and how Silas and his men were able to find you, or do I have to wait to read it in the Sunday papers?"

Violet laughed. "I'm hoping we have been discreet enough to avoid any sort of publicity," she said. "I can't see the men involved wanting to tell their story and I'm certainly not going to risk my reputation to entertain the general public. Least said soonest mended, is my view. The sooner it's all forgotten the better."

"Fair enough," John said, but do come upstairs and you can tell me and Alice about it over a cup of coffee if that's alright with you?"

"Of course," Violet said, relieved. "I have to explain it all at the police station this morning, but I've a little time until Gabriel arrives."

"Ah yes," John said. "The mysterious Mr Stone. I can't wait to hear about him and how he fits in. I trust he's young, handsome and rich, Violet. Or have you fallen for a dud again?"

Violet flushed. She had picked a few wrong 'uns in her day, but Gabriel was different and she wasn't sure she wanted to tell the family how she felt about him just yet, especially as she hadn't quite made up her own mind. Also, she didn't want to jinx it. She'd had too many dodgy relationships in the past.

"You'll be able to judge for yourself," she said. "He's coming here to accompany me to the station.

He's to make a statement himself to Inspector Penhalligan about his part in the rescue."

John chuckled and together they went upstairs to the parlour where Violet explained all that had happened to John and Alice while they waited for Gabriel to arrive. They didn't have to wait long. They'd been so engrossed in Violet's tale they didn't hear the knocking on the door downstairs, but the excited commotion in the kitchen let them know of his arrival.

Violet jumped up and rushed down to meet him. "We're upstairs," she said. "Come and meet John and Alice. Surely we've time for a cup of coffee before we go?"

"Coffee would be most welcome," Gabriel said, his smile widening as he looked at Violet. Her heart lurched as she took his arm to show him up the stairs. She couldn't help wondering what John and Alice would make of him. He was a great improvement on the men she usually walked out with.

When John and Alice greeted him Gabriel was as charming as ever. "So happy to meet you," he said. "Violet's told me so much about you."

John's eyebrows rose. He glanced at Violet.

"Only good things," she said.

"Pleased to meet you too," John said. "We, of course, have heard nothing about you."

Gabriel laughed. "Not much to tell," he said, "but I'm planning to be around for a while so there's plenty of time."

John shook his hand and nodded at Violet to show his approval. A swell of satisfaction rose up inside her. At last she'd done something right and the fact he'd

said he planned to be around for a while made her
spirits soar.

Chapter Thirty Four

Violet left the children with John and Alice so they could play with Amy while she went to the police station with Gabriel.

They waited in the hallway until Inspector Penhalligan came out to greet them. They both rose when he arrived.

"Good morning, thank you for coming," Penhalligan said. He showed Violet into his office. Gabriel went to follow but the inspector stopped him. "It's Violet I want to speak to," he said. "I feel she may speak more freely if we are alone."

Gabriel looked questioningly at Violet. "It's all right," she said. "I don't expect this will take long." She breathed a sigh of relief. She had hoped to speak to Penhalligan alone. She didn't want Gabriel to hear all the sordid details of her past with Bert. Not until she was ready to tell him herself.

Inspector Penhalligan called a constable over. "Constable Hughes will take your statement," he said to Gabriel. "Please make it as full and detailed as possible."

In the office Violet sat in the chair opposite the desk. As he took his seat behind it she had the opportunity to take a closer look at this man who she felt sure held her fate in his hands. He was wearing a well cut suit which she guessed he'd had made to measure. Gentle features in his thin intelligent face belied the tenacity with which she knew he would pursue his case. This was a man for whom justice was the imperative he lived by. If there was a murderer on the loose, Penhalligan would find him. Glancing round she noticed the cabinets piled high with files, the pictures of certificates on the wall, the odd photograph of men in uniform. A large blotter in front of his chair took up most of the desk. His pipe rested on a pipe rack and the smell of tobacco hung in the air like cobwebs. It was a reassuring scene.

"I know this is difficult," he said, his soft country burr making him sound almost caring, Violet thought. "I want to make it as painless as possible. Can you tell me what you remember about the abduction? What on earth were you doing in London's worst slum?"

Violet took a deep breath. "I was looking for Bert, the father of my children. Someone said he'd been seen there."

"But you haven't seen him for... how many years is it? Five or six. Why now, Violet?"

Violet was acutely aware that Penhalligan knew all about her past, all her family's secrets. She'd thought of him as a friend. It was no use trying to hide anything from him so she had to explain about seeing Bert, the note and her fear of his taking the children away. "He's their father. He'd have the law on his side, despite the fact that he couldn't care too hoots about them and only wanted them to make money out of."

"I see. So you went looking for him, why? What did you hope to achieve?"

"Not at first. First of all I took the children away, but then I feared he'd find us. I thought if I talked to him. Bert wasn't all bad you know, despite what people say about him. I loved him once." She coloured at the admission.

The inspector nodded. "He didn't deserve you," he whispered. Violet noticed the compassion in his eyes.

It reassured her. "So, you went looking for him. Then what happened?"

"It's a bit of a blur. I remember being afraid and wishing I'd never said I'd go with Silas and Knuckles. It was an awful place, smelly and full of rats and garbage. I don't know how people can live there."

"They live there because they can't afford to live anywhere else," Penhalligan said. "But go on, what happened next?"

"I only recall seeing some men appear from out of nowhere. They attacked Silas and Knuckles. I saw Silas go down, it was terrifying. The noise and confusion. I thought I'd die there, on the spot. Someone grabbed me and dragged me away. The last thing I remember is the smell of ether and a sweet taste in my mouth. I must have passed out. I woke up locked in a damp, dark room. I didn't know where I was. It felt like I'd been there for days when Jake Mullins came in and told me who he was and what he'd done."

"But why would he kill his brother and kidnap you? If it was a ransom from Silas Quirk he was after surely taking your sister, Hope, would be more profitable?"

Violet hesitated. Penhalligan was right. Hope would make a much more lucrative hostage than she would. She'd have to tell him what Jake, and by association Bert, had planned for her children. It felt like the worst sort of betrayal. She'd make sure he knew Bert had died because he wouldn't go along with his brother's plan.

"He was annoyed Bert wouldn't go ahead with their plan to use my children for his vile, repugnant trade. Pornographic photos indeed." Violet felt the rage she'd held inside her for so long coming to the surface.

218

Rage at Bert, rage at Jake and most of all at herself for getting into such an invidious position in the first place. Her face flushed and her hands curled into fists as she said, "Apparently Bert had agreed to this disgusting trade and then wanted to back out so Jake killed him. He had no right to Bert's children, so he took me instead. Pure spite. I hate him. I hope he hangs."

"So how did you escape?"

"I managed to slip out. The lock on the door was very old and rusty. It only took a bit of hammering with the clothes hanger from the wardrobe."

"But I still don't understand how you ended up in a brothel run by well-known brothel-keeper Carter Doyle. Apparently, that's where Silas and your friend Mr Gabriel Stone found you."

"I was lost. A woman, I can't recall her name, helped me. Or at least I thought she was helping me, but she was only helping herself." Saying it out loud again Violet felt stupid. Why had she been so gullible? "I think that's all I can say," she said. "Now I'd like to get back to my family. I've told you all I remember."

"Really?" He didn't sound convinced but let it go. "If you think of anything else…"

"I'll let you know." Relief flooded over Violet as she stood to go. She'd hated every minute of having to tell her tale of woe and now she was glad it was over. She had no intention of ever setting foot in the police station again – ever.

Just as she was leaving a uniformed officer came into the room to speak urgently to Inspector Penhalligan. Violet brushed past him as she walked out of the door.

Gabriel was waiting for her in the hall. Silas was there too, he'd made his statement to a constable who'd written it down. "Thank goodness that's over," Violet said as she joined them.

They'd just stepped out into the fresh air when Penhalligan came rushing after them. "I'm sorry," he said. "I have to detain you further. Jake Mullins's body has just been found in his rooms." He turned to Violet. "The rooms where you were held captive."

"What!" Violet gasped, thoughts running like wild hares through her head.

Penhalligan took Violet's arm. "I'm afraid I'll have to ask you to accompany me back into the station."

Violet's legs gave way. If it hadn't been for Gabriel catching her she'd have fallen to the floor.

A good hour passed before Silas and Gabriel were able to take Violet home.

"I'll need you all to have your fingerprints taken," Inspector Penhalligan said. "I need to confirm who was there."

"Gabriel and I never went there," Silas said. "We found Violet somewhere else."

"Then taking your fingerprints will allow us to eliminate you," Penhalligan said.

Violet protested. "I've admitted that I was there," she said. "So you won't need my fingerprints."

"It seems that the constables searching the room found a plank of wood with blood on it. We may be able to get some prints from it. In that case we will need your prints for elimination purposes."

"And if I don't want to have them taken?"

"Then we will assume that you have something to hide."

There was no getting out of it. Violet shuddered at the memory of swinging the plank at Jake and knocking him down, but she was sure he was alive and coming round when she ran out. Had she killed him? She'd never meant to. She feared for her life, surely that was justification?

The inspector led them back in and a constable took their fingerprints. After that they were allowed to leave the station, but Penhalligan made it clear that the investigation was ongoing and they may be required to return. All the way home Violet worried about what she had done. Now she would have to tell them the truth.

Chapter Thirty Five

Once Violet and the children had left with Abel, Peter stood, hands in his pockets, staring out of the window and kicking his heels. Hope realised how difficult the day would be for him. He liked playing with William, but now he'd gone out she saw the longing in his face for the freedom to go and roam the streets, find his friends and enjoy the sunshine in any way he pleased. Her heart went out to him. She put on her coat and bonnet. "We'll need to go to the bank first," she said. "Then we'll see about that headstone for your parents' grave."

Peter smiled, his whole demeanour changed at the promise of getting the headstone he'd wanted. He willingly went along with her. They walked to the bank to cash Silas's cheques. "It's your money," she told him, "but I'll need to draw it out for you as and when you want it."

Peter nodded but when they entered the bank he tugged at Hope's skirt. She glanced down and saw him ashen-faced with eyes saucer wide. He'd obviously never been into a bank before. She smiled to reassure him.

"It's like a church," he whispered.

"Yes, it is a bit," Hope said. To those who worship money, she thought.

It only took a few minutes to draw the money she needed. Then they walked to the churchyard where Peter's parents were buried. He led the way and Hope followed until they came to a grass covered mound near the hedge at the far end of the churchyard. The grave was marked with a simple wooden cross with the name *Hawkins* written in black ink on the upright.

Peter stood, head bent, lips pressed thin, tears shining in his eyes.

"Is this it? Your parents' grave?" she asked.

He nodded.

Seeing this small boy standing so bereft at his parents' grave Hope realised the enormity of his loss. The sorrow in his face tore at her heart. She saw his overwhelming grief. He'd been orphaned far too young and put into a home with strangers. How could anyone expect him to understand what was happening to him? No wonder he ran away. To him there was no alternative. Anger rose up in her at the injustice of it all. This poor, heart-sick boy had no family to rely on. She knew nothing could ever replace what he'd lost, but she'd move heaven and earth to try to make things better for him if it took every ounce of patience and understanding she possessed. "You wait here," she said. "I'll go and see the pastor."

She found Pastor Brown in the church vestry and asked him about Peter and his parents.

"The Hawkins – Martha and David? Yes I knew them," he said. "David worked on the docks. They died in a fire when Peter was about four. He was lucky to get out alive." Hope shuddered at the memory of the fire and its aftermath that had taken her parents.

"Does he have any living relatives? Anyone who could take care of him?"

The pastor shook his head. "According to the parish records he's an only child. After the fire everything that was salvageable was sold to pay for the funeral. The neighbours helped out. They were the only ones at the funeral. Peter was put into a home run by a charity but he ran away. He's been living on the streets ever since. I do what I can, but with so many children..." He made a helpless gesture and shrugged.

"So he has no one? No one who wants to claim responsibility for him?"

"Not as far as I know," the pastor said.

"So no one would object to my taking him in?"

The pastor smiled. "It'd be a blessing. A true act of Christian charity. One less child living on the streets. Who could object to that?"

"Good." Relief and joy flooded through Hope's veins. She could take him in and give him the love he deserved. "Peter wants to have his parents' grave marked with a headstone. I take it that would be in order?"

"Of course. That too would be an act of the greatest charity. Give the lad some closure. Somewhere he could come for comfort."

"Then I'll arrange it."

She thanked the pastor and put a sovereign in the poor box on the way out. Next she took Peter to the stonemason to choose the headstone. Once he'd chosen the one he wanted Hope asked the stonemason about the engraving.

"How about '*In Loving Memory*' on the top, then the name and dates, then perhaps '*Rest in Peace*'?" the stonemason suggested.

Hope looked at Peter. He nodded.

"Let's have the names and dates then," the stonemason said, taking a notebook and pencil out of his pocket.

"It's for Ma and Pa," Peter said.

"Fine," the stonemason said. "What were their names?"

Peter bit his lip and fresh tears brimmed his eyes.

"Martha and David Hawkins wasn't it, Peter?" Hope said.

A tear rolled down his cheek. He brushed it away with his sleeve.

"You can get the dates from the pastor," Hope said, "and please send the account to me." She took a card out of her bag and handed it to the stonemason.

The stonemason looked at the card. "Very well, Mrs Quirk. It'll take a couple of days."

"Excellent," Hope said. "The pastor will show you where it's to be placed."

Once that was decided Peter's solemn mood of the morning lifted. "Thank you," he said as they left the churchyard and Hope's heart swelled with gratitude for being able to give this small boy something he'd only been able to dream about.

They caught a hansom to Holborn. It had been some time since Hope had visited Harold Taylor's shop. Today, as she walked along High Holborn, her mind flooded with memories.

She recalled the first time she'd walked into the shop with Alfie to buy his new school uniform and how Mr Taylor had made them feel most welcome, despite their not being his usual class of customer. She'd warmed to this red-faced, mutton whiskered butterball of a man and felt immediately at ease in his company.

Alfie was old enough to choose his own clothes now, helped by Harold Taylor's expert guidance, so she'd not felt the need to accompany him. Harold and Margaret had become friends over the years and she had no hesitation in approaching him for Peter's new clothes. She knew from experience how he'd put the boy at ease as he had with Alfie when he was that age and starting a new school with unfamiliar requirements in uniform and behaviour.

Peter, walking along beside her, gazed eyes wide at the shops as they passed. She could imagine how new this would be for him and was determined that he shouldn't be discomforted by it.

A bell rang as she pushed the shop door open. An assistant came immediately to greet them. Seeing Hope the young man smiled. "Good morning, Mrs Quirk," he said, then seeing Peter by her side added, "and you, young sir."

Hope smiled. She guessed Peter had never been referred to as 'young sir' in all his life.

"You'll be wanting to see Mr Taylor," the assistant said. Before Hope could reply he put out his arm to direct them to the back of the shop where Harold Taylor had his workroom.

"Thank you," Hope said, relieved that no further discussion was needed. She was aware of Peter's unease and this smart, well-turned out young man would only add to it.

In the workroom Hope relaxed and she noticed that Peter did too. The workroom was much less forbidding than the shop. Here odd bits of fabric were strewn about, half-cut-out patterns and tacked together suits lay on benches around the room and Harold Taylor, in shirt sleeves and a bright yellow waistcoat, with a tape measure dangling around his neck, was a welcome sight.

The tailor stepped forward to greet Hope. "What an unexpected pleasure," he said, taking her hand. "And how is Silas? Keeping busy I trust?"

Hope assured him that they were both well.

"And who might this young man be?" Harold asked, his gaze flitting over Peter who stood there gazing back, his dark eyes wide and unreadable.

"This is Peter," Hope said, smiling at the boy dressed in Alfie's old suit. It was far too big, which would be immediately obvious to Harold. Although better than the clothes Peter had worn on the street it fell far short of the sort of outfit the tailor would provide for his customers.

"He needs a good suit, several shirts, trousers, I have a list." Hope reached into her bag and brought out a piece of paper which she handed to Harold.

"Hmm," he said. "It's quite a comprehensive list, but I'm sure we can manage it."

For the next half hour Hope watched Harold measure Peter. The tape measure seemed to have a life of its own as it flashed from his shoulders, to his arms and legs. Harold called out the numbers to a young lad who'd appeared from nowhere to jot them down. All the while Peter stood, unblinking, watching Harold going about his business. Not for the first time Hope wondered what was going on his head. His face gave nothing away. His thin lips were pressed together, his eyes wary. He wasn't stupid she was sure of that. He'd remembered Violet's message and the address well enough. What was he thinking now? What was he committing to memory about Harold and the shop?

By the time they left the shop Harold had found a couple of shirts and a suit that fitted Peter well enough. Alfie's cast-offs were bundled up in a parcel to be sent on with Peter's new outfits. Altogether Hope thought it had been a pleasant, rewarding morning.

She managed to wave down a hansom cab to take them to the Hope and Anchor. All through the journey

227

she couldn't help but notice how, as they left the West End, they left the bright lights behind them. The roads got narrower, dirtier and duller. The number of costers' carts and wagons grew as the fine carriages and cabs lessened. She wondered if Peter noticed it too.

When they arrived at the pub Elsie was in the kitchen rolling out pastry for the tarts she was making. Every surface was covered with trays of party food. "My goodness," Hope said, gazing round. "How many children are you expecting this afternoon?"

"The missus has invited the whole neighbourhood," Elsie said, rubbing the flour from her hands. "It'll be good to see the place full again."

Hope smiled. She knew how much Alice wanted the pub to become a place where friends and neighbours would be happy to come and spend an evening. She intended to make the pub the heart of the community and attract customers from all walks of life. Inviting the neighbours in for a children's party was a good way to do it.

"And who's this?" Elsie said, her gaze resting on Peter.

"This is Peter. He'll be coming to the party," Hope said, realising for the first time how difficult it was going to be to explain his presence without giving away his background and how he'd come to know Hope and Silas.

Thankfully Elsie didn't enquire further. "The missus is in the hall with her ma. Bin decorating it all morning," she said, a note of disapproval in her voice. "It's a lot of work to do." She sucked her breath in between her teeth. "She should be resting. Not good to do too much in her condition."

Her condition? Hope's heart turned over. Was Alice expecting again? It was the first she'd heard of it. She forced a smile to her lips although her heart wasn't in it. Of course, if that were the case, she'd be happy for Alice and John, but she couldn't help the stab of envy she felt. Everyone would be enquiring when she might start a family and the heartache would begin again. "Where are the children?" she asked. "Is Violet here? I really must speak to her."

"Miss Violet's not back yet. William and Rose are upstairs with Mr John. Keeping out of the way until the party's ready."

"Thank you. I'll just go up and see John, then I'll go and relieve Alice. Come along, Peter. Time to meet the rest of the family."

Upstairs Hope found John in the parlour going over the order book. He stopped what he was doing, put the book down and rose when she walked into the room with Peter. The look that flashed across his face when he saw the boy chilled Hope. It was quickly replaced by a smile that didn't reach his eyes.

"This is Peter," Hope said. She glanced around. "Where are William and Rose? I thought they were with you."

"They're in their bedroom playing with their toys. Perhaps Peter would like to join them."

"Yes. I'll take him along," Hope said, her heart hammering. Was it too much to expect that her family would welcome Peter as she did? If it hadn't been for him they never would have found Violet. Perhaps she ought to remind them of that.

At least William and Rose were happy to see Peter again. "Ooo," William said. "Now we can play marbles. You do have some marbles don't you?" He pouted. "I s'pose you can borrow mine if not, though it's better if you do have some."

Peter's face broke into a smile. The first Hope had seen that day. "In the street we used to play with stones," he said. "You know, throwing instead of rolling but it was still dandy."

Why can't we all be as accepting as children, Hope thought. She sighed. Rose was playing with her dolls with Amy. They seemed quite settled and glad to be back in their own room.

"I'll just be along in the parlour if you want anything." She said, mainly to Peter but William didn't miss the chance to ask for some milk and biscuits. Hope laughed. "I'll see what I can do," she said, her heart a little lighter.

Returning to the parlour sent her heart plummeting again.

"So that's the kid Violet told us about?" John said, a worried overtone to his voice.

"If you mean the lad that showed us where she was being held, yes, that's the boy. And we're all very grateful to him."

"Violet said you'd taken him in. She's worried you may have taken on more than you've bargained for. He's street urchin. You know nothing about him."

"I know he saved Violet and he's earned the reward Silas put up for finding her. He's an orphan who's lost the people he loves most in the world. He's on the street to avoid going into the workhouse. That's all I need to know."

"How do you know you won't wake up one day and find he's gone, and all your silver and jewellery along with him?"

"He's not like that. He wouldn't…"

"Oh no? How do you know? You can't take a boy off the streets and turn him into an honest, law-abiding gentleman just by buying him fancy clothes. Underneath the finery he's still a boy off the streets who's made his living by thieving and deception. Fine clothes won't change that. What makes you think he won't be off at the first opportunity?"

"I don't know how you can even think such a thing," Hope said. Tears of anger rose unbidden to her eyes.

"I'm sorry, Hope," John said, "but I'm not sure you've thought this through. You've allowed your heart to rule your head. You just need to think on… For the boy's sake as much as your own."

"I need to think on?" Anger rose up inside Hope at John's manner. Silas had agreed to Peter staying so it really was none of John's business. "Silas agrees with me," Hope said. "He said Peter could stay."

John's eyebrows rose. "Really?"

Actually Silas had agreed to Hope taking in the boy temporarily while he found out more about him. He'd agreed to take responsibility for his education and upbringing, if there was no one else. He hadn't wholeheartedly agreed with Hope about taking him in, but John wasn't to know that.

"Yes, really. You've obviously forgotten what a kind and generous man he is and how much we owe him for his help in the past."

John looked deflated. "I haven't forgotten, Hope." He sunk down into a chair. "It's the boy himself I'm thinking about," he said. "Hardly fair to him to take him in then regret it. You can't expect a boy who's been living on the street to be any different than he's always been – a thief and a liar."

231

"I'll never regret it," Hope said.

"And other people will never forget. They'll treat him differently. They'll soon see that he doesn't belong. And what about if you have children of your own? What will happen to him then?"

"I'll love him just the same. Just as Ma and Pa loved us all. You don't have to give birth to be a good mother," she said. She recalled her own childhood and the love Ma and Pa had given her. She could stand no more arguing. "The children asked for milk and biscuits. I'll get them some."

As she walked away Hope couldn't help wondering if John wasn't right. She hadn't given much thought to the future at all. Was she being unfair to Peter expecting him to fit in with her family when he's been free to do as he liked for most of his life? Expecting him to be something he wasn't? And John? He'd said 'if' she had children, not 'when'. Did he see her taking Peter in as the foolish whim of a woman denied children of her own? How she hated that description. She sighed. Too late anyway, she thought. This small boy with his crooked smile and independent way had stolen her heart.

When she returned with the milk and biscuits, her heart sunk again. As she approached the bedroom she overheard Peter telling William what fun it was to roll a drunk after throwing out time at the pub. "You wait till you see 'em stagger, then trip 'em up," he said. "If you 'elp them up they'll give you some'at. If not, you prig their wallets." Hope was horrified and even more horrified when she saw the look of fascination on William's face as he hung onto every word.

"Well, Peter. I hope you're not going to lead William astray," she said, sharper than she intended.

"Thieving's in the past and as long as you're staying with us that's where it will remain."

Peter shrugged and William stifled a giggle. Oh dear, she thought. Was John right? Had she taken on more than she bargained for?

Chapter Thirty Six

On the way home from the police station the streets were stuffy with heat. At Violet's request they stopped at a coffee shop for refreshment. "I can't face the rest of the family just now," she said. Fear bubbled inside her. Fear of what she may have done and what would happen to her now. If she'd killed Jake it was in self-defence. She was defending her honour; surely they couldn't punish her for that?

"I think you'd better tell us everything," Silas said as he set three cups of strong coffee on the table. "We'll both do everything in our power to help, but we won't be able to do that unless we know the whole truth."

So Violet told them about the room she was held in and prising the plank from the window then hitting Jake with it. "I swear he was alive when I left," she said. "He was moving."

"How many times did you hit him?" Silas asked, aware of Violet's temper.

She pouted. "A few, but I swear he was about to get up when I ran away."

"He may have died later from his injuries," Silas said. "I think we have to be prepared for an accusation of murder."

"No!" Violet was aghast. "It's self-defence at most."

"I agree," Gabriel said. "And I believe Violet may be right. It takes a deal of strength to kill a man. I'm not sure Violet could do it, even with the help of a wooden plank."

"And a rotten one at that," Violet said. "It broke in half when I hit him."

"I'll get the best lawyer in London to defend you if it comes to it," Silas said. "But if Gabriel's right and you didn't kill him, then someone else did. We need to find that someone."

Gabriel nodded. He put his hand over Violet's. Warmth flowed through her at his touch. Why oh why did they have to meet in such terrible circumstances. Any other time she felt sure she could enjoy his company, but with the threat of a noose hanging over her it all felt so terribly wrong.

Silas's brow creased into a frown. "How long were you in that brothel before we found you?"

Violet coloured at the memory. She shrugged. "I'm not sure. I was drugged, it's a bit of a blur. At least a day or two." She sipped her coffee. "I'm sorry I can't be more helpful."

"You've been amazing," Gabriel said. "I'm sure a lesser woman would have buckled under the strain long ago." He smiled and Violet's heart beat faster.

"Then we need to find someone who saw Jake alive after you left his place," Silas said. "It's a fair bet that he'd have come looking for you and asking around. Dead Man's Island's not a huge place. Someone would have seen him. We need to find that person."

"Yes," Gabriel said. "In his profession he must have made many enemies. Any one of them could have killed him."

"Do you really think so?" Violet said.

Gabriel stroked her cheek, his finger brushing the slight scar that resulted from the slap Carter Doyle had given her. "Don't worry, my love," he said. "We'll both move heaven and earth to prove you innocent."

"We'll take you to the Hope and Anchor, then I'll gather some men and go to Dead Man's Island and start asking questions," Silas said, picking up his coffee and swallowing it back in one go.

"I'll come with you," Gabriel said. "I know a few places we could visit on the way where there'll be men who know what goes on there."

They finished their coffee in silence, then made their way to the Hope and Anchor for the children's party. Violet had never felt less like going to a party in her life, but she put on a brave face for her children. They were the most important things in her life now. There was nothing she wouldn't do for them. If she had killed Jake then it was to protect her children and she'd done that. Now that both Bert and Jake were dead their future with the family was secure.

By the time they reached the Hope and Anchor the neighbours were arriving with their children for the afternoon party. Both the men were sullen. They went straight into the bar, leaving Violet to go to the party. Violet managed to shrug off her earlier mood. She was used to putting on an act for her audience. She'd learned that from Bert. "The show must go on,'" he'd say. "No matter how you feel or what you would rather be doing. People have paid good money to come and see a show and I'll be damned if you're going disappoint them." So, she'd put on her glad rags, made up her face, usually to hide the bruises, and gone on. In front of an audience the beatings, the put-downs, the cruel words, whatever hurt Bert had inflicted upon her, melted away like snow in August. She'd belt out her songs and all the cares in the world would be gone for a few hours. On stage she felt in control and the audience loved her. Now she had to do it again, only for her family, the hardest audience to fool of all.

"How did it go at the police station?" Hope asked as soon as she walked in. "Did Penhalligan believe you about Jake killing Bert? Is it all settled? Can we now go back to living our lives without fear of imminent arrest?"

Violet felt all was far from settled and arrest more imminent than ever, but she smiled and said, "I'll tell you later." She glanced around as the hall was filling with women with their children come for the party. "I will tell you one thing though. Jake Mullins is dead and Penhalligan thinks I killed him."

"What!" The shocked look on Hope's face revived Violet's spirits. She could still shock her sister. Who knew? Hope pulled Violet to one side. "Tell me now," she said.

Violet smiled at a family just arriving. "Later," she said. "Or you could go and ask Silas. He's in the bar with Gabriel."

"Fine. That's what I'll do then," Hope said. Violet didn't miss the annoyance in her voice.

Violet walked purposefully into the hall. Sun streamed in through the windows and once again Violet wished she'd worn a lighter suit. She smiled to herself. 'Show time' she thought. These were the local children who would go to the same school as William and Rose when they started in September. It was a good chance for her to get to know the mothers and for the children to make friends.

"This looks amazing," she said to Alice who'd just shown a woman with three children in. The murmur of conversation from the new arrivals was beginning to fill the hall, so she'd had to raise her voice a little to be heard. Streamers and colourful cut-out characters decorated the walls and the tables had balloons on strings floating above them. A side table held glasses for the lemonade and plates of fancy sandwiches and cakes enough to feed an army. "It must have taken you ages."

Alice grinned. "I had help," she said, "but I am rather pleased with it."

"Don't let her fool you," Alice's ma, standing next to her, said. "She's been working on this like a devil for weeks when she should've been putting her feet up."

Violet glanced at Alice and noticed her rosy glow which couldn't be entirely due to the heat of the day. "You don't mean…"

Alice blushed an even deeper red. "Yes. A little brother or sister for Amy."

Violet rushed up to her to put her arms around her and kissed her on both cheeks. "Congratulations," she said, although she was half-expecting it. She knew Alice and John were eager to have a large family. "When is the happy event?"

"After Christmas, hopefully," Alice said. "Late January if all goes well."

Late January, Violet thought. I could be dangling from the end of a rope by then. She pushed the thought to the back of her mind. "That's wonderful news," she said.

"What's wonderful news?" Hope asked, walking into the hall after talking to Silas.

"Alice's baby," Violet said, then wondered how Hope might feel about it.

"Oh yes. Excellent news," Hope said, although it was obvious her mind was elsewhere. "It'll be lovely for Amy to have a brother or sister."

"I'm so glad Violet's back to help me look after them," Alice said. "I don't know how I'd manage otherwise."

Violet smiled. Then Alice was called away to welcome in another parent with her child.

Hope put her arm around Violet. "I just want you to know that both Silas and I will be by your side whatever happens. We won't let them do anything to you. We'll fight just as we always fight anyone who tries to do us harm. I just wanted you to know that," she said.

Something inside Violet melted. "Thanks," she said. Words weren't necessary. She had family behind her and that was all that mattered. Suddenly she felt stronger.

Just then another family arrived and Hope, Alice and Violet were kept busy filling glasses of lemonade and organising games. It wasn't long before the hall rang with the clink of glasses, the hum of conversation, the sound of children's laughter, their shrieks and shouts and the thumping of feet as they ran around playing Blind Man's Buff, Ring-a-Ring of Roses, Lucy Locket and Are you there, Moriarty? When it came to Musical Chairs, the music provided by Alice's ma at the piano, Rose refused to play. "The boys are too rough," she said. "They keep pushing me."

Violet chuckled. "Well, push them back," she said.

She watched her children as they played. This was the best part of being a parent, seeing your little ones happy, laughing and enjoying themselves. Why does that have to change when you grow up? Why can't you always be as happy and carefree as children? she thought.

While she was watching them Violet noticed that Peter hardly joined in any of the games, despite William trying to include him.

"What's the matter?" she asked him. "Why aren't you joining in?"

"Can't play any of these games," he said. "I'm all right just watching."

She didn't miss how uncomfortable he looked as he spoke, the wistful look on his face or how different he was from the others as he stood a little apart from the games. It was as though he had been brought into a world he didn't quite understand or fit in and Violet was acutely aware of it. She wondered if Hope had noticed it too.

Later, when the children were hot and tired out by running around, they sat down to a feast of sandwiches, cakes and jelly. Peter joined in with the feast and again, Violet was surprised at how much he managed to eat.

Chapter Thirty Seven

Gabriel sat in solemn silence at the bar with Silas. He couldn't stop thinking about Violet and all she'd been through. Now the police inspector in charge of the case thought she'd killed the man who'd kidnapped her. It was beyond belief.

Violet had gone up even higher in his estimation. He'd seen how she put on a brave face for her children, like the trouper she was. What if she had killed Jake Mullins? It sounded to him as though he deserved it and he for one wouldn't blame her. Still, Silas was right. Inspector Penhalligan took a very different view of the situation. He sighed and sipped his drink. He thought about the rescue and holding Violet in his arms. It was the most exciting thing that had ever happened to him. Once again he gave silent thanks for having a man like Silas at his side.

He was about to say something of the sort to Silas when John joined them. Silas told him about the visit to the police station and the police finding Jake Mullins dead and how Violet was implicated.

"I can't believe it," John said. "Violet's not a killer. She might have a temper but she wouldn't kill anyone."

"I know," Silas said, "but try telling Inspector Penhalligan that." He swigged back the whisky John had poured for him. John refilled his glass. "I'm taking some men to the Island," Silas said. "I want to see where Jake Mullins lived and find out who else lives there. Someone must know what happened. I won't rest until I know the truth of it."

"What about you, Gabriel?" John said. "All this must make you want to think twice about having anything to do with our Violet."

"On the contrary," Gabriel said. "I find her more intriguing than ever. I'll do all I can to get to the bottom of it and find out what really happened and why. As far as I can see none of this is Violet's fault. We just need to prove it."

"That's very sporting of you," John said.

"I believe the prize is worth the effort," Gabriel said with a twinkle in his eye.

Silas patted him on the back. "Not sure you know what you're taking on," he said. "But I wish you well."

"Thanks."

Gabriel finished his drink and banged the glass on the bar. "I've made a few enquiries about that brothel and who runs it. I'll go back and see what I can find out. I'll meet you back at the club later."

"Good," Silas said. "I'll go and round up some men to come with us. It's not a place to go unarmed or alone."

Silas finished his drink and the men left the bar.

Outside Gabriel caught a hansom back to his hotel where he went in search of Harry the concierge. Before leaving to show Inspector Penhalligan where they found Violet, he'd asked Harry to find out all he could about the place. Harry was, as usual, a mine of information.

"Dead Man's Island is home to all sort of beggars, footpads, cracksmen, pimps, doxies, scriveners and murderers," Harry said. "A swirling underworld of filth that offers sanctuary to every kind of seedy criminal. That brothel's run by a man called Carter Doyle and his sister Sadie Sullivan," Harry grimaced. "It's not a place I'd like to think of any gentleman of my acquaintance going. Terrible reputation for drink, drugs and tarts. You can have whatever you like there, for a price. All tastes catered for." Harry shuddered. "Makes me skin crawl to think what goes on there it does. People like that, no better 'an animals."

"You mean children?" Gabriel asked.

Tears filled Harry's eyes as he said, "It's been known." Gabriel knew Harry had children and grandchildren who he loved dearly so anything like the trade Jake Mullins made his living from would be abhorrent to him.

"Have you heard of a man called Jake Mullins? A big man from all accounts and rough with it. In the same trade as Carter Doyle. Any information you can find about him would be well rewarded."

"Shouldn't be too hard, sir. I'll see what I can do."

"The thing is, Harry, Jake Mullins is dead. I'd love to know how he died and any gossip you can pick up about who may have killed him."

"If he's in the same trade as Carter Doyle they'd be in competition?"

"Yes, each as bad as the other, I'm sorry to say."

"In that case may he burn in hell, sir."

Gabriel reached into his pocket, brought out a wad of five pound notes, peeled two off and gave them to Harry. "I'd love know how he died. Was it a blow to the head, a fight or something else?"

"That'll be from the morgue, would it, sir?"

"Yes."

"Hmm." Harry stroked his chin. "The cook's youngest boy works as a porter at the morgue. I'll see what I can do, sir. Leave it with me."

"Thank you, Harry, Well done." Another five pound note found its way into Harry's hand.

The concierge tipped his hat. "Will that be all, sir?"

"For the time being. Thank you, Harry."

Upstairs Gabriel changed out of his suit into an older, more worn one. It was a bit warm for the August heat but he didn't want to stand out too much in the run-down area he'd be visiting. He roughed up his hair, put on his driving cap and changed his shoes to boots, scuffing them a little as he put them on. Then he went to meet Silas at the club. At least he had some idea of where to go looking for Jake Mullins's killer.

At the club Silas was ready to go. Knuckles and Eddie were going with him. Gabriel told him what he'd heard about Carter Doyle and the brothel.

"Well, if Violet escaped from Jake and then he heard of Carter Doyle offering a new girl with a bit of class…"

"He'd go there to look for her?"

"Precisely! That's where we'll start then. We'll visit the local pubs and see if anyone's heard anything about a fight between Doyle and Mullins."

"We need to show he was seen alive after Violet escaped," Gabriel said. "Any sighting would prove her innocence."

"Unless he was so groggy he went home and died later. It's been known."

"Is that where the body was found? His home?"

Silas shrugged. "So Penhalligan said. Still, it makes no difference. He could have staggered on for a day or even two before the blow killed him. Violet could still be blamed."

"Unlikely though wouldn't you say?" he said. He could see his dream of saving Violet, of being the knight in shining armour and slaying the dragon for her, slipping away. Why did Silas have to be so downright pessimistic? "I for one won't give up until I've found proof she didn't kill him."

"Well said," Knuckles said. "I never believed that little lady could harm a fly. If she did she was desperate. Let's go out and prove it."

They made their way to the river and took a ferry across to Rotherhithe. Gabriel noticed that Silas too had changed his clothes and wore a dark coat that could be mistaken for workman's. When they reached the bank at Rotherhithe they mounted the steps and walked along to the first buildings. Warehouses took up most of the riverside. Beyond them rows of terraced houses lined narrow roads. Filled with grubby, unwashed children, spilling over onto the doorsteps, they all looked as though they'd seen better days.

Gabriel felt a chill, despite the warmth of the day and his heavier jacket. Walking in the shadow along rubbish strewn cobbles, the air filled with the stench of rotting animal carcasses that lay in the gutters, he couldn't help but wonder what on earth he was doing here, blindly following people he knew little of to find out about a man who, by all accounts, got just what he deserved. Only a few days ago he'd been bowling along leafy country lanes, through the most beautiful countryside in England. Then he thought of Violet. It was her neck he was trying to save; suddenly it all became clear. Once again he was letting his heart rule his head, but in this instance he couldn't regret it. Violet's life was at stake. Nothing was more important than saving her. He didn't want to fall at the first hurdle.

Walking behind Silas he was glad of the man's bulk and heavier build. Gabriel was a thinker, Silas a man who knew how to handle himself in a fight. Gabriel was glad of that. He wasn't a fighter and felt completely out his depth in this terrible place. Silas's presence beside him was the only thing that made it bearable. He thought he'd like to get to know him better, only perhaps in happier times.

After a short walk they came to junction. "Let's split up," Silas said. "Knuckles, go with Gabriel and I'll take Eddie. We'll be less conspicuous that way. We'll find out what we can and meet up back here in a couple of hours."

The men nodded their assent and Gabriel and Knuckles walked to the nearest pub. It being early afternoon the bar was nearly empty. A couple of men sat by a window playing cards. The place was dimly lit and uninviting. Gabriel decided to leave the talking to Knuckles as his accent was bound to arouse curiosity. Knuckles ordered a pint of ale for each of them and asked about Jake Mullins.

The barman shrugged. "Sorry, mate, don't know 'im."

"Big man. Lives on Dead Man's Island. I thought he drank here."

"Na. Never 'eard of 'im."

"Thanks anyway," Knuckles said. Neither of the card payers spoke although they did look over. "Nowt doing here," Knuckles said to Gabriel, so they drank up and went out.

The next place was little better. One lone customer sat on a bench seat at a table with a dog beside him. He was reading a newspaper and occasionally picked up a piece of what looked like broken biscuit from a plate on the table and fed it to the dog. A half empty glass of ale stood next to the plate of biscuits.

The man looked up when they walked in. Gabriel smiled and nodded a brief greeting. The man went back to reading his paper.

Knuckles ordered them each a pint of ale. "An' one for yourself," he said to the barman.

The barman took a gin. Gabriel paid.

Knuckles glanced around as though looking for someone in particular. "Has Jake Mullins been in?" he asked.

"Who's asking?" the barman said.

Knuckles shrugged. "Just might have a bit o' business to put 'is way."

"You're a bit late for that. Last I 'eard he was brown bread."

Knuckles acted astonished. "Dead? Jake Mullins? How?"

"Well, 'e didn't die of old age," the barman chuckled.

Knuckles knocked back the rest of his pint. "Have another," he said. The barman pulled Knuckles another pint and got another gin for himself, a double this time.

Again Gabriel paid. "So what 'appened?" Knuckles said, egging the barman on.

The barman looked around and, as though satisfied that he wasn't being overheard, he said. "Wot I 'eard was that 'e got in a fight."

"A fight?" Who with?"

The barman shrugged.

"Tell me more," Knuckles said, indicating that he should help himself to another drink.

"Thank you kindly," the barman said taking another double gin and putting it aside for later. "Don't know much more. Only that a bloke came in 'ere the other day talking about how he's seen a fight. Right shook up 'e was. Must've been bad."

"Wasn't with Carter Doyle was it?" Knuckles said. "I know they've 'ad a bit of a barney in the past."

"Could've bin. Can't swear to it." The barman frowned. "Over some tart I wouldn't wonder. Usually is ain't it?"

"When was this?"

The barman shrugged again. "Days ago, maybe a week. Can't really say."

"So who was this bloke?"

"Dunno 'is name. Comes in off an' on. They call 'im Poke 'cos he always carries this sack around with him. Don't know what he keeps in it mind. But he never puts it down."

Gabriel and Knuckles exchanged glances. "Well, thanks," Knuckles said. Gabriel put some money on the counter and they walked out. It was a start. If they could find 'Poke' they could maybe prove that Jake Mullins died in a fight.

After leaving the pub Gabriel and Knuckles tried several of the lodging houses in the area looking for Poke but no one admitted knowing him or seeing anyone resembling him. By the time they'd tried the fifth one Gabriel was feeling decidedly queasy. He'd never in his life imagined that people lived in such places, although Knuckles appeared quite at home in the slums.

"Fair turns your stomach," he said at one particularly rancid place.

"I never knew people lived like this," Gabriel said, thinking of his father's immaculate hotels which would appear sumptuous by comparison.

"Aye. It's an education all right," Knuckles said. The filth and squalor didn't seem to bother him in the slightest.

When they got back to the Rotherhithe steps Silas and Eddie were waiting.

"How did you get on?" Silas asked.

Gabriel shrugged. "I suggest we take the ferry back to civilisation and compare notes there," he said. "I'm not sure my constitution can stand another hour in this place."

Silas laughed, but they took the ferry back. Gabriel's clothes reeked of ale, stale tobacco and rotting vegetation. He wondered what Violet would think if he turned up at the pub smelling so putrid. He shuddered at the thought.

Back in Wapping they found a coffee shop and Knuckles told Silas about the fight and the possibility that it might have been witnessed by a man known as Poke.

"That's pretty much the same as we heard," Silas said. "Trouble is no one knows where this Poke hangs out. Still, it does open up the possibility that Jake was alive and well when Violet escaped. Penhalligan can't argue with that."

"So how do we find this Poke and, even if we do find him, how do we persuade him to tell the police what he saw? I can't imagine he'll be willing without encouragement."

"You can leave any persuading to me," Silas said, and Gabriel had no doubt about Silas's powers of persuasion.

"From what we heard the most likely place to find 'im is the Waterloo slum," Knuckles said. "Most down an' outs end up there one way or another."

"That's true," Silas said. "We'll try there first thing tomorrow."

"The Waterloo slum? Sounds worse than where we were today, although I can't imagine it," Gabriel said, shuddering at the thought of wading through more muck and stench than they'd seen today.

Silas patted him on the shoulder. "It's a delightful place, but I'm afraid we're going to offend your gentlemanly sensibilities even further. It's not for the faint-hearted. I'll go with Knuckles and Eddie if you like. No need for us all to go."

"Wouldn't dream of it," Gabriel said. "I said I'll go with you and I'll stick with you until we find him, muck and misery or not."

"You're on. Till tomorrow then."

They finished their coffee and Silas, Knuckles and Eddie went back to the club while Gabriel went back to his hotel to change. If he'd rolled in the gutter he couldn't smell worse than he did. He'd have time to bathe and change before meeting Violet. It wouldn't do for her to see him, nor smell him as he was, stinking of the stench that clung to him.

Back at the hotel he bathed and changed then called on Harry to see if he had any news from the morgue.

"Not as yet, sir," Harry said. "But it's in hand. May take a day or two, but we'll get there."

"Thanks, Harry. You're a treasure," Gabriel said and went out to meet Violet.

Chapter Thirty Eight

Back at the pub the last of the families were leaving. Everyone said what a lovely time they'd had. "It's one we'll remember for a long time," a woman Violet recognised as the wife of one of local merchants said. "I remember the parties we used to have back in the days when Rose and William had the pub. They were good days and I'm glad you're bringing 'em back. About time this community had a place they could come together. Good on you and your husband."

Alice blushed with pleasure. "I'll tell John," she said. "He'll be pleased to hear it."

That was true, Violet thought. He was always going on about bringing in the customers. If the party had done that then it was money well spent, and, with the leaving gifts it was clear to Violet that a pretty penny had been spent.

"I guess you'll be doing the Chamber of Commerce Christmas Party, like in the old days," Violet said, the memory of those days playing in her mind.

"We have been asked," Alice said. "I hope you'll be around to lend a hand too. Wouldn't be the same without you."

"I hope so too," Violet said and she'd never meant anything more in her life.

Once the visitors had gone Violet, Hope and John made their way to the bar for drinks.

"What about the clearing up?" Hope asked.

"Leave it," Alice said. "It'll do 'till morning. I think we all deserve a sit down. Maisie comes in early to clean and Ma and Elsie will give her a hand."

Violet wasn't about to argue. Her feet ached and running around after a room full of boisterous children had tired them all out. Rose, William, Peter and Amy went upstairs to play. They seemed to have boundless energy.

"Now you can tell us what happened at the police station this morning," Hope said. "Silas only gave me the briefest details. Why does Penhalligan think you killed Jake Mullins?"

"Jake Mullins is dead?" Alice said. "Since when? This is the first I've heard of it."

"Yes, Silas told me," John said. "You were busy with the party, I didn't want to disturb or upset you."

"But that's terrible," Alice said. "I mean... not that he's dead, that's good, but to think Violet killed him..." She gazed at Violet. "You didn't did you?"

Violet shrugged. "I hit him with a plank of wood. He was alive when I left him. That's all I know. I don't think Penhalligan will be able to prove anything else. Even if he tries."

"Silas said they took your fingerprints, and his and Gabriel's."

"That only proves I was there. I've never denied that."

"But what will happen to the children?" Alice said, tears filling her eyes. "I mean... if Violet is put on trial... I can't bear to think of it."

"Now, now," John said. "Don't upset yourself, sweetheart. In your condition you don't need to be upset." Violet felt daggers in the look he gave her. "I think it best Alice goes for a lie down."

"I don't want a lie down," Alice said. "I'm not a baby. Please don't treat me like one."

"We're all hoping it won't come to that, Alice," Hope said. "Silas and Gabriel have gone out to find someone who may be able to prove that Jake was alive well after Violet escaped from him. We won't rest until we prove Violet innocent."

Violet refused to be down-hearted. "I've done nothing wrong," she said. "I'm the victim here. People seem to forget that."

"Of course you are," Hope said, but with little conviction. Violet guessed she remembered all the other times when they were growing up when she'd claimed to be the victim of whatever tragic circumstances she'd brought upon herself. "It's all Bert Shadwick's fault," Hope said. "He had no right to come after you and the children. If it wasn't for him none of this would have happened."

"It's no use crying over spilt milk," Violet said, anger rising inside her. Why did Hope always have to take the moral high ground? "Blaming Bert won't help anyone. I for one will carry on as though nothing has happened. I'll be looking after my children as usual. We can't let this spoil anything for them."

"Well said." They all glanced around as Silas walked into the room. "Business as usual, that's for the best."

The look of disapproval that flashed across Hope's face was fleeting. "Silas is right," she said. "Life must go on for the children with as little disruption as possible."

"That's what I said," Violet said, smothering an 'I told you so' smirk. She glanced at the door behind Silas. "Is Gabriel not with you?" she asked.

"He went back to his hotel to change, but he'll be joining us for dinner," Silas said.

"How did you get on?" Hope asked. "Did you manage to find anything of any use?"

Silas shrugged. "I'm not sure. We'll be going out again tomorrow. We hope to have better luck then."

With his arrival the happy atmosphere of the afternoon party had faded away and the evening was in danger of becoming dismal. Violet tried to lighten the mood. "Alice put on a lovely spread for the children," she told him. "And they all enjoyed the games. A sterling effort in view of her condition. What are you hoping for, Alice? A girl or a boy?" She'd had enough of worrying about what Inspector Penhalligan might think or do. She wanted to put the past few weeks behind her and get on with her life, such as it was.

Alice smiled. "I don't mind either, but John's hoping for a boy to carry on the business."

"Of course he is," Violet said, warming to the subject of the new baby. Anything to take their minds off her predicament.

"What's this?" Silas asked, beaming at Alice. "A new baby? Congratulations. When's the happy event?"

"Early next year," Alice said.

"That calls for champagne," Silas said. "Something to celebrate." He nodded to John to get the drinks but Violet didn't miss the resignation on Hope's face. She must be wondering when they'd be able to bring out the champagne on her account, Violet thought.

John disappeared into the cold store and brought out three bottles of champagne. "Let's take it upstairs," Alice said. "There are some sandwiches left and some of Elsie's famous pork pies if you'd like a bite to eat before you go."

"Lovely idea," Violet said. "And I'm sure the children will be able to cram in a few more cakes." She laughed.

She wasn't wrong. William and Peter finished off the sandwiches and pies and Rose and Amy picked at the cakes.

After they'd finished the champagne John said he ought to go and help Thomas in the bar. "He's been here all day," he said. "Good of him to do the extra time."

"I need to put Amy to bed," Alice said. "She's tired from the excitement of the party."

"I think we all are," Violet said. "Thank you for arranging it and inviting us. It's been something lovely to remember."

Everyone agreed and they all thanked Alice for putting on such a lovely spread.

Hope collected Peter and Violet rounded up William and Rose. Abel was with Silas and they walked home together in the warmth of the August evening. If only it wasn't for Jake's death hanging over them, Violet thought, it would have been the end of a perfect afternoon.

Chapter Thirty Nine

The next morning Gabriel dressed in his roughest clothes. He'd been promised a visit to a slum even worse than he'd seen already. He folded his good suit and put it in a bag to take with him. He'd leave it at the club when he went to meet Silas.

As he passed the long mirror in his dressing room he caught a glimpse of himself. He paused. He barely recognised himself. What on earth would his parents think if they saw him dressed like a workman? He could hardly believe it himself.

He thought back over the last few days, the sights, the sounds and even the smells. They were all foreign to him. Glancing around his comfortable, well-appointed bedroom he felt reassured. This was more to his liking. He walked over and opened the window. The morning air felt fresh and clean. The street below bustled with life. The clatter of hooves and the rumble of wheels on cobbles almost drowned out the cries of the costers selling their wares. Sounds that were missing in the slums. There carts were trundled along pulled by hand, the sound of the wheels softened by the mud and muck that lined every street. The narrow paths and alleyways were steeped in eerie, stagnant silence as though no one had the energy or inclination to move on or change anything. He found the thought depressing. He had never before had cause to consider how the poor of the country lived. In his world everything was neat and orderly. Everyone knew their place and were glad of it, or so he'd been brought up to believe. This other side of life was a revelation and not one he was very keen on. He sighed and turned away from the window, leaving it open to let in the morning air.

He picked up the picture of Violet and her children taken in Yarmouth, which he kept with him and sat on the bed. That brought a smile to his face. He thought over what she'd been through the last few weeks. Horrendous experiences that would have laid most women low. Certainly any lady of his acquaintance would have surrendered at the first hurdle, but not Violet. Her resilience amazed him as did much about her. She reminded him of a horse he'd once owned, high-spirited and dangerous. Temperamental and unpredictable, he was just as likely to throw you as let you on his back, but that's what made him so exciting. When you galloped him across the fields nothing in the world existed except you and the horse moving as one. He remembered the exhilarating sensation of being able to ride forever. He recalled the sense of power and feeling that everything was within reach, a feeling that was hard to forget.

He put the picture down. He'd do whatever he had to do for Violet. He only hoped they'd have better luck today and not come home empty handed as they had yesterday. He shuddered at the memory. Then he took a last look round, picked up his bag and went out to meet Silas and embrace the day ahead of him.

When he got to The Grenadier, Silas was already waiting with Knuckles and Eddie. "We'll keep together today," he said. "Where we're going we'll need safety in numbers." Gabriel guessed it was where they'd been attacked and extra care would be needed.

The day started out with drizzly rain and grey clouds scudding across the sky. They caught a cab to Waterloo Bridge, then proceeded on foot into the worst slum Gabriel had ever seen. The alleyways were lined with rough lodging houses where a bed in a room shared by up to twenty other people could be hired for tuppence a night.

Once again he was glad to have Silas ahead of him. Every inch of him oozed confidence, strength and power and his presence brought respect from everyone. Each time they made enquiries about a man known as Poke the lodging-house keeper would eye them up and down assessing what any information he could give them might be worth. If Silas offered a shilling, everyone claimed to have seen him, knew him or declared they'd 'just missed 'im'. People who did know him described him as a 'tinker' and said he'd either be looking for odd jobs or trying to sell his bits and pieces.

"He's maybe down by the river," one said. "It's low tide and he buys bits he can re-sell from the mudlarks along there. Mainly bits of tin or brass. That's best place to find 'im at low tide." Silas thanked him and gave him a shilling. "You'll know 'im if you see 'im," the man said. "'E'll be wearing an old army great coat and a battered black trilby. 'E'll be carrying a sack. Never ever seen 'im without 'is sack." It was the most promising account they'd heard all morning. Silas nodded and they moved on.

"Let's take a break," Silas said. "If what we've heard is true he'll be down by the river, so that's our next port of call."

They stopped at a stall on the corner by the docks and Silas bought them each a pie and coffee. He bought one extra and they walked to the bend in the river where the tide would be at its lowest. A stiff breeze blew over the water and Gabriel pulled his coat

258

closer around him. They saw Poke sitting on a low wall, gazing across the water, his sack by his side. One solitary mudlark stood knee-deep in the dirty water fishing around for anything that may have dropped off one of the passing barges or the boats going into the docks.

Silas nodded to Gabriel and indicated to Knuckles and Eddie that they were to wait out of sight. "Don't want to frighten him off," he said. Gabriel and Silas strolled up to him, as though looking for somewhere to sit and have their lunch. When they came to where he sat, gazing out, they sat each side of him.

"Nice morning for it," Silas said, putting his coffee on the wall and taking his still hot pie out of its wrapping. Gabriel did the same. Poke glanced from one to the other, then his gaze fell upon Silas's pie. Silas stopped as though considering something then passed the pie to Poke. Poke took it, broke it in half, wrapped one half in a grubby handkerchief from his pocket and put it in his sack.

"So what is it you're after?" Poke said in a lilting Irish accent. "I don't imagine you two fine gentlemen is here for the sake o' me health."

"Information," Gabriel said.

Poke turned to stare at him. He took a breath and a bite of the pie. It was several minutes before he spoke. "Now what information would a couple o' posh yokes be wanting from a harmless old man like me?"

Looking closer at his face Gabriel guessed he wasn't as old as he liked to make out. His coat was well worn, his chin dark with bristles and brown hair poked out from under his hat but he was no more than late thirties, early forties and fitter than he'd expected.

"We're looking for the man who killed Jake Mullins," Silas said. "I've heard that you saw him fighting with someone a few days ago. We'd like to know more about that fight."

Poke looked anxiously from one to the other. "You're not the polis?" he said half rising to his feet.

Silas and Gabriel grabbed his coat and pulled him back down again. "No, not the police," Silas said.

"Then why would you be wanting to trouble yoursel's wi' that?"

"Because a very dear friend of ours, a lady, is going to be blamed and we know she didn't do it," Silas said.

"Oh I see," Poke said, settling down again. "I'll tell you somat. It weren't no lady I saw fighting wi' 'im a few days ago." Poke took another bite of the pie.

"So who was it?"

"Ah now, that'd be telling."

Silas produced a gold half-sovereign and placed it on the wall between them. "I'll bet this half-sovereign you don't know," he said.

Poke swallowed his mouthful, licked his lips, glanced at each of them and picked up the half-sovereign. He slipped it into his pocket. "You lose," he said. He stood, grabbed his sack and walked away. He didn't get far. Knuckles and Eddie grabbed an arm each and marched him back to his seat.

"Let me be," he said, wriggling himself out of their grasp. "I'm an honest God-fearing citizen who's done nutin' wrong. I can't think what you'd want wi' the likes o' me."

"Can't you?" Gabriel said. "How about telling us about the fight you saw. I hear you've been telling all and sundry in the local pubs for the price of a pint."

"Oh, I see," Poke said, finishing off the pie he was still holding. "It's a business transaction you's after. Well, if'n I had the other half o' that there sovereign I'll tell you all I know."

"Which might not amount to a can of beans," Silas said. "Tell us first then we'll see and there's plenty more where that came from if you've a mind to make it official."

"Official? You don't mean the polis? I'll not blab to the polis. It's more'n me life's worth."

"The way I see it it's not worth a lot at the moment," Silas said. He nodded to Knuckles, standing in front of them. Knuckles balled his fist and punched it into his other hand in a threatening gesture.

"Begging your pardon, sir," Poke said glaring at Knuckles. "I'd as soon you didn't do that. It unsettles me nerves and I canna think straight when me nerves is unsettled."

Gabriel let out a sigh. "We're wasting our time here," he said. "He's no use to us. Might as well do your worst, Knuckles."

Silas stood up and Knuckles stepped forward.

"Carter Doyle," Poke said. "It's come to me now. I saw Jake Mullins fighting wi' Carter Doyle. I didn't see what 'appened. Made meself scarce. Can't swear to owt else but that's the truth of it."

"Okay," Silas said. "Now all we need is for you to tell the police what you saw."

"Oh, I couldn't do that, sir. Not and live to see me grandchildren."

"Grandchildren?" Gabriel said. "You have grandchildren?"

"Not as such, sir. But you never knows what the future might hold."

261

Gabriel stifled a chuckle. You couldn't stay cross with Poke for long which is probably how he'd managed to survive so far. He had a feeling Poke could blag his way out of any trouble. Looking more closely at his clothes he noticed that his coat, although now shabby, had once been quality and his boots too, although scuffed, had been well made and were not as bad as some he'd seen on the 'gentlemen of the road' that traversed the lanes of rural Norfolk. For a man who made his living by his wits he was better equipped than many he'd met on his travels.

Silas took a notebook and pencil from his pocket. "I'm going to write a statement about what you've told us," he said. "I want you to sign it. Will you do that?"

Poke looked from one to the other. "What I need is a little holiday," he said. "Wouldn't it be grand to sail away to Ireland to see me old grey-haired mammy afore she dies."

Gabriel took a five pound note out of his pocket and held it in front of Poke. Poke's eyes lit up.

"'Course I couldn't go dressed like this," he said. "It'd fair bring a tear to me mammy's eyes to see me so badly dressed."

Gabriel took out another five pound note.

Silas pushed the note he'd written in front of Poke. Poke took the pencil and signed his name, which turned out to be Seamus O'Malley. He ground his thumb into the dirt at his feet and pressed it to the paper.

"Ex-army?" Silas asked.

Seamus smiled. "Irish Fusiliers," he said.

Silas nodded and Gabriel gave him the two five pound notes. "Good luck," he said.

"Ta, I'll need it," Seamus said, pushing the notes into his pocket. Now that their business was concluded he stood, tipped his cap and strode away whistling, with his sack slung over his shoulder, his vacant, Irish beggar act gone completely.

Gabriel had the distinct impression they'd been had.

Chapter Forty

That evening over dinner Silas and Gabriel told Hope and Violet about Poke and his statement about seeing Jake fighting with Carter Doyle.

"We don't know when that was," Silas said. "He's very vague about the time. It may have been before Violet managed to escape. We just don't know."

"Well, it's a start," Gabriel said. "Surely Penhalligan can find others who knew about it and when it was, if he puts his mind and his men into looking."

"I'm just playing Devil's Advocate," Silas said. "Trying to work out the objections Penhalligan will have so we can find ways to get round them."

"It's good of you to try," Violet said. "I know from experience how dangerous those places are. Ask too many questions and you could end up in the river."

"We went mob handed," Silas said with a grin. "And we were ready for them if they did attack us. Still, with Jake dead I don't suppose anyone else will bother us. They've nothing to gain by it."

"Pity Poke wouldn't talk to the police though," Gabriel said. "I'm sure they could jog his memory more effectively than we can."

Silas shrugged. "He's ex-army. Could have more to lose than gain from a run in with the police."

"How do you mean?"

"We don't know how or why he left the army. Could have been any reason. They shoot deserters don't they?"

"You think he was a deserter?" Gabriel sounded incredulous.

"Either that or dishonourable discharge. Didn't seem like a fighting man to me. More like a man who avoids violence of any kind."

Gabriel shook his head. Hope and Violet glanced at each other. "I'm sure Violet appreciates all you're trying to do for her," Hope said. "But I'd prefer it if you didn't have to go round places like that asking questions. Perhaps we should leave it to the police."

"I'll go and see Penhalligan in the morning," Silas said. "After that it's up to him."

"I'll come with you," Gabriel said.

"There's no need," Silas said. "I think I'll be better going alone. We go back a long way. I'll be better able to persuade him."

"If you think that's best?" Gabriel said.

"I do."

The rest of the meal was eaten in silence. Daisy came in to clear the dishes and they retired to the drawing room for coffee for the ladies and port for the men.

"I've had a letter from Dexi," Hope said, searching for something she could talk about to lighten the atmosphere. "She's enjoying her visit to friends. She says the sea air is bracing."

"Knowing my sister that means it's freezing cold," Silas said. "Did she say when she'd return?"

"No. I expect she'll stay for another week if she's enjoying the company."

"I hear she's an excellent card player," Gabriel said. "Get in a game with her and you'll likely lose your shirt someone told me."

Silas smiled. "She's very experienced," he said.

265

"Talking of going home," Violet said. "I've been thinking it may be time for me to take the children back to the pub. It's their home after all."

"Oh no," Hope said, a little too quickly. "Surely you can stay a little longer, until this thing with Jake Mullins is sorted out."

"I'd like to take them home before they start school," Violet said. "They'll be able to get to know the local children and they'll need fitting out. I don't want them standing out or looking any different from the other children."

"I think it's best you stay," Silas said. "What if Penhalligan decides to take you in, even for questioning? You can't expect Alice to look after them. She's got enough on her plate, especially in her condition."

Violet shrugged. She supposed Silas was right, but she didn't want staying with Hope to become a permanent arrangement. "Where is Peter going to school?" she asked. "I assume he will be starting in September."

Hope looked flustered. "Yes, of course he'll be going to school. We haven't decided where yet."

"How will he cope with it, do you think?" Violet said. "I mean it won't be easy for him."

Hope looked at Silas but he said nothing. "I'm sure we'll sort out something suitable," she said.

The rest of the evening passed pleasantly enough. It was getting late when Violet said she'd go up and kiss the children goodnight.

"I'll have to be on my way, too," Gabriel said when Violet had gone. "I do hope you won't mind me calling tomorrow. I'd like to take Violet out somewhere special. A treat after all she's been through."

Silas and Hope looked at one another. It was clear that Gabriel had something special planned for Violet and they could only guess what.

"We have no objection at all," Silas said. "It'll be good for her to get out."

Violet came down to see Gabriel out. "I'll see you tomorrow," he said, "if you don't mind me calling."

"Of course I don't mind," Violet said. "As long as we don't talk about Jake Mullins or anything to do with him."

Gabriel smiled. "That's not what I had in mind," he said. He kissed Violet lightly on the cheek and made his way out.

Once he'd gone Violet felt bereft. It was as though his going had left an empty void on the doorstep where the fresh, clean smell of him lingered. She put her hand to her cheek where he'd kissed her goodnight, as though trying to recapture the touch of his lips, soft and warm as a summer breeze. She couldn't wait until tomorrow, when she'd see him again.

Later, when she'd retired to bed, she thought about Gabriel. Although, to be fair, thoughts of him rarely left her mind for long. His arrival had been so sudden and in such strange circumstances. What had brought him to London? He said he had business here, but seemed to have spent very little time attending to it while spending a great deal of time attending to her business. Her mind kept going back over what he'd said about Dexi too. He'd obviously been talking to someone about them, but who? Who did he know in London? And who else had he been talking about? When he looked at her she'd seen a depth of feeling clear in his slate grey eyes. Her pulse raced. She wasn't sure how she felt about that or about him. It had been fine when she was on holiday, the summer sun, the new surroundings, the feeling of impermanence. But at home? Back with her family? This was very different.

Chapter Forty One

The next morning Gabriel dressed with care. He wanted to look his best for the day ahead. What he planned was new to him. In the past his romances had always been light-hearted affairs with no thought of anything permanent. Why was being with Violet so different? Violet was important to him, that's why. In her he'd found a combination of everything that filled him with pleasure and satisfaction. She made him laugh. Life seemed so much more worthwhile in her company. He'd also found her stubborn, resolute and brave. He felt as though he'd found a part of himself that had been missing and finding it made him whole. He'd found the thing he'd spent all his life looking for and now he need no longer search for it. The problem was that he didn't know if Violet felt the same.

She knew nothing about him. He'd purposefully kept that back as it seemed appropriate to do so at the time because of the obvious difference in their social standing. It would have appeared to be bragging, but now he wasn't so sure. How would she feel when she found out he'd been lying to her and what would she think the reason for it? That he had her down as a gold-digger only after his money? Well she wasn't that. She wasn't aware he had any.

Was now the right time to tell her who he really was, the son of a successful businessman and an American heiress? He wanted to come clean and share everything with her; that would be the honest thing to do. He didn't want any secrets between them, but what if she didn't like what he told her? He'd be risking everything.

He went over what he knew about her. He'd met her family. They were honest, hardworking people and he liked them. He'd heard from Nesta about her singing career with Bert Shadwick, the father of her children. She'd told him how Bert had treated her too. That appalled him. He'd have wanted to kill him then for sure.

There'd been no need to tell him about the fierce love she had for her children. He'd seen that for himself. He had a feeling her children would always come first. Could he live with that? Then there was her dream of being on stage. He'd have to share her with an audience if she decided to pursue a career as a singer. That wouldn't go down well with his parents either, he knew that, but would it be fair to ask her to give up her dream for him?

He smiled at his reflection in the mirror and brushed his fingers through his flop of tawny hair. This falling in love business was complicated and he wasn't sure he could handle it. One thing he did know though, he'd never find out if he didn't give it a try.

The day promised fine weather. He'd arranged to take Violet carriage riding in the park in the morning as he thought she'd enjoy it. Then lunch in Brown's in town. The afternoon would be spent taking a boat out on the Serpentine and in the evening they'd dance the night away at one of the West End's most exclusive cabaret clubs.

All he had to do was persuade Violet.

He'd booked a carriage for the ride around the park and it was waiting for him outside the hotel. As he walked through the foyer Harry came up to him. He tipped his hat. "Good morning, sir, and a lovely one for a ride around the park."

"Good morning, Harry. Any news?"

"Indeed there is, sir. That little matter at the morgue you mentioned…"

"Yes?" Gabriel's heart leapt. Harry's next words could make or break any hope he had of being with Violet for the rest of his life. He took a deep breath and held it. If it was bad news he couldn't bear to hear it.

"Ahm." Harry coughed.

"Oh yes." Gabriel pulled a five pound note out of his pocket. Harry looked right and left before he spoke. "That man you mentioned, sir. Jake Mullins? Died of a knife wound as a result of an altercation."

"A knife wound? You mean he was stabbed?"

"It would seem so, sir."

Gabriel cupped his hands around a surprised Harry's face and planted a kiss on his forehead. "You know what that means?" he said when he'd let a stunned Harry go. "It mean Violet is innocent."

He ran out to the carriage, called out Hope's address and jumped in. "Fast as you can," he said.

When he arrived outside Hope's house he met Silas returning from his visit to the police station to see Inspector Penhalligan. "Good morning, Silas," he called jumping down from the carriage. "Beautiful morning it is too."

"Isn't it?" Silas said.

"I have some wonderful news," Gabriel said.

"As do I," Silas said as he opened the gate. They walked together up the path.

"I've heard from someone who knows someone at the morgue that Jake Mullins was stabbed," Gabriel said. "Violet couldn't have done it."

Silas grinned. "I know," he said. "Penhalligan told me. He had the pathology report. I gave him Poke's statement and he's sending his men to arrest Carter Doyle today. Once he's rounded up his gang they'll soon talk, especially if they see the threat of a rope at the end of it."

Silas opened the door. "Let's go and tell the ladies," he said and they went inside.

Hope was in the drawing room and when she saw Silas and Gabriel she called Violet down. Violet arrived with her hair loose around her shoulders. "I'm not ready," she said. "You won't mind waiting?"

"We've some good news to tell you," Gabriel said. "You didn't kill Jake Mullins and Penhalligan knows it. You're free of it."

Violet looked puzzled. "What?"

"It's all right, Violet," Silas said. "What Gabriel means is that we can prove that Carter Doyle killed Jake Mullins in a fight. Jake died from a knife wound, not from being beaten around the head with a plank."

Violet sank into a chair.

"You're no longer under suspicion," Silas said. "We can all get back to living our lives as normal."

"This calls for a celebration," Hope said. "Is it too early for champagne?"

"Not at all," Silas said and rang for Daisy to fetch a bottle from the cold store.

They were drinking to Violet's continued good health when William came into the room. "Hello, Uncle Gabriel," he said. "Have you come to take us out?" The expectation on his face was the first stab to Gabriel's heart. The carriage he'd hired stood waiting at the kerb. William must have seen it from the upstairs window. "Are we going out in a carriage?" he called. "I'll go and tell to Rose to get ready."

Gabriel didn't have the heart to disappoint him.

"Can Peter come too?" he asked.

"You need to ask Aunty Hope," Violet said. "She may have other plans for him."

"I'm sorry," Hope said. "I'm not sure Gabriel was planning take you and Rose either," she said, glaring at William.

Violet looked at Gabriel. "Do you mind?"

"Not at all," he heard himself say and wished he could kick himself. Why did he say that? He'd wanted Violet all to himself, but then, he supposed it would appear a little selfish when he'd have her all to himself for the evening.

"Are you sure you don't want Peter to come," she asked. "It would be a treat for him and William would love having him along. He's quite taken by him."

"No. I've arranged for a tutor to come and meet Peter with a view to teaching him all he needs to know before he starts school," Hope said. "I don't want him starting out behind the other children."

"If you're sure," Violet said. "Well, I'd better go and finish getting ready. I wish Hortense was still here. She has magic fingers when it comes to dressing hair."

Hope laughed. "Ask Daisy. She's very good too."

"Thanks, I will."

Once they were all ready Violet shepherded them out to the waiting carriage. The day being so fine the carriage top was down and they enjoyed a ride through familiar streets, jostling their way through the traffic.

"It all looks so different when you view it from here," Violet said. I feel like I've been elevated to the gentry." She laughed. "That'll be the day," she said.

Gabriel put his arm around her. "I had hoped to spend some time alone with you," he whispered.

Violet smiled. "I'm afraid we come as a package," she said. "I thought you understood that."

"Yes, but surely you have some time to yourself?"

"The children will be starting school soon. I want to spend as much time as possible with them before then. Is that so bad?"

"No. Of course not," Gabriel settled back. This was turning out to be more difficult than he'd expected. The news about Jake Mullins's death had elated him. Now Violet would be free and he intended to make the most of it.

When they got to the park the coachman whipped the horses into a canter and they enjoyed the thrill of the wind in their hair and the speed of the horses. "That was wizard. Can we go round again?" William asked when they slowed back to where they'd started from.

So they went round again. When the carriage drew to a halt only the promise of ice cream enticed William out.

"I'm glad we've stopped," Rose said. "It was too windy and now my hair's all messy."

Violet smoothed it down for her. "You look lovely," she said. "You have roses in your cheeks."

"Roses in my cheeks?" Rose asked. "Is that because I'm called Rose?"

"No, it's what people say when your cheeks are red," Violet said.

"Like your face goes when you talk to Uncle Gabriel?"

Violet blushed. "Shush now. Let's go for the ice cream. You like ice cream don't you, Rose?"

After the ice cream they walked to Brown's Hotel and Restaurant for lunch.

"Ooo. This is very grand," William said when they arrived outside. "Will they let us in?"

"Of course they'll let us in," Violet said, although the look she gave Gabriel questioned her assumption.

"I've booked a table," Gabriel said. "I booked for two but I'm sure they can stretch it to four."

"Of course," the maître de said, although the look on his face when he saw the children was less than welcoming.

"Are you sure?" Violet said. "This must be terribly expensive. We'd all be just as happy having something at the cafe in the park, wouldn't we, guys?"

The children both nodded.

"I wanted to take you somewhere special," Gabriel said. "But if you feel uncomfortable…"

"No. We're fine," Violet said.

The strained atmosphere as they ate their meal made Gabriel's heart sink. The children hardly spoke and when they did it was a whisper as though they were frightened to make a noise. Mostly they just sat, in funeral silence, staring around them. They were so obviously out of place here, yet he felt completely at ease. It brought home to him how very different their lives were.

"I'm sorry," he said. "This was obviously a mistake. We can go somewhere else if you'd rather."

"We're almost done now," Violet said. "Might as well have pudding. Do they have ice cream?" She bent her head and held the menu up to hide behind it so he couldn't see the expression on her face.

William brightened. "I'll have ice cream," he said. "Please," he added as an after- thought.

"Ice creams all round then," Gabriel said as loudly as he could to break the heavy silence of the place.

How come he'd never noticed before how stuffy it was and how gloomy. It was a lesson learned.

Once they were outside again his spirits rose as they walked back to the park.

"Do you like dancing?" he asked Violet. The children were charging ahead and out of hearing.

"Yes. I do. Why what had you in mind?"

"Tonight. I'd like to take you dancing, if you'll permit."

Violet grinned. "Yes please," she said.

When they got to the park they made their way to the boating lake where Gabriel hired a boat.

"Do you know how to row?" Violet asked, eyeing the boat suspiciously.

"Well, I'm no expert but I'll give it a go," Gabriel said. He didn't want to spoil the moment by admitting that he'd been a rowing blue at Eton and Oxford.

The children climbed into the boat and Violet sat on the seat next to them. Gabriel climbed in. "You'll have to sit still," he told them, "or you'll have us all in the drink."

The boatman gave them a push and Gabriel slid the oars effortlessly into the water. "You'll have to guide me, William," he said. "Warn me if I'm heading into the rushes or going to hit another boat."

William sat forward. Violet put her arm around Rose and leaned back as they glided across the sparkling water. "When I grow up I'm going to have a boat," William said. "And I'll go rowing every day."

"What about when it's raining," Rose said. "You won't go rowing then."

"Every day except when it's raining," William said.

Sculling across the water in the sunshine Gabriel felt at peace. This was something he could do and do well. Suddenly on this bright summer's day in the middle of Hyde Park, away from the rush and bustle of London with Violet and the children in this simple rowing boat, everything felt perfect. If only it could always be like this, he thought.

Chapter Forty Two

Once they'd gone Hope ordered some coffee for herself and Silas. "Good news about Jake Mullins's death," she said. "And I don't suppose having that Carter Doyle and his gang taken off the streets will be a bad thing either."

"No. Penhalligan said they'd been after him for ages but never able to pin anything on him. The statement from Poke helped but he'll need some of Doyle's men to talk. There's no way Seamus O'Malley's going to appear in court to back up what he saw." Silas finished his champagne. "Funny thing is, Gabriel had heard about it from someone he knows who knows someone at the morgue. There's more to that young man than first appears. For a furniture salesman from Norfolk he knows a lot of people in London, and influential people at that."

"Yes, Dexi said as much when she met him. Said something about the cut of his suit and his shoes. Swore blind they must have been made in New York. She doesn't miss much."

A broad grin spread across Silas's face. "Trust my sister to notice them. She's the best judge of character I've ever known. I'd back her judgement any day against my own."

"I only hope he's sincere with Violet and not toying with her affections. You know how naive she is when it comes to men."

"Yes. Not the best judge."

A string of Violet's past beaus ran though Hope's mind. Half of them cads and the rest useless idle louts.

"I had high hopes for Gabriel," she said. "Ah well. Let's hope we'll not be disappointed again."

Daisy arrived with the coffee and Hope asked Silas about Peter's schooling. "I've asked Alfie's tutor, Giles Larkin, to come and assess Peter for school. He's a bright boy and a quick learner. I'm hoping that, with additional tutelage, he may do well enough to pass the entrance exam for the public school, just as Alfie did. I don't want him going there on any terms except by merit." She poured the coffee and handed a cup to Silas. "What do you think? Should we send him to the local school, or maintain a tutor until he's ready for public school?"

"Whoa there," he said. "We haven't yet found out enough about him. He may have relatives we don't know about who may want him to live with them. You can't keep him, Hope. He's not ours to keep."

Hope's stomach crunched at the thought of losing him. "If he has relatives why have they not come forward? You've made enquiries and according to the pastor at his church he's an only child. The neighbours were the only ones at his parents' funeral. He's an orphan. All I want to do is offer him a home."

"From what I've heard he had a home. He was taken into a home for boys and he ran away. He chose to live on the street."

"Yes, chose the street rather than the orphanage. He was told that they were going to ship him to Canada with all the other homeless boys. He didn't want to go. This is where he belongs. His parents are buried in the local churchyard. That's why he wants to live here, to be near them and if that meant living on the street then so be it."

"But are you being fair to him, Hope? Taking him away from a life he knows…"

"To give him a better one!"

"Better for whom?"

Tears filled her eyes and Silas took her in his arms. "I know how fond you've become of him. I just don't want your heart to be broken if it all goes wrong."

"It won't." She sighed. She thought of her own parents. "It's not blood that makes a mother and father," she said. "It's the day to day caring and loving. That's what I want to give him. Something he lost when his parents died."

Silas held her close. "I know," he whispered. "But you know you'll never take their place in his heart?"

"No, but he may come to love us in time and caring for him will give me so much joy…" She lifted her face to look at him.

"How could I have been so lucky to have a wonderful woman like you for my wife?" he said.

She laughed. "If I remember rightly you pursued me relentlessly until I gave in."

"Ah, yes, so I did," he said and kissed her.

"So it's all right to employ Giles Larkin until the term starts?" she asked.

"Whatever you want, my love," he said. "If it makes you happy then so be it."

"I just want him to learn enough so he feels confident among the other boys."

Silas raised his eyebrows. "From what I've seen lack of confidence won't be a problem," he said.

Hope laughed and Silas took her in his arms and kissed her again. "Now I must be off to work to pay for all this extravagant tutoring I suppose." He finished his coffee and left.

Hope sighed with happiness. She missed Alfie now he'd grown and left home. She had no children of her own yet, although inside she had a faint hope, so fragile she dare not voice it. Having Silas's children would be a dream come true. At least with Peter she'd have someone she could nurture. Seeing him grow and flourish. Things may be difficult, there'd be obstacles to overcome, but she relished the challenge he presented. Silas had agreed, so all she had to do now was get on with it.

Giles Larkin, Alfie's tutor from his school, had agreed to come and assess the boy as a possible candidate for the entrance exam at Merchant Taylor's, the school Alfie had attended. "I can offer tutoring during the holiday," he said. "But only after hours during term time."

"He'll go to the local school until he's up to the standard required for public school," Hope told him. "I don't want him going there other than on merit. He's a bright boy. I'm sure he'll surprise you." After all he surprises me every day, she thought.

When Hope asked Peter about his schooling he shrugged.

"I can count up to a hundred," he said.

"Good. What about reading and writing."

"I can read. Never needed to write anything."

"What about going to school?"

"I go to the Pastor's school," he said.

"How often?" Hope asked.

Peter shrugged again.

"You know you have to go to school. It's the law."

"But not in the holidays."

281

"No, but in September you will be starting at the local school. Is that all right?"

"Why can't I go to the Pastor's school? They know me there. He doesn't hit us or beat us, not like in the other schools. I only want to go to the Pastor's school, if I go at all."

"I can assure you that the masters at the local school will not hit you or beat you. They'll answer to Mr Quirk if they do."

"Can I go out and play?"

"They have break times, yes."

"No I mean now. Can I go out and play now? William and Rose have gone out. Can I go and find some of my friends to play with?"

"I'd rather you didn't," Hope said. "Mr Larkin is coming to see if he can help you with your school work. You want to go to a good school don't you? Somewhere you can learn everything you need to know to become a successful businessman and make your way in the world?"

"I was making me way afore. I'm not a prisoner here am I? I can come and go as I please?"

Hope's heart sunk into her boots. Perhaps Silas was right. You can take a boy off the streets but you can't take the streets out of the boy. "Well, yes, but I hoped you would like it here and want to stay. You are happy here aren't you? I mean you don't want to go back and live on the streets?"

Peter shrugged.

She pulled him into her arms and hugged him. Then she held him at arm's length. "Peter, I want you to be happy but I also want you to be safe. We can keep you safe, well fed and educated. Isn't that what you want for yourself? What your mother and father would want for you?"

At the mention of his parents tears filled Peter's eyes. He slowly nodded his head. She hugged him again. "It will get easier, I promise," she said. "If you like we can go out this afternoon and see if the headstone we ordered for your parents' grave is in place. Is that all right with you?"

Peter nodded.

"Good. And you'll see Mr Larkin and show him what you have learned at the Pastor's school?"

Peter nodded again. Hope's heart lifted a little but she was acutely aware of the many difficulties that lay ahead of them.

Chapter Forty Three

When Violet and the children arrived back at Hope's house they were bubbling with excitement. The children ran in to tell Daisy about their day.

"We went on the pond," William said. "In a boat."

"It's a lake not a pond," Rose said.

Gabriel chuckled. "I'm glad you enjoyed it." He turned to Violet. "I'll be back at eight to pick you up."

"I'll be ready," Violet said although she had yet to decide what she would wear. He'd said they'd be going to a cabaret club in the West End. She had nothing suitable.

Upstairs she took everything out of her wardrobe and threw it on the bed. They were Nesta's cast-offs she'd brought back with her from Yarmouth. She thought of the gowns she had hanging in the wardrobe at the Hope and Anchor. Gowns she wore on Saturday nights when she sang. They were far more glamorous than the meagre selection she had at Hope's house. She rushed downstairs and found Hope in the drawing room with Peter.

"I have to go to the pub to collect something to wear for tonight," she said. "Gabriel's taking me out and I have nothing to wear. Can you see to the children?"

"Slow down," Hope said, rising from her seat. "You have to go to the pub?"

Violet felt herself beaming. "He's taking me to a cabaret club, ever so swish. I'll need…"

"Well, go, then, don't flap around here making dust. Don't worry I'll see to the twins."

"Thanks, Hope, you're a life-saver."

Outside Violet jumped into the first cab she saw to take her home. John, standing behind the bar drying the glasses, gasped when he saw her. "Violet, what on earth? What's happened?" He put the glass he was polishing down and rushed towards her.

"It's an emergency," she said. "I'm going out dancing and I have nothing to wear. I've come home to collect a dress—" She didn't get any further.

John stopped her. Laughter filled his eyes. "Violet," he said. "You scared me half to death. All this is over a dress?"

Violet smiled. "I wanted something special. One of my stage outfits. Gabriel's taking me dancing."

"Oh. I see." John bowed and held out his arm. "Go ahead, get your special dress and ask Alice to help you choose. You know how outlandish your choices can be."

Violet sighed with relief. He was right. Alice would know the best thing to wear.

Going through her wardrobe brought a plethora of memories. Where she'd worn this one, how she felt about that one. "What do you think, Alice. How about this one?" She pulled out a purple silk, low cut gown adorned with purple flowers at the neckline and on the hip. It rustled as she held it against her body and moved in front of the mirror.

Alice shrugged. "A bit... erm... you know..."

"Showy? Gaudy?"

"I always liked you in this one," Alice said pulling out an emerald green gown. "It brings out the colour of your eyes."

Violet sighed. "Don't you think it's a bit... you know... dated?" And dull, she added in her mind.

"Not really."

"It's five years old. The first proper dress I got after the twins were born. I wore it to Silas's New Year's Eve party. You know, when he proposed to Hope."

"Oh yes, I remember. We had a lovely evening, all of us." She paused, staring at the dress as though deep in thought. "Do you believe in lucky dresses? You know, the dresses you wear and always have a good time in. You can wear other gowns, better made, more classy and expensive, but you never get the same enjoyment."

"Oh yes I do." Violet took the dress. "Yes I always enjoyed wearing this. Perhaps it will be lucky for me tonight. What do you think?" She held the dress against her body and looked in the mirror.

"Perfect," Alice said. She turned and took a leaf green lace shawl dotted with sequins out of the wardrobe. "You could wear this with it, to liven it up a bit."

"Hmm. No. Still not sure." She bit her lip. "No I think I'll stick with the purple. It's my newest."

"Whatever you think best," Alice said, putting the green silk back into the wardrobe.

"Thanks, Alice. Wish me luck," Violet said. She'd asked the cab to wait and rushed out with the dress back to Hope's house where she was going to get ready. Back at the house Daisy helped her dress and did her hair. Once again she wished Hortense, Dexi's maid, was there to do it, but at least Daisy made a good job of it. By the time she was ready for Gabriel to call butterflies fluttered in her stomach.

"How do I look?" she asked Hope, twirling in front of her. "You look amazing," Hope said. "The King himself would be glad to take you out."

"I only hope Gabriel approves."

"He will."

Hope was right. When Gabriel saw her he whistled. "Wow," he said. "You're even more beautiful than I ever imagined."

Hope lent her a midnight blue velvet evening cloak and Gabriel escorted her out to the waiting hansom. When they arrived at the Royale Cabaret Club the uniformed doorman tipped his top hat as they walked in. Violet felt like a queen. She'd seen some glamorous places when she was on the stage, but they all paled into insignificance when she looked around, taking in the ornate, gilded surroundings. She left Hope's cloak at the cloakroom. Entering into the ballroom took Violet's breath away. Six crystal chandeliers lit the room. The white and gold walls reflected their light. A waiter showed them to a table by the dance floor and Gabriel ordered champagne.

Musicians, seated behind a low screen in front of a small stage at the opposite side of the dance floor, were already playing a slow waltz. A few couples glided around the floor, the men in tailored evening suits and bow ties, the women elegant in silk. Violet was in heaven. She didn't think anything could be better than this.

The champagne arrived in a silver bucket. The waiter placed two glasses on the table and poured champagne into each. Gabriel lifted his glass. "To us," he said. "The beginning of something beautiful." Tenderness shone in his slate grey eyes.

"To us," Violet said and sipped the champagne. It was the real stuff. The best she'd ever tasted. The next dance, another waltz, was announced. "Shall we?" Gabriel said, rising and holding out his hand.

Violet stood and he swept her into his arms. Soon she felt herself spinning around the dance floor being held so close she felt his breath on her cheek. He smelled of citrus and roses. She breathed in the smell of him, luxuriating in the warmth of his body against hers. She felt the strong muscles of his back through the fabric of his coat. Gabriel was an expert dancer and Violet had no trouble following his lead. When the music stopped her heart kept on dancing. This was the most magical night of her life.

The next dance was a foxtrot and Gabriel swept her into his arms again. This time, as she passed the band, the trumpet player winked at her. She thought perhaps he was just being overly friendly, but the next time they passed she took a closer look. Then she recognised him. He'd performed on the same stage years ago on the circuit. She recalled his face, but couldn't remember his name. Here he was playing in the band and she was dancing around in the arms of quite the handsomest man in the room. She couldn't help a chuckle escaping her lips.

"Anything the matter?" Gabriel said.

"No. I'm just so happy," she replied.

When that dance ended the band leader stood up "Ladies and Gentlemen," he said. "We are very lucky tonight to have a singer in the audience. I've been reliably informed that The Cockney Songbird is with us tonight." He pointed Violet out. "Perhaps she'd like to give us a song."

Everyone clapped and stared at her. "Go on," Gabriel said.

Shaking and completely unprepared she walked up to the front of the band. Not everyone knew the song she suggested, but the trumpeter, who she remembered

288

was called Ken, did and one or two of the others. She ran through the words in her head. It wouldn't do to dry up mid-way through. The band started. She let them pay a couple of bars then began. Once she got into it she sang the song, just as she did on stage in the theatre with all the winks, lifting her skirt as she walk around and making suggestive moves when she came to a bit that was pure innuendo. She heard the laughter from the audience as she came to the end of each verse. At the end of the song there was loud applause and cheering. She bowed and made her way back to her seat, still shaking.

Gabriel stared at her.

"What?" she said. "You told me to go on."

"Yes, but I didn't know you knew such bawdy songs."

Violet blushed to the roots of her auburn hair. She'd sung a music hall song full of sexual innuendo. The writers told her it was only the minds of the listeners that made it rude. The words themselves were perfectly acceptable. Obviously this audience didn't agree. "Well everyone seemed to enjoy it," she said.

"Yes. The men especially," Gabriel said.

"If you'll excuse me I need the powder room," she said and stood up.

Gabriel stood as she left. Inside her heart was pounding fit to burst. Hot blood coursed through her veins, perspiration trickled down her back. She'd enjoyed singing that song. It brought back so many happy memories. Some bad ones too, but she'd done it. She'd sung in one of London's top cabaret clubs and the people had loved it. She only hoped Gabriel felt the same.

The powder room was cooler than the emporium. A long mirror lined the wall above a row of sinks. She glanced at her reflection. Her face was flushed and strands of hair had fallen to curl on her forehead. She was glad to see a row of cubicles. She dodged into one as the door opened and two women came in.

"Well, what did you think of that?" one said to the other.

"Shocking," the other said. "Certainly brings the tone of the place down. They'll be showing burlesque next." Both laughed.

"I'm surprised at that Gabriel Stone bringing in such a trollop. I thought he'd know better," the first voice said.

"Yes. I bet his parents don't know what he gets up to in town." Once again they both laughed.

She heard the click of a compact or a handbag. "There, does that look better?"

"You look divine, darling. Come on, let's get Reggie and Jeremy up on the floor. They owe us a dance each."

Then they left. She stayed where she was until they'd gone. A quiet rage bubbled up inside her. Was that what people thought? Well, damn them for their narrow minded attitude. What was so wrong with what she'd sung? Everyone came into the world the same way as a result of the same thing. They couldn't deny that. Why be so coy about it? She gritted her teeth and glanced at her reflection in the mirror. She heard her mother's voice in her head "You're as good as them," she said. "Go on out there and show 'em."

"Yes, Ma," she said and felt a lot better.

Once she'd cooled down she made her way back to the table. Gabriel was standing talking to another man she didn't recognise, but she overheard their conversation.

"Slumming it tonight are you, Gabe? Brave of you bringing a toffer in here. I'd never have the nerve."

"She's not a toffer," Gabriel said. "I'll thank you not to use that language about–"

"Oh come on. You're onto a good thing there. Shame not to share it. I wouldn't mind giving it a tumble."

Rage flew up inside Violet. All she'd done was sing a bawdy song when she'd been asked to. This toffee-nosed, pigeon-livered gobshite was talking about her as though she was a whore.

She stepped up to him, took Gabriel's glass, full champagne, off the table and threw it over him. "I'll thank you to wash your mouth out when you talk about me," she said.

The man's nostrils flared, he grabbed her. "You little bitch–"

He didn't get any further. Gabriel swung a punch that caught him under the chin. He fell backwards. Someone grabbed Gabriel. Violet didn't stay to see what happened next. With tears streaming down her face she rushed out, collected Hope's cloak and ran to catch the first cab she saw. What had started out as a wonderful evening had ended up being the worst of her life.

Chapter Forty Four

When she got back to Hope's house she ran indoors and headed up to her room only to find Hope standing on the landing. "Violet? What on earth?" She rushed forward, put her arms around her and led her into the drawing room where she sat her down and poured her a large brandy. "What happened?"

"Oh, Hope, it was awful. They were awful, the people at the club. Snotty-nosed snobs." She took a swallow of brandy, sobbing into the glass.

Hope pulled up a chair next to her. "It couldn't have been that bad, Violet. Tell me about it."

Violet sniffed and Hope handed her a clean handkerchief. She wiped her face and blew her nose. "It was all right at first," she said. "Dim lights and Gabriel was lovely. We danced and even then I noticed the women. Oh. Hope they were all so elegant." She took another sip of her drink. "One of the musicians in the band recognised me and they asked me to sing."

"Nothing wrong with that. You have a lovely voice."

"I know. But the song, Hope. I sang *Inky Pinky Parlez Vous*', the rude version. I thought they were cheering, but now I realise they were jeering. I was so humiliated."

She blew her nose again. "Gabriel hated it, I know he did. And that's another thing. Everyone there knew him. They thought I was his... his... his...TROLLOP. One of the women in the ladies even said so." The memory brought on another bout of sobbing.

"Oh, Violet. I'm so sorry. I can't believe Gabriel meant any harm. I don't suppose he realised..."

"He knew. He knew what it'd be like for me. He set me up and made me a laughing stock. I hate him. I never want to see him again. He can take his mouldy cars and his friends and… and… and…" She took a gulp of brandy to steady her nerves. The warm liquid melted the lump in her throat. "I embarrassed him in front of his friends. That's unforgiveable."

"It's his friends who need forgiveness treating you like that. So you sang a risqué song. It's not the end of the world."

"No but it's the end of any hopes I may have had of him making an honest woman of me. I feel so ashamed."

Hope leaned over and hugged her. "You've nothing to be ashamed about. It's him should be ashamed of his friends for treating you so badly."

"What was I thinking, hoping there could ever be anything between us? I mean, a man like him. Why would he even look twice as someone like me? What am I going to do, Hope?"

Hope poured herself a glass or port. "You're going to dry your tears and remember who you are. You're wild and impetuous sometimes, Violet, but you have a good heart and generosity of spirit. That's what counts. Not how you talk or who you know."

"But I love him. I thought he loved me but he must have just taken pity on me when he saw me looking for a cab at the train station. He must have seen that we're not wealthy and rich as him and his friends. He led me on. He's had a good laugh at my expense. I don't suppose I'll ever see him again and I feel so… so… wretched. How could I have got him so wrong?"

"I think we all got him wrong. I mean, I can't believe he thought of you like that, Violet, I saw him with you and I've never seen a man so smitten."

"Really? You really think he liked me, just a little bit?"

"I think he liked you a lot, Violet. I remember how distraught he was when he heard you'd gone missing and how eager he was to find you. He went out with Silas every day. He must have seen how you live and that you weren't well off but he wasn't going to let the difference between your class stand in his way. If he loves you he'll take you as you are, faults and all. If he's not prepared to do that then he's not the man for you and the sooner you forget him the better."

"I don't think I'll ever forget him."

Hope sighed. "Dexi once told me you have to get used to having your heart broken. It happens all the time."

Violet picked at the purple silk of her dress, remembering how she'd swished it about as she sang and winked at the men in the audience. "And another thing," she said. "Alice was right. I should have worn the green."

Hope put a hand to her mouth as though stifling a laugh. Violet looked at her and they both burst out laughing.

"There, that wasn't so bad was it?" Hope said. She poured Violet another brandy. "Go to bed. Get a good night's sleep and things will look better in the morning."

"I doubt it. The children will be disappointed and sullen and I'll have a hangover. How's that going to be better?" She sniffed and wiped her nose again. "You married Silas and he had money but it didn't come between you did it?"

"No. But we married for love. I'd have married him rich or poor. It didn't make any difference to me. I married the man not his money."

"Just as I would have, I mean, if he'd asked me. I wasn't after his money. I didn't even know he had any until tonight. Why do I always get it so wrong, Hope? What's wrong with me?"

"There's nothing wrong with you. You've made mistakes in life, who hasn't, but you've learned from them and they've made you a better person. If Gabriel's too stupid to see that then he doesn't deserve you." She finished her port and put the glass down.

They heard a loud knocking at the front door. "I expect that's Silas forgotten his key again," Hope said. She went to the window. "It's Gabriel."

"Oh no. Don't let him in. I don't want to see him."

"Of course you do. I expect he's come to see you're all right."

"Tell him to go away."

"I'll do no such thing. Wipe you face and try to look calm, even if you don't feel it."

"I can't see him looking like this." She took a small mirror out of her bag. Her eyes and nose were red from crying and her hair had come awry, several curls of it sticking to her forehead. She heard Hope open the door and let Gabriel in.

"Is Violet here?" he said. "I've come to apologise. I can't think what she must be feeling and it's all my fault. I should never have—"

"She's upstairs, but I warn you she's not happy about what happened tonight."

Gabriel rushed up the stairs. Violet stood and went to the window, pretending to be interested in what was going on outside although she could see nothing. "Oh it's you," she said and turned to face him. "What have you come for? I'd have thought you've got better things to do. Shouldn't you be out riding to hounds and chasing some unfortunate fox, or shooting defenceless birds out of the sky? Much more fun than spending an evening with a *trollop* like me."

"You're not a trollop. I've never thought that. Miles was out of order and I had great pleasure in letting him know it. What he said was unforgiveable. I've come to apologise."

"But he was right wasn't he? Why did you take me there, to a place like that? You must have known what would happen. How out of place I'd be, what people would think?"

"I didn't care what people thought. I just wanted it to be special for you. I wanted you to have a wonderful evening."

"And you lied to me. You're not a furniture salesman are you? You've been stringing me along pretending to be something you're not in case I was only after what I could get out of you."

"I never thought that. Never, but in my position–"

"Your position! What about my position. An unmarried mother of twins. I bet that went down well with your friends. You must have had a good laugh at my expense. Well, thank you very much." She turned away from him to look back at the window.

"No, Violet. No. It was never like that." He walked towards her. "I was looking to buy furniture; it just seemed easier to let you think that way so I could be myself, not the son of somebody rich. You've no idea what it's like being me with the weight of expectation on my shoulders. Being with you gave me a freedom I've never felt before. I wanted to be that furniture salesman. An ordinary man making a living."

He paused and turned her round to face him. "I felt alive when I was with you. You opened my eyes to things I'd never dreamed about."

"Yes, the slums around Waterloo and Dead Man's Island."

He laughed. "I love you, Violet. I'd rather live in a slum with you than in a palace without you." He ran a finger over her tearstained cheek. "You're exciting, unpredictable, beautiful. Being away from you was dull beyond measure. When you left Yarmouth it was as though the sun had gone and taken all the beauty of the earth with it. I missed you, Violet. You and your children. Without you my life's not worth living."

He dropped down onto one knee, took a small box from his pocket and opened it to reveal the most fabulous diamond ring Violet had ever set eyes upon. "Marry me, Violet, and make me the happiest man alive."

Her breath caught in her throat. A rush of love filled her heart so full she thought she might burst with the strength of it. "Really?" she said, unable to believe her ears or her eyes. She felt sure she must be dreaming.

"Really," he said. A beaming smile filled his face.

"Oh yes please," she said pulling him up to embrace him. She removed her mother's wedding ring from the third finger of her left hand, and slipped it on to the right. As she did so she felt her mother's presence. She knew she would have been proud of her. Proud and pleased for her.

He slipped the ring on her finger and kissed her. She almost fainted with the joy of it. "Let's tell the others," she said as quickly as she could in case he should change his mind.

Silas arrived home in time to join the party. He opened the champagne and Violet woke the children to tell them about their new father-to-be.

"Does this mean that we'll all be living together forever?" William asked.

"Yes," Gabriel said.

"And will you buy a car so we can go out for rides?"

Gabriel laughed. "I expect that can be arranged," he said.

Rose went up to him and hugged him. Then she kissed him on the cheek. "I like you," she said. "I'm glad you're going to be our new father."

Gabriel's heart melted. He loved his new family. All he had to do now was tell his old one.

By the time Gabriel got back to his hotel dawn was breaking. He stopped for a while to watch the sun rise its rays creeping over the rooftops, lighting up the streets. The city was waking up to a beautiful day. He'd never felt happier in his life.

At the reception desk he sent his parents a telegram:

Engaged to a wonderful girl called Violet. Coming home this weekend. Letter follows.

Back in his room be started to write. He found it difficult to put his feelings into words. Violet wouldn't be his parents' first choice as a suitable bride for their son and heir. He wanted to make it clear that he intended to marry her with or without their approval, although he fervently hoped it would be with. Once he'd decided on the wording he wrote and told them how much he loved Violet, a young widow with two children, and he felt sure they would love her too.

Chapter Forty Five

The next morning Violet packed up her things and moved back to the Hope and Anchor. "It's my home," she said, "and now there's no danger of me being taken in, or the children being taken away I can go back."

Hope was sorry to see her go and she'd miss the twins terribly. Peter too would miss them. She had to do her best to make him feel at home. "You'll be going to school soon yourself," she said when she found him hanging around the kitchen getting in Mrs B's way. "You'll make lots of new friends then."

"I had lots of friends before," he said. "Street boys stick together. We look out for one another." Hope's heart crunched. Again she wondered about the wisdom of taking in a boy off the streets, then recalled that being on the street usually ended in death, the workhouse or prison and she knew she'd done the right thing.

"Mr Larkin will be here soon to go over your school work," she said, in a bid to take his mind of his loneliness.

Peter huffed. Then she heard the front door open. Surely it can't be Silas, she thought, home so early in the day.

She went out into the hall just as Silas came in carrying a small bundle of brown and white fur under one arm. Abel followed him in carrying a dog basket, collar and lead and various bowls.

Silas put the bundle on the floor and a small brown and white puppy waddled its way towards Hope. Peter, standing behind her stepped forward. "It's a puppy," he said crouching down and holding out his hand.

"Well spotted," Silas said.

The puppy bounded forward towards Peter. A broad smile lit up Peter's face. "Can we keep him?"

"You can," Silas said. "But you have to be responsible for him. Feed him take him for walks etcetera."

"Oh I will," Peter said lifting the puppy into his arms. The puppy licked his face. Peter laughed. It was the first time Hope had seen him laugh and her heart swelled with joy.

"What's his name?" Peter asked.

"You can call him what you like. He's your dog."

"Really?"

"Yes," Silas said. "He's a terrier. Strong, fearless, intelligent, reliable and intensely loyal. A bit like myself."

Hope giggled. She went and linked her arm through his.

"I think I'll call him Patch," Peter said. "He has a patch over one eye. Look." He held the puppy out and sure enough there was a patch of black over one of his deep chocolate eyes.

"Wonderful," Hope said. "He's so adorable." She turned to Silas. "That was very clever of you. How did you know?"

"What? That he'd miss the twins and you'd miss Violet? We all will. They did seem to fill all the empty spaces in the house didn't they?"

"Yes," Hope said. "But a dog?"

"Every boy should have a dog. I was a boy myself once, a long, long time ago." He looked at Hope. She pushed a stray lock of his raven dark hair back behind his ear. "You still are, at heart," she said. She could see that he'd make a wonderful father. Perhaps now wasn't the right time to tell him her news. It was early days yet, and she wasn't completely sure, but if her calculations were right she'd be making him a father of his own son or daughter by next summer.

"Come on, let's get him settled in," Silas said.

"Can he sleep in my room?" Peter asked.

"Yes."

"Oh. No," Hope said. "I've just remembered. I had a letter from Alfie. He's coming home. He's finished his course and they've got him a job as a junior clerk at an accountancy firm in London. He'll want his room back."

"Does that mean we have to share?" A worried look passed over Peter's face.

"No. You can have the room Violet's just moved out of. It's bigger than Alfie's room. I think you'll be quite comfortable there."

Abel and Hope helped Peter move his stuff into the room across the landing that Violet had just left. It had a nice view over the garden and Peter loved it. "You can keep all your bits and pieces in here," Hope said, "and invite friends round if you like."

"Really?"

"Yes," Hope said. "You're part of the family now."

Peter smiled. He stroked the puppy in his arms. From the look on his face she could see he'd found something he could really care for. Hope had never seen him look happier.

Chapter Forty Six

Back at the Hope and Anchor later that morning Gabriel arrived full of excitement. "I telegraphed my parents," he said. "They can't wait to meet you." That was true. His mother had threatened to get the first train to London until Gabriel telegraphed to stop her. "I thought we could go up this weekend."

"This weekend?" Violet swallowed. It all seemed a bit sudden and real. Of course she'd have to meet his parents but she'd been hoping to spend more time with him before then, getting to know all about them and him. She realised how little she knew. "What about the children?"

"They'll come too. They are part of the family."

Violet kissed him. "Thank you," she said. "Although I don't know what your parents will think."

"They'll think I'm the luckiest man alive when they meet you," he said and pulled her into his arms to kiss her again. "Now I'll go and arrange the tickets."

Once he'd gone Alice helped Violet sort out her things for the weekend. "He told me his mother's first instinct was to catch the train to London and come and see me for herself," she told Alice. "Thankfully she was persuaded not to. Can you imagine, his parents turning up here unannounced. Whatever would they think of me?"

"They'd think that Gabriel was lucky to find such a warm-hearted, hard-working bride. After all, look at the Society girls and useless debutants he could have ended up with."

Violet laughed. "You always cheer me up, Alice. But do you really think they'll like me?"

"Of course, my dear. What's not to like?"

Violet thought of the times she'd appeared on stage, not always in the best places, the rough boarding houses they'd stayed at while touring, the drinking, and worse that the other performers relied on to get them through the acts, especially when they were booed off stage. Then there were the children, born out of wedlock with a stage magician and well known conman for a father, not to mention her latest escapade, kidnap and ending up having to be rescued from a brothel. Oh yes. There was plenty not to like.

Gabriel's parents lived in Yorkshire so they went by train.

"Are we going to the seaside?" William asked.

"No. We're going to stay in a big house in the country," Gabriel said. "They have sheep and goats and cows."

"Do they have a motor car? Can we go for a ride?"

Gabriel smiled. "Yes. My father does have a motor car. If you're very good I'll see if he can be persuaded to take you for a drive."

"We are good, aren't we, Rose?"

Rose nodded. After that the children were happy to sit and look out of the window as the countryside sped by. All through the journey Violet worried. "How much did you tell them about me?" she asked.

Gabriel smiled. "Well I thought it best not to mention that I'd rescued you from a brothel," he said with a glint in his eye.

She punched his arm. "I'll never live that down will I? But it wasn't my fault."

"I know that. That's why I think it's best forgotten," he said glancing out of the window. "Still it does make a jolly good story."

She punched him again. "What did you tell them?"

"I told them that I'd fallen in love with a beautiful girl who's done me the great honour of agreeing to become my wife. I said I'm the luckiest man alive who doesn't deserve you and I want to spend the rest of my life making you happy. That's all they need to know." He put his hand under her chin and tilted her face to look into her eyes. "The rest will remain a secret just between us," he said and planted a kiss on her lips.

Violet's whole being filled with love for this man sitting beside her. "If we weren't on a train…" she said with a twinkle in her eye.

Gabriel pulled her into his arms and kissed her anyway. It was only William staring and Rose pulling Violet's skirt that stopped them going any further.

When they arrived at the station Gabriel's parents had sent a carriage for them.

"I suppose I'll have to get used to this luxury," Violet said, remembering the first time she saw Gabriel was while she was waiting at a railway station for transport.

The coachman greeted them warmly. "Good to have you home, Master Gabriel," he said. He nodded to Violet and smiled at the children while he loaded their luggage.

Violet hoped the family would be just as welcoming.

The Gables, Gabriel's home, sat at the end of a long drive. As soon as they entered through the gates the children stared. "Do you live here?" William said. "It's very grand."

"It's just a house," Gabriel said. "A home, just like where you live."

"No," William said. "It's nothing like where we live."

Violet took a breath. Gabriel had told her about his family, their background and their business so she'd expected something fine, but not nearly as impressive as the mansion that stood before her. The carriage drew up in front of a porticoed entrance. Two footmen came to open the carriage door.

Gabriel squeezed her hand.

She needn't have worried. Gabriel's mother was just as gracious as he said she would be and his father kissed Violet's hand. "My you're a beauty," he said. "If I was twenty years younger I'd be giving my son a run for his money." Mirth twinkled in his eyes.

"And these are our children," Gabriel said. "Or will be."

"Oh my," his mother said. "Aren't they adorable?" She kissed both William and Rose, which made William squirm and Rose giggle.

His mother put her arm around Violet and guided her into the house. "Let the men take care of the luggage and the horses," she said. "Gabriel's told us nothing about you. I want to hear all about you and your children." She rang a bell and a maid appeared. "Tea please. In the drawing room."

Violet didn't know what to say, except to compliment her on the magnificent house and gardens. She was quite thankful when Gabriel joined them. "Now, Mother, you mustn't monopolise Violet," he said. "Plying her with questions. She'll be tired from the journey. There's plenty of time to get to know her. We're here for the weekend."

Gabriel showed them upstairs to the nursery where two beds had been made up for the children. There were cupboards, a chest of drawers and a colourful rainbow painted on one wall.

"It's lovely," Rose said, touching the frilled net curtains.

"Can we play with the toys?" William asked, seeing a box of soldiers on a side table.

"If you're careful," Gabriel said. "The parlour maid Ginny will be looking after you. Is that all right?"

"I don't need looking after," William said, his voice filled with indignation. He shrugged his shoulders. "But I suppose Rose might."

They left the children with Ginny to help them unpack and Gabriel showed Violet to her room. It was along the corridor from his. "When you're all unpacked come down and I'll show round the garden," he said.

It was only when they walked around the grounds with the children ooing and aarring at everything they saw, that Violet realised how different Gabriel's childhood must have been from her own.

Gabriel's sister Ruth and her husband came for dinner that evening. The meal was a formal dinner, much more formal than Violet had ever attended but with Gabriel by her side she felt equal to whatever they threw at her. She needn't have worried. Breeding and a lifetime of good manners prevented anyone doing anything to raise a ripple around the table. It was only afterwards when his sister managed to corner her in the drawing room that Violet found out what they were really thinking. The others were playing Bridge and she'd declined to play with them.

"So, you're the surprise my mother was getting het up about," Ruth said. "She was fit to burst when she got Gabriel's telegram."

"So, what was she expecting?" Violet asked

Ruth laughed. "Well it was so sudden, so out of the blue, she quite expected a gold-digging tart after his money. A tart who'd got herself pregnant to force Gabriel to marry her."

Violet's jaw dropped. Anger flared in her eyes. "I can assure you I'm no tart and I'm not after his money. He can keep it as far as I'm concerned. In fact I never even knew he had any. And as for being pregnant…"

Roth glanced round as the murmur of conversation at the card table died. Violet hadn't realised she'd raised her voice.

Gabriel stood up and came over. He had a face like thunder. Before he could say anything Ruth stepped back, holding her hands up in defence. "I'm sorry," she said. "I never meant…"

"Is that what everyone thinks?" Violet said.

Gabriel put his arm around Violet. He gave his sister a look that would stop a galloping horse. "Anyone who insults Violet insults me," he said. "If she's not welcome here, neither am I."

"No, no, no," his mother said, rising from the table an anguished look on her face. "No one thinks that. I don't know where Ruth gets her ideas. We all just want to welcome you into the family, don't we, George?" She turned, with panic in her eyes to Gabriel's father, who also stood up.

"Indeed," George said. "I'm sorry, Violet, you must forgive us. Your engagement came as a surprise to us all. That son of mine kept you very quiet. Not that I blame him, didn't want to lose you I suppose. But,

308

now that we've met you and your charming children we can see why he wants to make you his wife. I hope you won't hold our earlier suspicion against us."

Violet's shoulders dropped as her anger ebbed away. She supposed she shouldn't blame them. Their stations in life were so different, she understood their wariness. Hadn't Nesta warned her about giving her heart to Gabriel when she knew nothing about him? "I love Gabriel," she said. "I love him for the man he is, not where he comes from. The man I fell in love with was a furniture salesman from Norfolk. I'd love him if he had nothing. I hope you believe me and, in time, you'll come to see that I'll make Gabriel a wonderful wife."

"Well said." Ruth's husband rose from the card table, clapping his hands. "Now can we all have a drink and get on with the game?"

Violet laughed and the whole atmosphere relaxed. Gabriel held her close and she knew that as long as he was with her she could do anything.

The next morning Gabriel's father, after William's constant pestering, took Gabriel and the children for a drive in his motor car while Violet walked around the garden with his mother. Violet told her about meeting him while they were on holiday and Gabriel coming to London to find her. She didn't mention anything about the kidnap or Bert's murder. She simply said the children's father was dead. They talked about the wedding and the plans they'd have to make.

When they got back Violet had trouble getting William away from the garage. "When I grow up I'm going to have lots of motor cars," he said.

By the time they returned to London she felt she was already part of Gabriel's family.

On Monday morning Gabriel came to the Hope and Anchor to show Violet the announcement his parents had placed in *The Times*. It read:

Mr and Mrs Addison Stone
of The Gables, Hitchinhampton, West Yorks.
are proud to announce the Engagement of their
son,
Gabriel Joshua Addison Stone
to Miss Violet Amelia Daniels
of The Hope and Anchor Public House,
London.

Violet swallowed when she read it. It all appeared so formal and so real. Her heart fluttered. It *was* real. She was going to marry Mr Gabriel Joshua Addison Stone.

On a beautiful day in May 1906, Violet and Gabriel were married in the little church on The Gables estate. Hope was matron of honour, Rose and Amy bridesmaids and William and Peter page boys. Alfie carried the rings on a velvet cushion. John gave Violet away while Alice sat in the congregation nursing their little boy, Alexander, who was four months old. Dexi came over from France and brought Violet the exquisite oyster satin wedding dress she wore. The latest Paris fashion.

Daisy held Hope and Silas's baby girl – Olivia Esmé Quirk who was just one month old. She had to jig her up and down and shush her to stop her crying. Olivia Esmé had the loudest, most persistent cry of any baby they'd ever heard. It was obvious from the start she was a little lady who wouldn't be ignored. After the service Hope put her down in the pram with a bottle to settle her.

The reception was held in a marquee on the lawn. Gabriel's father told everyone how pleased they were that their son had found the happiness he deserved. John made a short speech saying how proud their parents would have been to see Violet settling down at last. He spoke about the importance of families and hoped they'd remain as close as they'd always been.

Nesta came with some of Violet's old theatrical friends. "You've done well for yourself," she said looking around. "It's no more'n you deserve." She nodded at Gabriel to show her approval. "Always did like 'im. Thought you'd make a good pair."

"And we'll be neighbours," Violet told her.

Her eyebrows shot up. "Why? Where's you gonna be living?"

"In the Addison Grand Hotel in Great Yarmouth."

"Really?"

"Yes. We'll be managing it for Gabriel's father. I can't wait. I've been there and from the top floor you can see out over the bay and the pier. You can see The Pavilion where me and Bert…" She paused as though lost in memory. "Happy days," she said.

"Aye. Some of 'em," Nesta said.

"The hotel's got a hundred rooms, a restaurant and a ballroom." She sipped her champagne. "Bit of a step up from the Hope and Anchor."

Nesta nudged her. "Get you. I'm so glad. It'll be grand having you near to talk over old times. Perhaps even take up the singing again?"

Violet laughed. "The only singing I'll be doing is for Gabriel in the privacy of our own home."

"Go on. You won't be able to resist. 'The Cockney Songbird' sings again. I'd go and see it."

Violet laughed, remembering the last time she sang in public. It wasn't a happy memory. She saw Silas talking to Gabriel's father. They were discussing the usefulness of a motor car in town. Funny, she thought, how time moves on. Hard to believe she once envied Hope her happiness. Now she had a lifetime of happiness ahead of her and she didn't envy anyone. She wandered over to where the children were talking to Gabriel, their new father.

"Are we a proper family now?" William asked, tucking into the third bowl of trifle.

"Yes," Gabriel said. "We're a proper family now."

"Are we going to live here now?" he said. "Only I've left all my things at home."

Gabriel smiled. "No. We're not going to live here. We're going to live somewhere very special."

"Oh go on tell them," Violet said, almost bursting with excitement herself.

"You remember where your ma and I first met?"

"Yes. At the seaside. Are we going to live at the seaside?" his eyes widened. "Really?"

Gabriel laughed. "Yes. Your mother and I are going to manage a hotel on the seafront. What do you think of that?"

"Yippee. Can I go in the sea every day?"

"Well. You'll have to go to school, but after school maybe."

"Not every day," Rose said. "You won't go in the sea in winter."

"Every day except in winter," William said.

"And what about you, Mrs Addison Stone?" Gabriel said turning to Violet. "Will you go bathing every day?"

Violet laughed. "No I'll be much too busy running the hotel with you."

He put his arm around her and pulled her close to him. "That's not the only thing you'll be doing," he whispered. "I can think of lots of other things you can do."

Violet giggled as he kissed her and wished they could go to the hotel now so she could spend the night in his arms. It was where she'd always longed to be and now all her dreams were coming true. Everything she'd gone through, all the troubles of the past melted away in his arms. She really was the luckiest girl alive.

About the Author

Kay Seeley lives in London. She has two daughters, both married and three grandchildren, all adorable. She has been a writer for several years, writing novels, short stories and poetry.

A Girl Called Violet, is her fifth novel set in nineteenth century London's East End. Kay writes with passion and inspiration in this evocatively written tale about a girl's struggle to keep her children safe. Love, loyalty, tragedy and betrayal all play their part in this gripping story. Perfect for Cookson fans.

Kay Seeley's three previous novels, The Water Gypsy, The Watercress Girls and The Guardian Angel were all shortlisted for The Wishing Shelf Book Award. The Guardian Angel was a #1 best seller. Kay has had over fifty short stories published in women's magazines including The People's Friend Magazine, Woman's Weekly, Take-A-Break Fiction Feast and The Weekly News. Her stories are available in her three short story collections: The Cappuccino Collection, The Summer Stories and The Christmas Stories.

She is a member of The Alliance of Independent Authors and The Society of Women Writers and Journalists.

Visit her website www.kayseeleyauthor.com

Acknowledgements

Once again I thank my family for their unstinting support and listening to me droning on about my books. Many thanks.

I also need to thank Lorraine Bell for beta reading and Helen Baggott for editing, both of whom have helped make this a better book.

My thanks also go to writing friends for their invaluable support. Most of this book was written during lockdown which gave me lots of time but did feel somewhat isolating.

Once again thanks to Jane Dixon-Smith for the amazing cover.

But most thanks of all go to my wonderful readers who make it all worthwhile.

If you enjoyed this book you may enjoy Kay's other books:

A Girl Called Hope

A heart-wrenching saga of love, loss, courage and resilience.
Book One in the Hope Series

In Victorian London's East End, life for Hope Daniels in the public house run by her parents is not as it seems. Pa drinks and gambles, brother John longs for a place of his own, sister Violet dreams of a life on stage and little Alfie is being bullied at school.
Silas Quirk, the charismatic owner of a local gentlemen's club and disreputable gambling den her father frequents, has his own plans for Hope.
When disaster strikes the family lose everything and the future they planned is snatched away from them. Secrets are revealed that make Hope question all she's ever believed in.
Can Hope keep them together when fate is pulling them apart?
What will she sacrifice to save her family?

A captivating story of tragedy and triumph you won't want to put down.

The Guardian Angel

When Nell Draper leaves the workhouse to care for Robert, the five-year-old son and heir of Lord Eversham, a wealthy landowner, she has no idea of the heartache that lies ahead of her.

She soon discovers that Robert can't speak or communicate with her, his family or the staff that work for his father.

Robert's mother died in childbirth. Lord Eversham, a powerful man, remarries but the new Lady Eversham is not happy about Robert's existence. When she gives birth to a son Robert's fate is sealed.

Can Nell save him from a desolate future, secure his inheritance and ensure he takes his rightful place in society?

Betrayal, kidnap, murder, loyalty and love all play their part in this wonderful novel that shows how the Victorians lived – rich and poor. Inspired by her autistic and non-verbal grandson, Kay Seeley writes with passion and inspiration in her third novel set in the Victorian era.

A love story

The Water Gypsy

Struggling to survive on Britain's waterways Tilly Thompson, a girl from the canal, is caught stealing a pie from the terrace of The Imperial Hotel, Athelstone. Only the intervention of Captain Charles Thackery saves her from prison. Tilly soon finds out the reason for the rescue.

With the Captain Tilly sees life away from the poverty and hardship of the waterways, but the Captain's favour stirs up jealously and hatred among the hotel staff, especially Freddie, the stable boy, who harbours desires of his own.

Freddie's pursuit leads Tilly into far greater danger than she could ever have imagined.

Can she escape the prejudice, persecution and hypocrisy of Victorian Society, leave her past behind and find true happiness?

This is a story of love and loss, lust and passion, injustice and ultimate redemption.

The Watercress Girls

Annie knows the secrets men whisper in her ears
to impress her. When she disappears who will care?
Who will look for her?

Two girls sell cress on the streets of Victorian
London. When they grow up they each take a different
path. Annie's reckless ambition takes her to Paris to
dance at the Folies Bergère. When she comes home she
takes up a far more dangerous occupation.

When she disappears, leaving her illegitimate son
behind, her friend Hettie Bundy sets out to find her.
Hettie's search leads her from the East End, where
opium dens and street gangs rule, to uncover the
corruption and depravity in Victorian society.

Secrets are revealed that put both girls' lives in
danger.

Can Hettie find Annie in time?

What does the future hold for the watercress girls?

A Victorian Mystery

Kay's Victorian Novels are also available for Kindle in:

The Victorian Novels

BOX SET

Romance, mystery and suspense come together in these heart-pulling tales of love, loyalty and sacrifice. Beautiful evocative writing and compelling characters bring Victorian London to pulsating life. These three historical novels and their feisty heroines will grab you by the heart-strings and won't let go until the last page.

Contains:

The Water Gypsy
The Watercress Girls
The Guardian Angel

http://bit.ly/2TVNBS3Uni

You may also enjoy Kay's short story collections:

The Cappuccino Collection
20 stories to warm the heart

All the stories in *The Cappuccino Collection*, except one, have been previously published in magazines, anthologies or on the internet. They are romantic, humorous and thought provoking stories that reflect real life, love in all its guises and the ties that bind. Enjoy them in small bites.

The Summer Stories
12 Romantic tales to make you smile

From first to last a joy to read. Romance blossoms like summer flowers in these delightfully different stories filled with humour, love, life and surprises. Perfect for holiday reading or sitting in the sun in the garden with a glass of wine.
A stunning collection.

The Christmas Stories
6 magical Christmas Stories

When it's snowing outside and frost sparkles on the window pane, there's nothing better than roasting chestnuts by the fire with a glass of mulled wine and a book of six magical stories to bring a smile to your face and joy to your heart. Here are the stories. You'll have to provide the chestnuts, fire and wine yourself.

Please feel free to contact Kay through her website
www.kayseeleyauthor.com She'd love to hear from you.

Printed in Great Britain
by Amazon